Red

A novel by Kim Jones

Kim Jones

Copyright © 2013 by Kim Jones

All rights reserved.

This book is a work of fiction. Names, characters, places, and incidents are the product of the author's imagination or are used fictitiously. Any resemblance to actual events, locales, or persons, living or dead, is coincidental.

Editing provided by Mandy from Raw Books Editing.

Cover Designed by Hang Le

Photographer: Perrywinkle Photography

Cover Model: Tosha Straley

DEDICATION

Lisa and Jessi... This one is for y'all. I didn't have a place in the plot to put your ignorant, psycho-babble bullshit. So, I figured what better place than front and center?
#teambestfriend

Prologue

Regg
Present Day

It's been three months since I've seen Red. The phone call Luke got Saturday morning had me thinking the worst. To say I was relieved when I found out she'd been locked up is an understatement. I was afraid she was dead. I knew she'd been hitting the dope pretty heavy. Luke never said anything demeaning about Red, but he did confide in me about her addiction. Still, I never thought any less of her. Sometimes life makes you do stupid shit. I know because I've done my fair share of it.

I'd dated a few girls, but they never measured up. I even went as far as dating girls who looked like her, but they were nothing in comparison. When you meet someone who has a fire that burns as bright as Red's, it does something to you. That's what happened the first time I laid eyes on her. She did that something to me. She has a gravity about her that pulls me in. She makes me want to live in a world that thrives off of her energy. She makes me want something more than what I have.

A little over a year ago, I thought my life was complete. I had everything; a good job, money, a full patch with my club. There was literally nothing else that I wanted. And then I saw her. She was so fucking beautiful. Waves of red hair, bright hazel eyes, an infectious smile and a personality that was sexier than those long, tan legs of hers. She walked with confidence, spoke with pride and made everyone in the room feel better by just breathing.

I've never been so affected. I've never desired anyone or anything so much. I wanted more of her. This was the first woman I'd seen who exuded raw sex appeal, but she wasn't flashing naked in my mind. I just wanted to talk to her. I wanted her to smile at me. Even if she didn't, I just wanted her in the same room so I could admire her beauty and let her presence possess me. She's what was missing from my life. When she looked at me, it was like we'd known each other our whole lives. Ten minutes was all it took for us to build a connection. In that time, I knew I would do anything to have her. Now, I had my chance.

***

Luke sits next to me at the back of the courtroom. He's trying to look calm, but I know better. I shoot a wink at the girl in front of us and wait for her to turn around before nudging his arm.

"You alright?"

"I don't know if I can do this, man. I've seen her like this before. It's bad." His voice is low and I know it's taking all he has to keep it together. He runs his hands through his hair, drawing the attention of the girl in front of us again. I motion with my finger for her and her giggling-ass friend to turn around. They look confused, so I give them my best 'mind your own fucking business' face. It works.

"This is my fault, Regg." Here we go.

"Luke," I say, grabbing his shoulder until he meets my eyes. Those baby blues that make all the bitches go crazy are now dull and lifeless. "This ain't your fault. She's a big girl. You can't make her do anything she don't wanna do. You did the right thing by stepping back. Getting locked up was the best thing that could happen to her." My words do nothing to ease his mood. I'll have to dig deeper and fuck, I don't want to.

"Do you trust me?" I ask, hating that I have to.

"With my life." No hesitation.

"With Red's?" This time, Luke hesitates but eventually answers.

"Yes." I hate seeing my brother go through this. I convinced him that I was doing this for him. It wasn't a lie. I would cut my own heart out and give it to my brother if it made his whole again. Red had done some damage to Luke. She is the sister he never had, and her fuck-ups always fall on his shoulders. He feels like he's responsible for her. If I can take that burden from him, I will. And it would be a lie if I said I didn't want it. Red needs a man in her life. She has Luke, but he's a brother. She needs a man to take care of her. Protect her. Be with her. I'm that fucking man.

"Then trust me, brother. I got this. I promise." The conviction in my words breaks through to him. He lets out a breath and nods at me.

"I know you do." Finally. I focus my attention on the front of the room while Luke notices the girls sitting in front of us. Good. He needs the distraction.

When the side door opens, I hear her before I see her. Red is laughing, and I can't help but smile at the sound.

But I can physically feel my face fall and my heart nosedive when she comes into view. This is not my Red. This is only the shell of the woman I met a year ago. When I last saw her, I could only see a slight difference in her appearance. She'd lost some weight, but she still had her spirit. Now, she just looked broken. Even though she's smiling, you can tell she's in another world. I'm not even sure she knows what's going on.

She's thin. Too thin. Nothing but a sack of bones in an orange jumpsuit. The chains on her arms and feet are heavy in comparison to her frail body. They pull at her wrists, causing her to slouch over from their weight. Her feet shuffle across the floor slowly. When she lifts her head, thin red hair frames her sunken face. Even though I can't make them out perfectly, I can tell that her eyes have lost their sparkle. But, even at her worst, that magnetic pull is still there and I want nothing more than to go to her. I want to rip those fucking chains off, carry her to my truck and drive her away from everything that's ruined her. I want to heal her. I want to help her find herself. Then, I want to find the motherfuckers that did this to her.

I stare at the back of her head, wishing I could stand beside her. The judge speaks to her and I listen for her voice, but I can't hear it from where I sit. I grind my teeth, waiting for the moment I can take her with me. I feel Luke's hand on my shoulder, but I refuse to look at him. This is why he's so upset. This is what he'd witnessed only a few weeks ago. No wonder he felt guilty for not doing something then. As much as I wanted to blame Luke, I wouldn't. Red wouldn't have gone if he'd asked her and she wouldn't have stayed if he'd made her. This was for the best. It had to happen like this.

I listen to the judge as he gives his speech about some bullshit work program. He makes eye contact with me, and

I nod. What he says doesn't matter, though. Nothing can keep me from getting what I want. I'll rip through this place like a mad man. I'll bring hell to Forrest County. I'll tear the roof off this motherfucker with my bare hands for what's mine. I'm here for one reason- Red.

And I'm not fucking leaving without her.

Chapter One
Southern Charm

Red
One Year Ago

"Heads up, Red. LLC's in the house," Lucy, my stripper sister from another mister tells me.

Dammit. So much for that bump. I stuff the clear baggy containing the finest, white powder in the South into a drawer and turn to the next best thing. Vodka. Not that cheap, rotgut vodka that gives you the shits either. This was the good stuff. Kauffman Luxury Vintage Vodka shipped straight from Russia to Pete's Gentlemen's Club in Biloxi, MS in a beautifully wrapped box with my name on it. I toss a few ice cubes in a glass, fill it to the brim and take a sip, sighing at the familiar burn as it travels through my body.

"You're not up for another twenty. Go say hi, I'll get your outfit together," I stare at Lucy from across the room as she adjusts her pigtails in the mirror. I will dress in just about anything, except pigtails are a deal breaker for me. But Lucy, with her petite figure, girlish voice and blonde curls, wears them well.

"You always were my favorite." I blow her a kiss, grabbing my robe from the back of my chair before going in search of the infamous LLC.

LLC, or Luke, and I go way back. At the age of fourteen, I was placed in the foster care of some of Hattiesburg, Mississippi's elite. My new parents had no problem sending me to the finest private school around. Luke went there too. He was the smoking hot jock, and I was the orphan outcast. After he caught Jimmy Daniels trying to force his hands down my pants behind the school cafeteria, he beat his ass, and then we shared a cigarette. We've been friends ever since. Even after I ran away from the best home life I'd ever had just after my sixteenth birthday, we kept in touch. He was like my big brother. And he still is. Too bad I don't see him differently, the man is mouthwatering.

"Well, if it isn't the heartthrob Luke Carmical," I call from across the room, drawing everyone's attention to the sexy beast in leather sitting at the bar. "Congratulations sir, you are the winner of about twenty pairs of wet panties, compliments of Biloxi's finest female entertainment."

"There's my girl." I walk into his waiting arms, squeezing him tight before placing a quick kiss on his lips. "How you doin', Red? You look good." I curtsy dramatically then give him my best smile. Which is really the only smile I have when it comes to genuine happiness. A full teeth baring smile that causes my nose to scrunch up and my eyes to almost become invisible. It doesn't take much to get that smile outta me, but it doesn't say anything less about giving it to Luke. He deserved it.

"And who do we have here?" My eyes go to the blonde guy who sits completely relaxed on the stool next to Luke. The side of his mouth curls up into a smile and I'm surprised to find it so attractive. He looks more like a schoolboy than he does a biker, but the cut he wears proves that he is indeed a Devil's Renegade.

"This is Regg. Regg, Red." I stick my hand out and he engulfs it with his own. His hand is warm, strong and he has the most perfectly manicured fingernails I've ever seen on a man. My eyes scan his body, appreciating his thickness compared to Luke's tall, cut frame. His shoulders are wide and broad, giving me the impression that he is some kind of body builder. His forearms are huge and I find it almost crucial to touch them. The black, leather cut he wears looks new, so do his patches.

"Nice to meet you, beautiful," he says with a thick, southern drawl. Laughter dances in his big, brown eyes and I can't help but give him my signature, mega watt smile.

"Gotta love the charmers. Tell me, does that actually work on women?" For some reason, teasing him just feels...right.

"Judging by the way you can't seem to take your hands off of me, I guess it does." I look down at my hand, still latched on to his and laugh.

"And here I was thinking my heart palpitations, ragged breath and lustful desires weren't noticeable," I say, using my best southern belle accent. Regg laughs and the sound is comforting. It's as if I've known him for years. He pulls my hand to his lips and kisses it, keeping his eyes trained on me. The hair from his goatee should tickle my hand, but instead it sends desire coursing through my body. It tickles all right, just not where it should. Shit, I gotta lay off the booze.

"Be careful, Red." He releases my hand, smiling up at me. "I'm pretty easy to fall in love with." I throw my head back and laugh. His cheesy ass pickup line gives my hormones a lethal injection, and my lustful desire disappears. I appreciate a man with good humor, reminds me of myself. I slip my arm around his shoulders and look at Luke.

"I like this guy." Luke rolls his eyes and takes a pull from his beer before answering.

"Famous last words." And although Regg and I are laughing, there is not a trace of humor in Luke's statement.

The guys promise to stay and watch the show, and against my better judgment, I satisfy my internal craving with the line of cocaine Lucy already has laid out for me when I return to the dressing room.

"You got two privates after your performance. I figured you might need it," Lucy says, confirming that she really is my favorite. I lean down, press my finger against my left nostril, and inhale the fine powder, making sure not to leave one tiny speck of residue.

I look up at the song list and smile, *Cherry Pie* by Warrant- one of my favorites. It was a classic, and I found that when people can sing along, they become more involved. That means a good payday for me. Especially since the house is packed, the customers are drunk and there isn't an empty seat at the stage.

My eyes land on the plastic, red mini-dress that has been laid out for me. It isn't right. This crowd needs something a little different. It's Friday night and half the men at the stage are wearing suits. Being here is the perfect ending to a shitty forty hour week for them, before they go home to play their roles as father and husband. And it is my duty to their wives and children to send them on their way in a great fucking mood.

Red

    I drain my glass, refill it and take it with me to sip on while I shoot the shit with the guys behind the curtain- something I always do right before I go onstage. My bodyguard and lifelong friend Corey greets me with a nod. Corey and I were in the system together from a young age, and have always been close. He is a massive man with caramel colored skin and big hazel eyes that darken when he gets pissed. He played football for the New Orleans Saints for a year before blowing out his knee and landing a job here. His role in this industry is to keep the men in check when they get too touchy feely and to make sure we are walked to and from our cars. Not that he needs to be paid to do that for me, Corey is one of my best friends. Hell, he is like family.

    "What's up, Red? You ready to give these boys a show?" He always asks the same question, and I always give him the same answer.

    "I'm ready to get paid." I touch my glass to his water bottle and we take a drink in celebration of the good life. Pete's Gentlemen's Club has been around for years. I was eighteen when I made my debut, and it was with Pete. I'd turned down some pretty great offers, but money is nothing when you find a place you love. Plus, I wasn't doing too bad here. In four years, I'd danced in the laps of men ranging from celebrities to drunken frat boys, and almost all of them had come back for seconds. My face covers the billboards that advertise for Pete's. My voice is the sexy, sultry one that plays over the radio. I'm the crowd favorite, and I have a waiting list for privates. The money is good, the drugs are aplenty and this two story, eight thousand square foot building is my home.

    The emcee makes my introduction and I hand Corey my glass, shooting him a wink. He is all business now, stone faced and ready to kick anyone's ass who even thinks about putting their hands on me. I straighten my long sleeved, oversized men's button up shirt, check to make sure my hair is still tightly secured inside the clip that's high on my head and adjust my fake, black framed glasses. My shoes are eight inch, clear platform heels that will accompany my thin, black g-string as the only articles of clothing I'll walk off the stage wearing. The music begins and I feel the familiar rush of adrenaline as it progresses through my veins. That, mixed with the cocaine, has me tripping on a high I know I'll regret all too soon.

    I'm all smiles when I waltz through the black curtain and head straight to the shiny, metal pole that centers the entire room. I pull myself up, letting the cheers from the crowd fuel me as I do just as Warrant asks me to- swing it. The muscles in my arms and legs are strong, allowing my limber body to rely on them to hold my weight. I climb to the top, then use the support of my wrists to keep me airborne as I spread my legs out, my ass faces the crowd and gives them a sneak peak of the bare cheeks beneath my shirt. I shake my ankles, causing my ass to shake as a result. When the catcalls ripple throughout the room, I loosen my grip and slide faster down the pole, landing in a split at the bottom.

    I turn to my left, crawling my way over to the men on the far side of the stage. I crook my finger at one of them and he stands, a big, goofy grin covering his face as his eyes glaze over with lust. I grab him by his head, burying his face in my cleavage. He is there all of two seconds before I push away from him and stand. He sticks his lips out on a pout and I wink before ripping my shirt open, exposing my all natural D cups. No sense in teasing them any longer. I only have three minutes to make bank, and by the money that litters the stage, I know my choice to go braless was the right one.

I work the front of the stage, dancing and rubbing my hands suggestively over my body. The feeling is heightened due to my high and I fight to keep from rubbing my pussy in search of release. My eyes drift to the leather clad men at the bar. Luke sits with his arms crossed, scanning the men at the stage with a murderous glare on his face while Regg looks at nothing but me. His eyes are hooded, the cute smile he once wore is now a sexy smirk and instead of ogling my bare chest, he meets my eyes. I'm not self-conscious about my body. There is no room for doubt on the stage. But, his appreciative stare has a different effect on me than any other man's in the room. He doesn't look at me like I'm some potential quick bathroom fuck or a poster girl for masturbation. He looks at me like he wants me. And not just in the bathroom, but in his bed, on the back of his Harley and in his arms.

Holy fucking shit. I'm losing my mind.

I continue the show, removing my glasses, and freeing my long, red locks. I flip my head over, pulling my bottom lip into my mouth on the way back up. I watch his lips part and make out the word 'damn,' before I drag my eyes away, fighting the shy smile forming on my face. I'm going through the motions, dancing, splits, pulling my hair, but all I'm thinking about is the way he looks at me.

What the fuck is wrong with me? Men always look at me like that when I am on stage. I'm a fucking stripper. My purpose is to dance, theirs is to look. I finish out the song, making sure to concentrate on everyone that isn't him. When I walk off, Corey is there waiting with a drink. I greedily grab it and let the slow burn of vodka wash away any and all thoughts of Devil's Renegade Regg.

Chapter Two
My Best Friend and His Best Friend

Ten Months Ago

"Red! Phone!" I close my eyes, silently sending up a prayer that whoever in the hell is calling me at five in the morning doesn't want anything more than to bid me goodnight. I'm on my twelfth and final hour of work; the last thing I need is for someone to ask me to cover their shift. I drag myself to the phone at the bar, the result of my all night binge is catching up to me and I know I'm about to crash.

"Yo," I say in greeting, declining the bartender's offer for another drink. That's the last thing I need.

"Hey, babe. Long night?" Luke's voice fills the phone and despite my sore cheeks, I smile. Most of the girls wear a sexy, sultry look when they dance. I always smile, but twelve hours of it is taking its toll on my face. I'll no doubt have crow's feet by the time I am thirty.

"Is it that obvious?" Luke's low rumble of laughter has me smiling again. It's been almost two months since I've last seen him and his presence is missed.

"I just wanted to check on you. Haven't seen you in a while." Luke doesn't attempt to hide the concern in his voice. After five nights of constant work, endless drinking and line after line of powder, my exhausted body demanded sleep. And at his house, I got it. It wasn't unusual for me to show up at his place on my days off and claim his spare bedroom. I sleep better when Luke is around. He is like my security blanket. He isn't always in the room, but his presence is always there. Here lately, I'd fought my demons on my own. Luke was a busy man. It was time for me to become less dependent on him and more on myself.

"Yeah, I know you got a lot going on with the club and all. I'm proud of you, by the way." Luke's hard work has paid off and I know it won't be long before he has the reins.

"Thanks, Red. But, you know I always have time for you." His words cause me to frown. Luke is such a good guy. I will never understand why he took on a burden like me. "Come see me. I'm off today. We'll hang around the house and catch up. I'll cook for you." I laugh at his offer.

"You mean you'll buy something for me to cook."

"I mean, if you insist." His playfulness has me missing him more. There are no clocks in here, but from my experience, the ache in my feet and the 'I don't give a fuck' in my system, I know it's quittin' time.

"I'll be there in an hour."

My shitty little single wide isn't much, but it's home. The trailer park is full of people ranging from senior citizens to gangsters and everywhere in between. On any given day, it's not unusual to find a cop or a hearse blocking the small, gravel drive. Thankfully, this morning there is neither. It reminds me of the home where I spent six years of my childhood. I don't know why I stay here. I can afford to move, but instead, I'd rather stay here and taunt myself with memories that still give me nightmares. I thought over time they would make me stronger. But, strong is something I'm not.

I drag my sorry ass out of the car, fishing my keys out of my pocket to unlock the flimsy door. It would only keep an honest man out. Hell, a child could kick the damn thing in. The smell of stale smoke and last night's supper hangs heavy in the air. Damn fried food. The lingering odor of fried chicken will be here for days.

I take a quick shower, scrubbing the sweat and filth from my body before brushing my teeth, and throwing on a pair of sweats and a tank. One of the great things about mine and Luke's relationship, there's no need to impress. He's seen me at my worst and my best, but he most often sees me like this. I throw a few things in a bag, grab my tennis shoes and sprint through the house, trying to prevent the smell of cooking oil from clinging to my freshly laundered clothes.

When I'm safely in my car with the doors locked, I look back at the fading brown siding of the mobile home. Staying on top is hard. I've worked my ass off to be in the spotlight. My face on a billboard and tips from horny men are all I have to show for it. I don't have a nice home or a nice car. My old Mustang is on its last leg, and a new used car is in my near future. But, I have to keep working. I have to keep up the fight to stay where I am. Girls walk through the doors of Pete's everyday looking for a job. And most of them have the potential to replace me. They're prettier, smarter and easier to get along with than I am. But, as long as I'm pulling the big numbers, the guys assure me I'm not going anywhere.

I pull the envelope containing my check from my purse. Maybe I'll have enough to put a deposit down on an apartment. Luke is in the real estate business and has offered to help me, but I refuse to take any charity. I make enough money to get myself out of this shit hole, I just have to back off the coke for a while and drink cheaper Vodka.

Pay to the order of: Denny Deen

Denny Deen. A name just as tainted as my career. Actually, being 'Red the Stripper' was an improvement over who I was before. I don't know why the great state of Mississippi gave me a name like Denny Deen. I guess Jane Smith was already taken. Like always, when I see my name printed in front of me, I think of my mother. I wonder what she was like. I wonder if she had red hair too. I would give anything to meet her, but chances are she's a lot more fucked up than I am.

I'm exhausted. Getting lost in my thoughts does this to me. As does long nights of work and sudden realizations of how shitty my life is. I'll forget tomorrow, and then sometime next week, I'll be reminded again.

I rest my head on the steering wheel, knowing what I have to do. Guilt begins to settle in my gut. I know Luke ain't stupid, but if he is aware of my addiction, it isn't because he's ever seen me do it...this time. He helped me get clean a few years back, but I've fallen off the wagon-so to speak. Luke hates drugs in all forms, and I refuse to be high around him. If I did it now, I wouldn't be worth shit by the time I got to his house. The high would only last about thirty minutes, and considering the amount I've already ingested, the inevitable crash would only be worse. But, if I don't do it, I won't make it there. Thoughts of getting some decent sleep, Luke's protection and his face have me pulling my stash from the hidden compartment beneath my console.

I measure out a line on the square mirror, put the straw to my nose and inhale. Before it has a chance to take effect, I pour the remaining powder out and snort the rest. I tell myself it's because I don't want to have it at Luke's place, but I know the real reason. I fucking want it. I slide my finger over the residue and rub it on my gums, then hide the mirror and straw before turning the key and listening to my car purr to life. Jimi Hendrix is on the radio, Biloxi, Mississippi is in my rearview and I'm back to floating in the clouds. And it's exactly where I want to be.

***

Luke's house is located just across the Forrest County line. A long gravel driveway lined with pines leads you to a beautiful log cabin home surrounded by tress and nothing but bright morning sky. It's peace on Earth. The huge shop behind the house serves as a clubhouse for the Devil's Renegades MC. The club was originally formed in Lake Charles, Louisiana, but has branched out to several other states and cities including Hattiesburg, Mississippi. This is the chapter I'm sure Luke will be President of very soon. I feel pride swell in my chest at the thought of my best friend wearing that P patch so proudly.

I grew up around the club and consider myself biker trash just as much as orphan trash. The foster home I was moved to when I was nine had ties to the MC. I wasn't sure of their exact connection at the time, but now I assume it had something to do with the drug trade. When the man serving as my dad sent me to the clubhouse on a delivery, I came face to face with the scariest man alive. Pops, the chapter president, took the bag from me and made me promise to never bring anything to them from my dad again. I didn't know how I would explain that when I got home, but I never had to.

From that day on, the club always seemed to look after me. Birthdays, Christmas and Easter might not have meant much at home, but the club always made it special for me. When I met Luke, he insisted I meet his grandfather-his idol. You can imagine my surprise when I found out it was Pops. Luke's father tried to keep him away from his grandfather as much as possible. He feared Luke would be influenced and take the same path and end up like Pops. Realizing he couldn't keep him away, Luke's dad gave up. It's a small world when you realize the boy who once saved you is the grandchild of the man who also saved you. I guess life has a way of showing you where you belong.

I pull up and Luke's outside waiting. His comfort attire of nothing but basketball shorts has me rolling my eyes. The boy never wears a shirt. Not that he should. I'm sure if he did, women would be rioting in the streets, demanding him to take it off.

"I should have known your hour would be two," Luke says, pulling me into his arms for a hug.

"Yeah, yeah, yeah. Get my shit, will ya." He grabs my bag and leads me inside. The scent of his home is clean, masculine and nothing like mine. The place gives a whole new meaning to the term 'bachelor pad.' Not a thing out of place or a speck of dust can be found. I am such a shitty housekeeper, that I'm sure he'll be ready to kill me by the time I leave.

I stop just inside the kitchen and stare at the counter lined with ten different boxes of cereal. It was a luxury I wasn't offered growing up, and when Luke found out he always made sure to have plenty on hand when I came over. The reminder of the hunger pains I endured as a child has me unconsciously rubbing my stomach. I feel the tears building in my eyes as my mind floods with flashbacks. Years I lived in a home where dinner was served when the mom wasn't high or wasn't on her back. Men paraded in and out of our house as if it were a brothel. And some of them had a fetish for young girls. I can still smell the stench of their sweat and feel the roughness of their hands.

"Hey," Luke's soothing tone cuts through my thoughts, but it's not enough to make them disappear. The happiness inside me is gone. My endorphins are asleep, and will stay that way until I force them out with another hit of coke. Now, I'm just a pool of sadness, depression and exhaustion. I sob in my hands, my fatigued body fighting hard to keep me on my feet. Just before my legs fail me, I'm in Luke's arms. He talks to me, tells me I'm safe and he is here. He lies with me on the couch, his strong arms holding me close to his chest. The fear begins to fade. The sobs begin to die. And in the arms of my best friend, I finally give in to sleep.

***

Someone beating on the door wakes me what could be days later. When I look at the clock, I see it is after nine p.m., and I realize the pounding I hear is only in my head.

"Son of a bitch," I mumble to the darkness. I look around, patiently waiting for my vision to adjust. I'm not in the living room anymore; I'm now in the comfort of Luke's spare bedroom. I force myself up and to the bathroom that adjoins it, and find two pain relievers and a bottle of water on the counter. Luke is always so prepared.

I scrub the sleep from my eyes, letting the cold water from the tap shock me fully awake. I slept all damn day. No wonder I felt like shit. I toss the pills to the back of my throat and nearly drain the whole bottle of water before brushing my teeth and going in search of the only thing that can pull me out of my slump. Cereal.

I stumble out of my room, glancing around the den as I make my way to the kitchen. Luke sits on the end of the couch, his legs reclined out in front of him on the ottoman while he watches T.V.. When he sees me, he gives me his trademark smirk.

"You look like hammered dog shit." I give him the finger, ignoring his laughter. Fruity Pebbles call to me and I fill a huge bowl before curling into his side on the couch. "Feel better?" I give him a nod, already lost in the movie. Steven Seagal will marry me one day. I am sure of it.

My constant crunching in Luke's ear doesn't seem to bother him, but it bothers the hell out of me that he's staring.

"What?" I ask, not pulling my eyes from the big sexy ninja on Luke's T.V. screen.

"Can I have a bite?" He had to be joking. I look at him and he is staring greedily at the huge bowl in my hand. And he most definitely is not joking.

"Um, no." I continue eating, ignoring his stare. Or at least trying to.

"Just one?" Fuck.

"No, Luke. You know how funny I am about milk." It's true. I can eat after people, smoke after people, drink after people, but there was something about milk that totally grossed me out when it was shared.

"You're an ass," he huffs, trying to move away from me but he has nowhere to go. Because I really am an ass, I scoot closer to him. He makes some kind of grunting noise and I smile at my ability to annoy him so easily. I hear the kitchen door open and the heavy sound of footsteps.

Shit.

I'm braless, in a white tank, baggy jogging pants and look like hell. It could very possibly be Steven Seagal and now I will have to work harder to make him fall in love with me. Or maybe just fall into my bed. Either is fine. But the image that comes into view isn't ol' Steven at all. It's Regg. He doesn't speak as he walks through the house, into Luke's bathroom and closes the door.

"What in the hell is he doing here?" I whisper to Luke, wishing like hell I had put on a bra. My words are harsher than I intended which earns me a look from Luke that tells me he thinks I'm crazy.

"He's my best friend, Red. Why wouldn't he be here?" My face falls at his words. Hell, my whole body sags. As does my heart.

"I thought I was your best friend," I say, poking my lip out. It's not exaggerated either. Luke gives me his charming smile that has dropped the panties of every girl in a fifty mile radius, except mine. My frown deepens. He knows I hate that smile. He gives me a wink, which I hate too before telling me words that do nothing to lift my spirits.

"You're my best *girl*-friend."

"It's not the same," I hiss, just before Regg walks back into the room. I focus on Steven Seagal, the one man who won't let me down.

"Red, I mean if you wanted to see me all you had to do was ask. I wouldn't have kept you waiting this long if I knew you were here." Regg is all smiles blocking the T.V. and thoughts of him replacing me as Luke's BFF are forgotten.

"Well, I know what a busy man you are." I shoot him a wink and he takes the seat right next to me. He doesn't look confused about me being right up under Luke, I guess he's aware of our relationship.

"Is that Fruity Pebbles?" he asks, getting way too excited. And just like Luke, I ignore him too. "Can I have a bite?" He leans over into my personal space, way too close to my delicious food.

"No. Go away," I snap, but he is undeterred. Bastard.

"Please?" He pokes his lip out and I would laugh if not for the seriousness of the situation. This is my cereal we are talking about.

"Dammit," I grumble, trying like hell to get out of the hole I've made in the couch as gracefully as possible. "I wish y'all would just leave me alone. Here," I go to the other end of the couch, sitting down and throwing my feet into Regg's lap. "Why don't you rub my feet?" I'm only joking and half expect him to push them away, but he takes my foot in his hands and begins massaging. Shit, that feels good.

"Look at those little pigsters," He smiles, pulling on my toes.

"What in the hell are pigsters?" My cereal is forgotten as I stare curiously at Regg who looks completely absorbed in my feet.

"Toes. Pigsters." So help me God, if he starts... "This little piggy went to the market." You have got to be kidding me. What is he? Seven? He throws his head back on a laugh, before resuming my foot rub and talking to Luke. "I'm staying home this weekend. Little brother's got a game Friday night. It's his freshmen year and I don't wanna miss it." Luke nods and talk of football starts between them and for some reason, I want to know more about Regg's family. He has a brother. Does he have any other siblings? Does he come from a good home? Does he have a girlfriend? No. He couldn't have a girlfriend. A flirt like him would never settle down.

I shovel cereal into my mouth, appraising him from across the couch. Regg is a good looking guy. Boyish, yes, but no less good looking. My eyes travel to his leather cut, and I can't help but wonder if he would still be attractive if he wasn't wearing it. There is something about leather vests on a man that can change his appearance from average to mouthwatering. Not that Regg is mouthwatering, I mean he is, but I don't see him that way. He is just cute. Well, more than cute, but I ain't attracted to him or anything. Am I?

Shit, I need to watch the movie. Seagal is fixing to kill someone with a condom and a spatula. I should really give him my undivided attention. But, damn that laugh. And that smile. And the boy can give a mean foot massage. I shift at my thoughts and he tightens his hold on my feet. *No, baby. I wasn't going to move them.* I snort at my stupid conversation with myself and it earns me silence and a look from both Regg and Luke.

"You don't think so?" Luke asks, genuine concern on his face. Shit. What in the hell were they talking about? I play it safe and shovel another spoonful of cereal into my mouth. "Red," Luke's voice is demanding and I look up. "I value your opinion. Do you think it's a bad idea?" How in the hell do I manage to always get myself into shit like this?

"Maybe I just don't understand everything. Tell me again. Start from the top." My ability to bullshit my way through anything is one of my best qualities, but Regg's smirk tells me he knows my game.

"She don't even know what we're talking about." Observant little shit. He really needs to mind his own business.

"Do you think the club would benefit from a new bar in Hattiesburg?" Luke asks, not bothered by Regg's assumption. Well, hell yeah. Of course. There isn't but a couple now and Hattiesburg is steadily growing.

"I think something like a bar would only be beneficial if you catered to the right environment and had the right location. Something across from the University that had dancing and karaoke would no doubt be a success. But, just a beer bar, not so much. Hell, the club would drink up all your profits." I look back down at my cereal, but can still feel Regg's eyes on me. I glance up to find him smirking. He shoots me a wink before turning back to an oblivious Luke. I sigh and I'm not sure if it's from the cereal, Seagal winning the fight or the skilled hands of Devil's Renegades Regg.

Chapter Three
Old Violins and Pork Chops-The Way to Regg's Heart

Eight Months Ago

I'm back at Luke's and it's the best sleep I've had in two months. I stretch, looking over at the clock to see that I've been out for over twelve hours. I feel something on my forehead and reach up to find a small sticky note covered in Luke's handwriting.

Red,
How much do you love me? Is it enough for pork chops?
   -Luke

Now that I'm standing in line at the grocery store behind a woman with three screaming kids, I'm beginning to think I don't love him that much. Maybe he should have sent his best friend to get it. Maybe he could cook it too. Oh, and maybe he could console all the hearts Luke breaks. Lord knows I'm tired of dealing with all of them crazy bitches. Since we were teenagers, my job has been to become best friends with Luke's latest crush. When he is finished with them, my job is to let them down easy and give them a shoulder to cry on. It is hard to be a player and a good guy. Or at least that's what he tells me. What an ass. And still, all the girls love him.

It's after six and Luke is already home when I pull back up at his house. Good. The little shit can help me with the fifty-six dollars' worth of groceries I bought for his ass. I stumble through the kitchen door bags in hand, after deciding I better tote it in myself since I got no response from the six car horn honks. I call out to Luke again, and still no response. If he was ignoring me, I'll kill him. I look out the back window and see the bikes lined against the wall of the clubhouse. Well, that makes sense.

I cut up the potatoes before putting them on to boil and going in search of Mr. Luke Carmical. If I didn't tell him when dinner would be ready, chances are he'd stay out here all night. And I wasn't fixing to slave in the kitchen for him to eat cold food.

I pull open the door of the clubhouse and immediately become depressed at what I hear.

"What the fuck are you listening to?" I say to no one in particular. I scan the room and my eyes find Luke sitting at the bar, looking over some papers. He gives me the finger without looking up. It's our best form of communication. "Shit, it makes me want to kill myself. Excuse me, sir?" I say to the young guy behind the bar. He looks up at me confused. "Do you have a rope? I suddenly want to hang myself."

"Blasphemy!" I turn to the voice across the room and find Regg pointing an accusing finger at me. He throws his pool stick back on the table and walks over, shaking his head. "Shame on you. This is Johnny Paycheck. Good thing you are on your feet or we would force you to stand in his honor." Oh, fuck me. I roll my eyes and start towards Luke, but Regg grabs my arm before I can get to him. "Dance with me, beautiful." I can't help but smile at him as one strong arm circles my waist. He holds me close, taking my left hand in his right. He moves me across the floor in true cowboy fashion. Damn, he can really dance.

"This song is depressing," I tell him, my grin widening as he dramatically closes his eyes and mouths the words.

"This song is like every other classic country song-a story. See, I know you are all citified, so I'll break it down for you in a language you can understand." I shake my head, wondering why in the hell I'm letting him lead me around the floor. But, I can't argue with the fact that being in his arms feels pretty damn good. "You have to visualize the story. Imagine it's a music video. Not one of them hip hop ones you're used to, but one that's full of emotion. Like a scene from a chick flick. Let the song build, then when it reaches its climax, picture something romantic happening."

"I'm not pickin' up what you're puttin' down." I'm already bored with his meaningless talk, but I believe I can stomach the song a little longer as long as his grip on my waist stays in place.

"I'm gonna show you. Reckon you can act?" I laugh at his question and earn myself a huge smile.

"I'm a stripper. Of course I can act." My hand involuntarily squeezes his shoulder, and shit, the muscles. I swear he is hard as a rock. On his arms, of course.

"Right. Well, you ready to make a music video?" I laugh again, my cheeks hurting from the permanent smile on my face. Regg is a funny guy.

"Sure." I'm still only half-ass letting his words register in my brain. He seems like someone who could ramble on about shit for days. I watch his face turn serious as we come to a sudden stop in the middle of the room. I almost lose my balance, but his grip tightens, holding me in place.

"So, I ask myself, I said 'John, where do we go from here?'" The rest of his words are lost in my laughter, but he keeps on. Then, the music starts and suddenly I can't laugh anymore. And I don't want to. But, even if I did, I can't because his mouth is on mine. The opening of my lips allows his warm satin tongue to slip inside my mouth. Holy fucking shit. The hair of his goatee tickles my chin as he kisses me with the passion of two lovers. One hand is on my neck and one around my waist, and somehow, mine has ended up in his hair. Too soon, he pulls away, his intense brown eyes staring into mine as his thumb grazes my jaw.

"Listen, Red. Listen to the music, feel the climax of the song." I nod, wishing he would just shut up and kiss me again, but I don't want to look any more of a fool than I already do, so I listen. He starts speaking again, telling me that he was looking in the mirror, talking to himself. I don't know the whole song. Maybe it's just the moment, but the words he speaks are poetic, and when the music starts and he kisses me again, I feel it. I feel the climax of the song and intenseness of the moment. And it's beautiful. I kiss Regg back, with just as much passion as he first kissed me and I don't give a shit what I look like. I'm an actress for all he knows.

Fireworks are exploding inside of me. Electricity is pulsing through my veins. He makes me feel so wanted. He kisses me like I'm his long lost lover that he's just been reunited with. Son of a bitch, it's good. He's good. The moment is good. I want him to kiss me forever. I want to feel his lips on every part of my body. Just the thought of how his mouth would feel on my neck, my shoulder, the inside of my thighs, has me moaning into his mouth. I feel his hand tighten in my hair at the nape of my neck. He likes the sounds I make-the audible pleasure he pulls from me.

He ends the song with the sweetest feather like kisses against the corners of my mouth. My heart is racing, my breathing is harsh and there is a downpour of arousal happening in my panties. "Either you're a good actress, or you're already falling in love." My eyes go from half mast to wide open at his words. He is smirking, obviously pleased with himself and I wonder how many girls he's used that line on.

"I was gonna say the same about you." Really, Red? That's the best comeback line you got? That's almost as bad as 'I carried a watermelon.' I seriously need to work on my game. I pull out of his grip, forcing my own smirk that looks more like the result of a stroke than anything else. My lips are still numb from his kiss. This guy is good. Too good.

"So, you cookin'?" he beams and I want to slap him.

"For Luke? Yes," I answer, praying like hell that my legs will cooperate and move me away from him. I wander over to Luke, fighting so hard to ignore Regg's effect on me that it's beyond obvious and the look on Luke's face says he knows.

"Is it cool if Regg stays for supper?" Luke's smile is evil and it makes me want to slap him too. I shrug noncommittally.

"Sure. It'll be ready in twenty." I leave the clubhouse with two thoughts in my head. I hope Regg kisses me again and where can I buy Johnny Paycheck's entire fucking album.

***

"Holy shit, Red." Well, I think that's what he said. The mouthful of food is affecting his speech. I look at him, waiting to hear what else he has to say. After he swallows, takes another bite, wipes his mouth, take three gulps of tea and burps, he continues. "This is the best food I've had in years. Damn, babe. It's good." I curl my lip at him, still bothered by the fact that I cooked seven pork chops and he has consumed three, Luke had three, which leaves me with only one. Jerks. I was a two pork chop kinda girl.

"You're a pig," I say, wishing I had even just half of a pork chop to finish off my potatoes and butter beans.

"I could be your pig. And you could feed me this slop anytime." He wiggles his eyebrows, and even though I don't want to, I smile.

"When you leaving?" Luke asks, still hovered over his plate as if me or Regg might steal a bite. It's possible.

"Tomorrow. I have to be at work by six, so I'll probably be leaving here around noon."

"When will I see you again?" His question reminds me of something I've yet to tell him.

"I have a really good opportunity in New Orleans. It's only for a few weeks as a fill in, but I'm thinking about taking the job." Liar. Actually, I've already accepted their offer and leave as soon as I finish my shift tomorrow. Luke looks concerned as he pushes his plate away and I know where the conversation is going.

"Corey going with you?" I nod, ignoring his intimidating stare and hoping that this is the only question I'm gonna get from him. "Red?" His demanding tone reminds me that Luke likes verbal answers, not head nods.

"Yes, Luke, Corey is going with me. Yes, Luke, I'll be careful. Yes, Luke, I know New Orleans is dangerous." I feel my temper rising and I feel like a bitch for acting like this, but sometimes I just need Luke to be a friend. Not a daddy. I watch Regg as he leaves us and I wish he would have stayed. He would likely have been able to say something funny and lighten the mood. As of now, the tension is way too thick for my liking.

"I worry about you, Red. Are you back on the drugs?" And there's the snap. I jump up from the table, grabbing the dishes and throwing them in the sink before unleashing the red-headed beast on his ass. And only because what he is assuming is true.

"What kind of fuckin' question is that, Luke? You're an asshole. Don't start judging me." I'm seething, and even though I'm only angry with myself, I'm taking my wrath out on him-the only guy who gives a shit about me in this world.

"It was just a question, Red. But now, I know the answer. Keep that powder out of your fuckin' nose." He is still sitting at the table, and I'm sure it's to keep him from throwing shit if he stands.

"And keep your nose out of my fucking business." I stomp from the kitchen and to my room, gathering all my shit in my pathetic, little bag so I can continue on with my pathetic, little life. See, it's here that I realize I pity myself. It's here that I know that what I'm doing is wrong. And it's here that even though I'm aware of my actions, I still don't give a shit.

So, I do the two things I'm so good at when it comes to hurting my best friend. I run. I run far away. And when I'm out of sight, I stick the straw to my nose and inhale. I inhale line after line until Luke is a memory and the feeling of loneliness doesn't matter anymore.

Chapter Four
The Big Easy

Five Months Ago

They call cocaine the rich man's drug. They say this because the high you get is only for a short amount of time. About twenty to thirty minutes. People who need it more often than that are said to have a 'big nose.' So, when you're snorting the rich man's drug with a big nose, shit gets expensive. Since I've been in New Orleans, I've made plenty of money, but it's all gone to coke. That all changed when I met Prissy and Chip.

Prissy strips with me at Lover's Cabaret. Her friend Chip, is a notorious drug dealer in the Fifth Ward. And he looks nothing like one. Where Prissy can be identified as a stripper on any given day, in any attire, Chip looks like a high school football coach. He is a well built, attractive middle aged man who gives you the impression that he lives in a nice home with a wife, two kids and a dog. But the truth is that he lives in an apartment, with his grandmother, in Slidell, Louisiana. Prissy hooks him up with clients and Chip hooks them up with dope. It is a flawless system and a turning point for me and my addiction.

"You're gonna overdose on that shit, ya know?" I roll my eyes at Prissy, before snorting my sixth line of the night. "Look, why don't you let me get you some H. The high is better, it lasts longer and it will save you a shitload of money." Even before I answer her, I see Prissy start punching buttons on her phone.

"Heroin? Um, no. I don't do that shit," I tell her, determination ringing loud in my voice.

"Oh, because doing coke is so much better? Don't be stupid, Red. Look, when your high wears off in, what? Ten minutes? Try a little of this. If you like it, I'll hook you up. If not, then keep spending your hard earned cash on that shit." I've heard horror stories about Heroin and how easy it is to overdose. The last thing I want is to die at twenty-three, in a strip club, with powder on my nose.

"I think I'll pass. Thanks though." I hear the song end just as Claire, the last performer, comes running into the dressing room. She looks happy. Ecstatic. Which tells everyone here that someone important is sitting at the stage.

"Cleveland Browns' running back Brandon McDonald and three of his teammates are at the stage. Red, you're up, you lucky bitch. I'm sure they're waiting on you." And I am sure they are too.

After I rocked the stage, the rest of my evening was immediately booked with privates. The football players requested me, personally. Because I'm a good friend, I encouraged them to allow Prissy to accompany me too. I knew she could use the cash and it is always more fun when there were two of us.

I pull the jersey they asked me to wear over my head, and exchange my clear shoes for a pair of black, knee high boots. The heel is just as tall, but there is something about the boots that makes me feel sexy. And these boys are paying for sexy.

"Red," I watch Prissy approach, bringing with her what she already knows I don't want. I start shaking my head,

Red

but she cuts me off. "Seriously, just try it. Half a line and you're good for six hours. I promise. I snort a whole line and I'm good." For good measure, she tilts her head and snorts the longest of the two lines on the mirror until there is nothing left. "We are gonna be back there for hours. Trust me. You need this." She wipes her eyes, rubs her nose and stares at me, waving the small glass mirror around in my face. I wish I could tell you I said no, but you already know that I didn't. With one last sigh, and one prayer to the Heroin gods, I snort the small line. And it might have been my worst mistake, but it was the best feeling I'd ever had.

I spend two more months in New Orleans, and on my last night, I get a surprise visitor. Part of my arrangement for taking the job was that they provide me with a studio apartment that I share with two other girls. It is small, but located in the heart of the French Quarter and only a short walk to Bourbon Street where Lover's Cabaret is located.

Chip and I had become close friends…with benefits. Meaning that I got a discount and he got me. We don't talk about our pasts, our families or go on dates. We get high, fuck and occasionally, I make us pancakes. It is a good relationship. Or it was until Chip became possessive. He didn't want me giving privates anymore and has been asked several times to leave the club. Every time I try to break up with him, he shoves more powder in my face. It is the solution to all of my problems. It doesn't matter how crazy he gets, one line and I don't care what he does.

I am up to snorting a full line of H, at least twice a day when I am working, and totally crashing on my days off. And still, I am aware of what I am doing. But, I don't see myself as an addict. I am just enjoying life. Or at least that's what I tell myself. There is nothing fun about my life.

I can't sleep, I can barely eat and the strain of my job and the long hours I work are taking their toll on me. Not to mention Chip and the endless supply of dope that comes with him.

Chip and I have just finished a line when my doorbell rings. Being the gentleman he is, Chip told me to answer it. Being the idiot I am, I do. And low and behold, I open the door to find Luke Carmical staring back at me. The look of shock doesn't go unnoticed by me as I cinch my robe tighter and try like hell to make myself fat.

"Hey, Luke!" My smile is fake and as much as I want to be high, I try to force normalcy into my stance, eyes and voice. It isn't working.

"You're fucked up. What are you taking, Red? Look at you!" Because I have nothing to say, I keep my mouth shut. "Is someone in there?"

"Yes, Luke. I have company and you came at a really bad time. I'll call you tomorrow?" My attempts at keeping him out of the apartment don't work, and I wonder why I even tried. He easily pushes past me until he finds my bedroom and the man lying naked in my bed.

"Who the fuck is this?" Really?

"That's Chip," I say, wishing like hell I hadn't just snorted that line. If only I'd have waited a little bit longer.

"Red!" Luke's voice booms through the room and it's almost like it hits me in slow motion. Shittttttttt. I just want to be high. This is a really good one.

"What?" I feel him grab my arms, and I watch him as he searches for track marks. Nope honey, won't find any of those. I follow him back to my room where he throws what I think are Chip's pants at him before telling him in an eerily calm voice to get the fuck out. Chip looks at me and I repeat Luke's words, only they're not quite as mean. "You need to leave." He mumbles something, and I think he calls me a bitch, but I'm not sure. The next few minutes are a blur, but I do remember seeing blood and someone lying unconscious at my feet. When I can't make out the face of the man, I realize that maybe I've taken just a little too much this time.

    I wake up in a hotel room which isn't uncommon after a night of partying. Not remembering how I got here isn't uncommon either. Usually when this happens, I don't pick my brain for memories because I'm afraid of what I might find. But, the voices I hear tell me that this is a memory worth digging for. I recognize Luke and Corey's voice, and eavesdrop on the conversation.
    "How the hell could you have let this happen?" Luke is pissed, but his tone is low. Almost a whisper.
    "What the fuck was I supposed to do, Luke? She's a grown woman. You know what happens when you try to intervene." Corey's voice is full of regret and I feel myself sink further in to the mattress as the guilt lays heavy on top of me. I hear Luke sigh and envision him running his hand through his hair.
    "She is not going to listen to me. She's gonna push me away like she's always done." What a lying asshole. I've never pushed him away. If anything, I've always pulled Luke in closer. I want to sit up so I can scream at them, but the next voice I hear freezes me.
    "What? Are y'all scared of her? Hell, I'll take her home with me. I can get her off that shit." Regg. Motherfuckin', charmin', smilin' Regg. And I'm sure I look like shit. I open my eyes and realize that I am alone in the room. Another room adjoins this one and the door is halfway closed. That must be where they are. Slowly, I crawl out of bed, feeling like I've been hit by a truck. I look down to find myself in Luke's shirt and nothing else. I smell good too. Like soap.

Shit. I probably threw up on someone. No, I bathed when I got off last night. Maybe. Hell, I can't remember.

I open the door silently and slip out, pressing the elevator button harder than necessary. Soon, I'm in the hotel lobby wearing nothing but a t-shirt. But, it's New Orleans and nobody gives me a second look. Lucky for me, a taxi is outside when I step into the cool mid-spring air. I slip in to the back seat and give the driver my address. If they ran into the street looking for me, I didn't know. I never looked back.

I promise the driver payment if he will wait for me, and he does considering it is his only shot at getting any money. I find my apartment empty, and only the blood spattered sheets left as a reminder of last night. I pack a bag, grab my cash, throw on some clothes and write a note to Prissy before running back downstairs to the waiting cabbie. This time, I do look back. And as I wave goodbye to The Big Easy, I make myself a promise that I will never go back.

Chapter Five
Fancy Meeting You Here... With her

Three Months Ago

I knew the day would come. Beyond a shadow of a doubt, I knew that one day, Pete's would find someone younger and prettier to take my place. And not only was she here to take my place, but I was supposed to train her too.

"It's just temporary, Red. Until you can get your shit together," they told me. 'They' being the management team. I smiled about it, blaming it on the fact that they were jealous of my success. This new 'Brittany' hadn't been offered to go to New Orleans to work in an establishment as nice as Lover's Cabaret. But, I guess for Pete's, she was enough. Oh, well. Out with the old and in with the new.

There was talk that I was struggling with my addiction. I'd fainted on stage and they blamed it on the drugs. In all reality, it was my blood sugar. I'm sure if they were to research my family history, they would find it was common. I'd also accused a few people of stealing my stuff. It was true, I just knew it. There was no way I snorted all that blow in one night. I'd trashed the dressing room and that earned me a week without pay.

But, just like they always did, they turned to their 'go to' girl when shit got busy. And that girl was none other than me, Red. As I dance, the saying 'There's no place like home' has no greater meaning than right now. My fans, my stage, my home. This is where I belong. Not in some fancy strip joint in New Orleans, but here back at Pete's with Lucy, Corey and the rest of the gang. The only thing I got out of New Orleans was a few extra bucks, a shitty lay and a lot of nights I don't remember. Oh, and Heroin. That little jewel I couldn't leave behind.

After rocking the entire room, earning double in one set what the other girls did all night, I figured I would be getting my job back. Brittany, being the sweetheart that she is, congratulates me on an awesome performance. I want to tell her to eat shit and die, but I refrain. To celebrate, the girls decide that I deserve a night on the town.

The Sunday following my kick-ass performance we decide to do something out of the norm for us. We didn't want to go to another club, we wanted something a little more subtle and normal. So, dinner and a movie it is. Carmella, a veteran stripper just like me, and Lucy chose the restaurant, a bar and grill. Brittany-evil little bitch-chose the movie. A romantic comedy. I have a feeling I am gonna need an extra bump just to get me through without choking the shit outta her.

The girls pick me up from my house around six-thirty. Dressed in white jeans, rope wedge sandals and a sheer, neon pink sleeveless top, I am ready for my night on the town. Flipping my long, red hair over my shoulder, I take a minute to model for the girls when they tell me how amazing I look. I'd be lying if I said I didn't take extra care in getting dressed just to outshine Brittany. She still looks amazing in her black jean shorts and white blouse, but she doesn't hold a candle to me.

I am three vodkas in when I notice the beautiful redhead walking hand in hand with none other than Devil's Renegades Regg. I take a moment to take her in, noticing that she is about my height, my size and has long, red hair that she wears in waves down her back. Just like me. Is it a coincidence? Regg is dressed in a black Henley and jeans that are ripped from wear, not because he bought them like that. Something about this makes them even more sexy. His blonde hair sticks out of the sides of his plain, black cap, and he looks like he hasn't shaved in a few days. I watch the muscles in his forearms flex as he pulls a chair out for the girl before taking the seat across from her, putting his back to me.

"Red," Lucy says, elbowing me to get my attention. "What the fuck? You look like you've just seen a ghost." Maybe in some way I have. Was this God's way of telling me that the girl could have been me in a different life? I order another drink, forcing myself back into the conversation at the table. But, strip club gossip and talk of Justin, the new bartender, isn't enough to keep me focused. My eyes wander back over to the table where Regg and that *damn girl* are sitting. I'm not jealous. Not even a little bit. For some reason, I'm just sad.

I duck my head under our table, pull out the small baggy and stuff a little powder under my long acrylic pinky nail. I inhale it, and then run my finger along the inside of the bag, gathering a little residue before rubbing it over my gums. By the time I come back up, I feel the sadness leave. Now, I'm happy for Regg. I look over at the girl one more time, watching how her eyes light up when Regg talks to her. She seems nice enough, and I'm glad he found someone worthy of him.

To show off a little, I pick up the check, slapping down a hundred before anyone has time to object. It's a fool move considering it's my light bill money, but I don't want Brittany to have any inkling of my struggles. Her gracious thank-you almost makes me want to puke, but I smile and wave it off like it's no big deal.

We exit out the side door to smoke before the movie. Doing this allows me to avoid Regg and the feeling is bittersweet. I want him to see me, but because I don't know what I would say, it is probably for the best that I steer clear of him.

"So, Red." I roll my eyes before painting a smile on my face to see what the fuck it is Brittany has to say to me. "LLC. Reckon you could hook me up?" It takes everything I have in me not to smack the shit outta her. I feel the tension around us grow thick as Lucy focuses her attention on anything that isn't us. Carmella, on the other hand, loves drama. She throws her hand on her hip, her dark hair swinging around her shoulder, as she waits to see if I need her to handle this shit for me. I shake my head and her full, red lips poke out on a pout. She loves going 'hood' on bitches. Or at least that's what she always tells me. She also took a week without pay when she helped me destroy the dressing room, looking for my 'stolen' goods. She was a ride or die and I owed her one for it.

"Luke isn't really the type to 'hook up,'" I say, using my fingers to quote her words. It was a lie, of course. Luke is definitely the fuck em' and leave em' type, but she didn't need to know that.

"Renee, a friend of mine, told me that his cock is huge. And he has this thing called a punishment fuck that leaves you walking funny for days. She says he'll ruin you for any other guy." She's way too excited. I have to end this now. No way am I letting Luke fuck the girl who has taken my place on the billboard next to the "Welcome to Biloxi" sign. Or the girl who has replaced my sexy voice on the radio. Or the one who is slowly but surely taking all of my customers.

"First off, Renee is a slut. She'll fuck anything. Second, Luke doesn't hook-up with my co-workers and third, you're really not his type." Lies, lies, lies. Well, one of them is. Renee is a slut and Luke doesn't hook up with my co-workers. But, Brittany is definitely his type. Long legs, long hair and a big mouth were the only credentials you need to fall in to bed with Devil's Renegades LLC.

"Well, tell him I asked about him anyway. And let him know, that if he ain't the hook-up type, I'm totally open to settling down with someone like him." Brittany is a heartbreaker. It is written all over her. Even if I didn't hate her, I would do everything in my power to keep her away from Luke. She is the kind of girl he could fall in love with. And then I'd have to kill her-which isn't entirely a bad idea.

"I'll let him know," I lie, flicking the butt of my cigarette dangerously close to her pretty little feet.

"I say we go get our tickets," Lucy, my lovely peacekeeping friend suggests. It's the best idea I've heard all night.

Walking through the thick glass doors of the mall, I'm too invested in my conversation with Carmella to notice who is also standing in line to get tickets. But, like always, he makes his presence known whenever he's around.

"Red?" Regg asks, pulling my attention to him and the girl wrapped around his arm. Damn, she's pretty. His eyes move up and down my body, silently appreciating what he sees. When he reaches my face, I can't help but beam at him.

"Hey Regg!" I say, my enthusiasm not the least bit forced. He pulls away from the girl to give me a tight hug.

"You look good. You ain't tryin' to get skinny on me, are ya?" I laugh at his words. I've lost a little weight, but hardly anyone has noticed. Considering I haven't seen Regg in a couple of months, it figures that he would.

"Never!" I let him hold me at arm's length, enjoying the way he looks at me, and the bubbles of excitement in my belly. He seems to remember where we are and releases me, turning to introduce me to his date.

"Red, this is my friend Taylor. Taylor, this is my friend Red." I don't like the way he said 'friend' about me or her. There was an underlying meaning to the term on both our parts. I flash a smile, taking her fragile hand that I could easily break. Judging by her handshake, this girl doesn't have a backbone. I am sure that if she thought she could disappear, she would. She looks intimated. Good.

"Nice to meet you, Taylor. Watch out for this charmer. If you ain't careful, you'll be falling in love." I wonder if Regg used that line on her like he did on me. Judging by his nervous laughter, he didn't.

"It's really nice to meet you too." Her niceness is genuine and should have me feeling like shit for hating her. But, I don't. For some reason, I can't get the thought that it should be me with Regg out of my head.

"Red! Come the hell on before all the good seats are gone," Carmella calls, pulling me back to the real world where I am a stripper out for a normal evening and Regg is a normal guy out doing normal shit with a normal girl who could probably offer him a hell of a lot more than I could.

"See ya around, Regg." I give him a wink and he rewards me with that sexy ass smile of his.

"Be good, darlin'." Darlin'. I wonder if he calls *her* darlin'. Probably not. He probably just calls her Taylor or 'hey girl.' This thought has me happy and leaving him with the comfort of knowing that the special word, is reserved only for me.

"You want some popcorn, darlin'?" You've got to be shittin' me. Only five minutes have passed since I've seen them and now, here they stand, behind me in the food line. And he's calling *her* darlin'. I want to throw this big ass, gut-busting coke that is sure to give me a kidney infection in his face. I want to order all the popcorn so him and 'darlin'' are forced to eat snowcaps and M&M's. Chances are though; those are her two favorite things. I force a smile on my face and turn to look at the picture perfect couple.

Her arm is looped through his and his hands are shoved down in the pockets of his jeans. Damn, he looks good.

"You following me, Regg?" I ask, flirting like the psycho slut bitch I am.

"Always, babe." Babe. We're back to the formalities. Calling me babe is like calling me by my given name. Nothing special about that shit. I don't respond, I just fake a laugh and saunter away, swinging my hips so hard I'm surprised I don't knock one outta socket.

"Who is *that* guy?" Brittany asks, and really, she shouldn't have. It's enough that's she's taken the spotlight. Then, she wants to hang out with my friends. Then, she asks about Luke. Now, she wants to take the only thing that's rightfully mine, but yet I don't have. And if I can't have him, nobody else will either. Except for maybe Taylor. I can't do shit about her. Well, I could, but I'd probably go to jail.

"That *guy* is none of your fucking business," I snap, earning me a look from both Lucy and Carmella. I stomp into the theatre, trudging my ass all the way to the back center seat. Lucy sits on my right, and Carmella takes the seat on my left, separating me from Brittany, or Top Cunt as I now plan to call her. When Regg and Taylor walk in, it's too much for me to handle. Because I was on the last row, any seat they take is below me, forcing me to look at them. When he puts his arm around her shoulders, it's my undoing. Without another word, I get up and leave.

    I can't make it to the bathroom fast enough and nearly rip a girl's throat out when she tries to step into a stall before me. Luckily, I only have to shoot her a murderous glare and she throws her hands up and steps back in surrender. Once inside, I dig through my purse, pulling out my compact mirror and spilling the remaining cocaine out onto it. I need something stronger, but I won't be getting my weekly supply until tomorrow, so this will have to do. I grab the pen from my purse, gutting it until I have nothing left but the plastic cylinder. I don't measure out a line because there is no need. Even though there is plenty, it is never enough.

    I flush the toilet, taking advantage of the loud noise to snort the powder from the mirror. By the time I leave the bathroom, I don't care about Brittany, or Taylor. And I damn sure don't give a shit about Devil's Renegades Regg.

Chapter Six
Goodbye Angel, Hello Demons

Last week

"Red!" Shit.
"You're up in five."
"K." One more dance. Just one more dance and then I can get the hell outta here. I tear through the endless supply of makeup, fake lashes and cosmetic jewelry covering my dressing table. *It has to be here somewhere.* I am still searching when Corey yells at me from the other room, notifying me of my two minute warning. Fuck it. I pull open my money drawer, sort through the bills until I find the straightest one with the least amount of ass sweat on it. I roll it tight, creating the perfect cylinder shaped straw, then lower my head to snort the line of powder that calls to me from the glass table top. Ahh... My guilty pleasure.

I stand, dab the corners of my eyes and grab my helmet. Before I step on stage, the numbness in my face starts to take effect. I can almost feel those tiny little endorphins dancing around in my brain. I picture them wearing Oompa Loompa costumes, their little legs working overtime to make sure they do their damndest to make me happy. I can't help but smile at the thought. I love those little fuckers.

"It's firefighter appreciation night, y'all. And we've saved the best for last. Ladies and gentlemen, put your hands together for the lovely Red." The emcee's announcement booms through the speakers, and the applause is deafening. They came here for a good show, and I'm a sure thing.

The sound of sirens fills the room as the song *Fire* by the Ohio Players has every drunken firefighter in the house fully amped. I look at Corey and shoot him a wink.

"Let's make it rain in this motherfucker." It's show time.

The management at Pete's has cut me back to three days a week and they are shitty days too. Dayshifts full of regulars who tip the minimum and bore you with small talk. I've lost a lot of weight. I've lost a lot of customers and almost everyone's respect. Oh well, their loss. I'm not doing anything to hurt anyone. I am just having a good time. My friends don't hang out with me anymore, but that is fine too. There is only one I miss. Luke.

Tonight, I am off the H and on the Cocaine. I need to bring my full game to prove I can handle it. I am filling in for Lucy who has come down with some sort of summer flu, and the weekend is too busy to be short someone. After the show, Corey informs me that the stage hasn't seen that much money on a Friday night since I stopped working it weeks ago. Now, I am sure I'll get my job back.

If I had listened to what else Corey was trying to tell me instead of chugging my drink and waving him away, I would've known that Luke was waiting for me in my dressing room. And had I known that, I never would've gone in there. But, I did and there he sits and the look he wears tells me that he wasn't impressed with what he saw.

"How you doin', Red?" he asks, clasping his hands so tight in his lap that his knuckles are white. I shrug and take another sip of vodka. "I thought you'd call when you got back in town." Instead of standing there like I should and just letting him talk, I do something I'll never forgive myself for.

"You know, I thought I might call too. But, I didn't. Wanna know why? Because I'm tired of snobby motherfuckers like you looking down their nose at me." I know it is a low blow, but the truth is, that bag of powder in the drawer right behind where he is sitting means more to me than he does in this moment. And all I want is to piss him off enough for him to leave so I can get what I've been craving since the last hit I took. Which was about ten minutes ago.

"I've never made you feel like you were beneath me. It's the voices inside of your head, your demons, that you're letting replace who you really are. You're-,"

"I'm, what?" I snap, cutting him off. "I'm the same person I've always been, Luke. This is all about me and my shortcomings. What about you? You don't think I know you're working for fucking Charlie Lott?" I watch in pure satisfaction as the horror registers on his face. Charlie is a known mafia affiliate who likes to use MCs as his enforcers. "That's right. Word has it you're his new bitch. What are you doing for him, Luke? I heard he had you-,"

"Enough!" Luke's on his feet and in my face in a split second.

"Looks like I struck a nerve." I smile at him, my angel. My angel who was once my friend but who is now a stranger to me.

"You don't know shit, Red. And even if you did, you're too fucked up to understand. If this is what you want, you got it. But, don't come crying to me when you hit rock bottom 'cause I won't be there." Even as he says it, I can see the regret in his eyes and hear the doubt in his voice. I wish I had a comeback to hurt him. I wish I had something to say to cut him. But I don't. I just hang my head in defeat and tell him the truth before walking away from the only true friend I have in this world.

"Don't worry, Luke. Hitting rock bottom is something I'm used to."

After that night, my life became what I knew it was always destined to become-worthless. I lost my job at Pete's. Turns out, I wasn't a fill in at all. It was their way of telling me goodbye. Corey encouraged them to let me have one more night of fame before they ripped the rug out from under me. What a night it was. After my shift, the management called a meeting, gave me two grand in severance pay and sent me on my way. It hurt. I'd given them five of my best years, only to have them shit on me at my worst.

I became more dependent on drugs and didn't care if the sun rose or not. I didn't know one day from the next or whether it was morning, noon or night. I'd lost not only my career, but my passion too. My shitty trailer became my prison. I would sometimes go days without food until Corey showed up and demanded I eat. I would as long as he made me one promise, to not tell Luke. And like the good friend he was, he kept his word.

The night I was arrested turned out to be the lowest point of my pathetic life. I'd run out of powder, money and booze. Chip promised to give me what I needed if I promised to show him and his friends a good time. I was out of practice, but dancing was in my blood. I knew I still had it in me to perform, and for a little Heroin, I'd do almost anything.

Dressed in a white, leather dress that barely covers my ass, and a pair of eight inch stilettos, I drive to the

Imperial Palace Casino to meet them. Two lines, three drinks and one lap dance later, things take a turn for the worse.

"I want you to fuck him," Chip tells me. 'Him' is a vein bulging, nostril flaring, steroid junkie who already has a problem keeping his hands to himself.

"I don't think so, Chip. I don't fuck people I don't know. I'm not a whore." Why I don't run, I'll never know, but I don't.

"You're a stripper. I'm sure you've sucked plenty of cock for an extra twenty and rode just as many for a little more. You've snorted a hundred dollars worth of shit tonight; I think you owe it to us both." This motherfucker has to be out of his mind. I grab my purse and head for the door, but 'Roid Boy' blocks my exit.

"Get the fuck outta my way," I growl, or hum, or lip sync. My ability to speak is diminishing rapidly. I have to get out of here before I end up ass raped by Chip and his friend. But even as my mind is telling me what to do, my body refuses to respond.

"Why don't you lie down and relax?" I'm nodding, my body already splayed out on the bed before I can register what is happening. I am floating. I can feel my dress being pushed up my hips and just the skin on skin contact is almost enough to make me come. It is the best high I have ever had and in that moment, I don't care what they do to me because I know it is going to feel amazing. Nothing can hurt me in this moment.

I feel my panties being slid down my legs, while Chip convinces me that this is what I want. I hear a ringing sound in my ears, a commotion in the room and moments later, I am alone.

I don't know how long I lie there looking at the ceiling, counting the swirls in the design of each tile. I don't know why the guys left, but as soon as my body can function, I know I have to get outta here. I need to be gone before they come back, or worse, the police show up. I get up, rake the remaining three lines of Heroin into the cellophane wrapper from my cigarette box, stuff my panties in the trash and walk out into the hallway of the Imperial Palace Casino Hotel.

I hitch a ride with a couple of guys from Hattiesburg that I meet on the Casino floor. Persuading them isn't hard to do. On the ride there, I give each of them a lap dance in the passenger seat-just like I'd promised. The only time we stop is for them to swap drivers. Because the drugs heighten the sensation I feel rubbing against them, I take my clothes off and dance for them naked. The feeling at the time is amazing, but the act is nothing shy of disgusting.

They drop me off downtown, outside of a small club that is already closing for the evening. The guy at the door lets me use the bathroom and I inhale half the baggie before stumbling back into the empty street. I don't know why I am in Hattiesburg. I don't know why I chose my hometown to be the place I visit tonight. Maybe it is in hopes of running into Luke and begging for his forgiveness. Maybe it is because there is nothing left for me in Biloxi. Or maybe it is divine intervention. Whatever the reason for me being here, possibly saves my life. Because when I round the corner, there the law sits. And here I am, dressed like a prostitute, at four a.m., higher than a Georgia pine and holding a baggie containing a line of pure, East Coast Heroin I would never get the privilege of snorting.

Chapter Seven
Court Day, Dooms Day, A Bad Day for Me

Present Day

"Case number 45874, the state of Mississippi vs. Denny Deen. Are all parties present?" The Bailiff's booming voice echoes over the room as I fidget with my hands. *If only I had something to calm my nerves.* I look down at my white, slip on shoes issued to me by the Forrest County Sherriff's Department. They're quite comfortable. I don't know why everyone bitches about them. And they totally match my neon orange jumpsuit and silver ankle chains. The handcuffs are a nice addition too. A cute hairstyle, some makeup and a little jewelry would make this a really nice outfit. Maybe I could use this in my next scene, if I ever decide to dance again.

I pled guilty to the charge of possession of a controlled substance even before they put me in handcuffs. There was no need in denying it. I was caught. When I got to jail Saturday morning, I refused to call anyone because there was no one to call. First thing this morning, they notified me that I would be going to court today. It is unusual, considering my court date should be at least thirty days out, but I am sure someone has pulled some strings somewhere. I just don't know who would do it.

I look up into the eyes of Judge Glen Harvey. He stares at me expectantly and I have no idea what he just said. I clasp my hands together, trying to contain their shaking and clear my throat.

"Sir?" I ask, forcing a smile.

"I see you plead guilty, Miss Deen." He sounds bored. He should be. We've done this several times. Only this time is a little different. I might have overstayed my welcome in his courtroom.

I am sure my sentence will go far beyond community service or a simple fine. This isn't my first offense, and I am pretty doubtful that he might shed any mercy on me.

I watch him study me for a long time, then remove his glasses and rub the bridge of his nose as if he really is struggling with his decision. I've seen this look once before when I paid him off. He didn't want to let me go, but money talks and bullshit walks. And my money talked me right out of the shit I'd gotten myself into. Now, I am broke and almost positive a bribe wouldn't work anyway.

"Miss Deen," he starts, then takes a deep breath while thumbing through a stack of papers I'm sure are my prior offenses. "Over the past five years, I've seen you in here more times than I care to count. Frankly, I'm tired of seeing you. It seems there is only one solution to your problem, and this time, you're not going to like it." I close my eyes, and try to control my breathing. The shaking in my hands is no longer a sign of withdrawal. Now, it's just nerves. I swallow the lump from my throat and open my eyes to find the Judge focused on something in the back of the room. The hair on the back of my neck stands up as I slowly turn to see what it is that holds the Judge's attention.

"Oh, shit." I hear the words as I say them but nobody seems to notice. Or maybe I don't notice that they notice because I can't take my eyes off the men sitting in the back of the courtroom. Luke Carmical is here in all of his six foot two glory and standing next to him is none other than Devil's Renegades Regg. But today, Regg isn't a biker. Today, he is dressed in a blue, long sleeved, button down shirt, tucked into a pair of jeans that hug him in all the right places. A mess of blonde hair covers his head and is a shade lighter than the neatly trimmed goatee that surrounds his mouth. His face is serious but his brown eyes are soft, and I'm sure that's not for me. I haven't seen Regg in months and after the way I treated his best friend, I'm sure he isn't too happy with me.

Luke looks impeccable as always. His face is impassive and I'm thankful he's here. It's probably just to watch me crash and burn, but that's okay too. I feel my face redden when I think about my own appearance. I've been in custody for two days and Friday's mascara still clings to my eyelashes. My hair is a grease pit oily enough to fry chicken in and I'm pretty sure I smell like the dead. I was offered a shower, but I'd refused. Once I found out I was going to court, the smart-ass deputy wouldn't let me go back on my decision. I guess it was his way of paying me back for calling him a limp dick prick.

"Miss Deen," the judge says, demanding my attention. "I think the best option for you at this point is a work program that works with our youth, and is headed by a good friend of mine." When the word 'friend' leaves his mouth, his eyes look to the back of the room, causing my spine to straighten. Luke has paid him off. It sounds wonderful-my best friend spending his hard earned money to get me out of jail. But, I know my freedom will come at a price for me too. One I am sure, I am not ready to pay.

"Your honor." The judge looks at me and this time I start pleading for something I never thought I would. "I would rather serve my time in county." It isn't so bad there. The food is decent and I already know I can get something for my nerves inside. Going without drugs for almost forty-eight hours is already having an effect on me.

"Really? And why is that, Miss Deen?" The judge seems somewhat surprised by my request and I use this to my advantage. I force the tears to burn my eyes, but hold them so that they don't spill over. I don't want to overdo this.

"I've done some pretty bad things in my life. It's no secret that here lately I've acted in an unruly manner." I fake a sigh, replaying my words in my head. Yep. They were good. I fidget with my hands before letting one lone tear fall down my cheek. "I deserve to do my time. It's not fair for anyone else to be responsible for me. It's time that I suffer the repercussions of my actions." Perfect. Damn, I should have been an actress. But, the truth is, I will do anything to stay away from Luke. I'm not ready to give up my way of life. Just the thought of Luke forcing me through his version of rehab has my heart nearly beating out of my chest. And I damn sure don't want Regg to see the hell that is sure to ensue when I hit rock bottom. I've been there before. It's nasty. I would rather just do my year in county, where I'll make trustee in thirty days and spend the rest of the year washing cop cars and running the dispatcher's errands.

The judge slams the file in his hands shut and repositions himself in his chair. "I don't think you realize what you're up against, girl." Well, there go the formalities. "You think a drug as powerful as heroin in the possession of someone with a record like yours is only going to earn you a year on easy street? I'm thinking three to five upstate." Upstate was Central Mississippi

Correctional Facility. Or CMCF. Or Parchman for women. Or bad fucking news. However you want to look at it.

I feel that lump of bile I've been swallowing creep back up my throat. I feel tears burn the backs of my eyes and this time, they're not forced. I stare at the floor, but the softness in the judge's tone has me looking at him once again.

"You need help, Denny. You don't deserve to be locked up with criminals. You deserve another shot at life. You're a good person with a good heart. I know life has been cruel, and because of that, I am going to do what I believe is in your best interest." His pockets are lined, and his decision is made. There's no need to hold my breath in anticipation of what he's fixing to tell me, but I hold it anyway. Maybe I will pass out and they will take me to the hospital where I will escape and move to California. And I won't be running from jail or Regg, I'll be running from embarrassment. It's bad enough that I'm in this situation. I didn't need my life story out for everybody to hear. I don't want pity, and I'm sure if I were to look around, pity would be on every face in the room.

"Denny Deen, I hereby sentence you to community service through the Youth Challenge Work Program under the direct supervision of Reggie Rawls for the next ninety days." My head snaps up at his words. Reggie Rawls? Could him and Devil's Renegades Regg be one in the same? The judge continues speaking, telling me the hours I will have to devote to the program, the days I'll have to spend under supervision. Regg's supervision.

"You will report to a clinic of my choosing for scheduled drug tests on the first and third Tuesday of every month with the possibility of random testing, also at my time of choosing." Ninety days. Ninety fucking days. I know the program is bullshit. If it exists, I won't be attending it. If the club has paid off the judge, he would have just dismissed my case; saying it was under false pretenses or some other bullshit. "If at any time you test negative on your drug screening you will be immediately sentenced to serve out a minimum five year term at the Central Mississippi Correction Facility for Women. Case dismissed."

    The slamming of the gavel causes me to jump. He just sentenced me to my doom. Parchman might have been the better choice. I don't know what is scarier, three to five years in the pen, or three months in hell.

    I ride back to county in the back of a cop car while the paperwork is being processed. There, they give me the clothes I was brought in with to change in to. I look down at the skimpy, white dress that looks more like a tube top and frown. Next to it lies my eight inch platform stilettos, an array of cosmetic jewelry and a half empty pack of Marlboro Lights. I look pleadingly at the woman behind the cage and she offers me a sad smile.

    "Take the clothes, honey. But you can wear what you have on home." I offer her what I can manage of a grateful look and gather the items in my arms. Regg is waiting for me when I walk outside, but he doesn't say anything. He walks me around to the passenger side of a lifted, Chevy Z71 and opens the door while I climb in. Without asking, I let down the window and light a cigarette. The hot September air blows against my face as I close my eyes and let the nicotine calm me. The radio is on, the truck is loud and the wind is howling. But, I can't hear anything over the one question screaming inside of my head.

    How the fuck did I get here?

Chapter Eight
Who Needs Rehab When You Have Regg-hab?

"Red." The sound of my name on Regg's lips wakes me, and I open my eyes to see a large, white house looming in front of me.

"Where am I?" I ask, sleep still thick in my voice.

"Home." Home is a trailer with no skirting and a leaky bathroom faucet. This is not home. Memories of court and the shit Regg and Luke pulled has anger building inside of me. Who the hell did they think they were?

"Let's get one thing straight, Reggie." I draw out his name as I turn sideways in the truck to look at him. "This is not my home and you are not the boss of me. Nobody asked you to do what you did. So, whatever shit you and Luke have brewing stops now. I'm calling my friends, they're coming to get me and I'm leaving." Immediately I start searching for my cell phone that I already know I don't have. Fuck it. I'll walk.

"Let me give it to you straight, Denny. This is your home for the next ninety days. I may not be your boss, but I am responsible for you. You're right. Nobody asked me to do this, I offered. Luke is my brother and I'll do anything in my power to help him. You don't have any friends. Those junkies you were hanging out with, they probably don't even realize you're gone." I glare at Regg, my hazel eyes challenging his brown ones that are full of determination and something I know so well-disappointment.

"Fuck you." I jerk on the handle of the door, my clammy hands fighting with the lock as I struggle to get it open. I feel sweat bead across my upper lip as I try to focus on opening the door and not ripping the son of a bitch off the hinges. I know the drugs are almost out of my system. I can already feel my body starting the grueling process of withdrawal.

Anger consumes me, blinds me and has me beating on the window screaming when the door opens. I fall out of the truck, thankful for the seatbelt that keeps my face from hitting the gravel. But it's not a seatbelt holding me. It's the huge ass forearm of Reggie fucking Rawls.

"Let me go!" I scream, finally finding my footing and pushing against his chest. His arm releases me and he takes a step back, his face completely void of emotion. "Just leave me alone!" I step forward, giving his chest another shove that does nothing but cause pain to shoot through my wrists. I turn from him, stumbling down the long driveway that seems to go on for miles. When the world around me begins to blur, I slow my pace and then have to stop all together to keep from passing out. Shit. If I just had a bump. Just one. I could get through the rest of the day. I could walk right out of here and back to my life.

"In less than an hour there are gonna be a whole lot of people here, Red. So either you can come inside and deal with this shit, or you can try to run. But, there's only one way in and one way outta here, babe. And unfortunately for you, that same road you're taking to leave, they're gonna be drivin' down very shortly." I place my hands on my knees, gulping in mouthfuls of air that never seem to quite make it to my lungs.

Sure enough, the Youth Challenge Work Program was bullshit. The only program I would be attending was the 'Devil's Renegades We'll Get You Off That Shit' program and it was under the direct order of Regg. This was the pisser of club life. Nothing happens that everybody doesn't know about and everybody wants to help. And they would be here, all of them-telling me they love me, telling me what a fuck-up I am and promising me that they would be here if I needed them. Because there is no one else to take my anger out on, I spin on my heels and focus all of my rage on Regg.

"Why would you do that? You don't want to help me, you want to make me look like a fool." Even from a distance I can feel Regg's tension. His eyes narrow and he starts towards me.

"I would never make a fool out of you. And to prove it, I'm gonna do for you what you obviously don't have the willpower to do for yourself." He dips and his shoulder connects with my stomach in one swift motion. The sudden movement has my stomach flipping and I open my mouth in hopes of vomiting all down the back of Regg's jeans. When nothing happens, I start screaming, kicking and punching him with as much force as I can manage.

"You motherfucker! Put me down! I hate you! I fucking hate you!" I'm like a cat that's been backed in a corner. I'm pissed and I'm coming out fighting. I do everything in my power to hurt Regg with not only my fists, but my words too. I tell him what a piece of shit he is. I tell him he is dead to me. I threaten to take his life. I scream so loud that my throat hurts, but the pain makes me feel like a fighter, so I scream louder. My head bobs back and forth. The rushing of blood to my brain causes a heavy ache behind my eyes. But still I fight. I watch the strands of my stringy, dirty hair sway back and forth in front of my eyes, and that pisses me off too.

These people-my family are coming to see me, and instead of supporting me from a distance, they are gonna be up close and personal while I'm at my worst. And I hate them for it. But right now, I hate Regg more. My fingernails dig into his ass. Between my screams, I try to lock my teeth on anything within reach, but I can never make contact. I hear the sound of water and look down to see the white, claw feet of a tub.

"What are you doing? Stop!" I scream, but it's useless. I'm flipped back over and before I can adjust to my upright position, I'm drenched in a spray of freezing cold water. My breath is taken from me as I fight against the strong arms that force me to remain in the tub. The water is so cold it hurts, but the shock of it clears my head and reality seeps back in. When I can form words, I stutter out a plea that I pray like hell doesn't fall on deaf ears.

"P-please." Instantly, the cold water is turned off. I dig my nails into the arm around my waist, using it as a support while I try to catch my breath. Warm water pools at my feet, filling the tub. With his arm still around my waist, Regg guides me until I'm sitting, completely submerged in the water that does nothing to keep my body from shaking. My eyes zone in on the stainless steel faucet in front of me, focusing all of my attention on it and nothing else.

I don't know how long I sit there, but eventually I regain control over my breathing. I'm still shaking, and it's not from the cold. This is my body's reaction from the lack of heroin. Soft, brown eyes come into view and they are still just as determined as they were before. But there is no disappointment in them, only promise.

"You're gonna get through this, Red. I know it." I stare at him, feeding off of his faith in me and trying to find some in myself. I concentrate on his face until he becomes nothing but a blur. Then the tears start to fall. I try to blink them away, but they pour down my face in hot, heavy streams that sting my cheeks. "I'll stay and help you if you want me to." I feel my eyes widen in panic. Just the thought of being alone in this moment with only me and my demons has my grip on his arm tightening further.

"Don't leave me," I manage, hoping he sees the desperation in my eyes. And for once, hoping that he takes pity, something I've never wanted from anyone, on me and stays.

"I'll stay. I promise. But, you have to let go of my arm." A slow, sexy smile moves across his face and my eyes follow his down to my fingernails that are dug deep into his skin. I loosen my hold and he removes his arm, but keeps a reassuring hand on my leg. I let him strip me, bathe me, and wash my hair while I turn my attention to the slow, steady drip of the faucet.

Drip.

Drip.

Drip.

Even when I'm wrapped in a towel and lifted into his arms, I envision that faucet. I sit on the edge of a bed, my eyes staring off into nothing, while Regg dries my body that suddenly feels battered and bruised.

"I don't want to see anyone," I say, looking down at him as he kneels between my legs to dry my feet.

"I know." He doesn't look at me. He just continues his task before standing and slipping a t-shirt over my head. Taking a seat beside me, he readjusts his hat and lets out an exaggerated breath. "They're coming because they care. I know that's not what you want to hear, but you need to at least make an appearance. This is your family, Red, and they're not going anywhere." I pick at the red polish on my acrylic nails, feeling a small hint of satisfaction at each piece I manage to flick off. "Tell you what. I'll make you a drink and maybe that will help calm your nerves a little." Just the mention of a drink has me off the bed and heading downstairs.

For the first time, I notice Regg's house. It's a colonial style home that is void of any décor. The walls are white, the floors are hardwood and each step creaks and groans as I make my way down them. I push through a swinging wood door and find myself in a massive room that stretches the length of the entire house. Deer mounts line the walls along with turkeys, a hog, several bobcats and too many guns to count. A camouflage sectional is centered in the room in front of a T.V.. To the right of it is a massive brick fireplace and to the left a pool table and a loveseat. In the corner of the room, an array of liquor bottles line a mini bar and I can almost smell the vodka before I even see it. Without bothering to look at the label, I grab the first bottle I see and start pushing on doors until I find one that leads to a kitchen. I open almost every white, wooden cabinet door before finding the glasses. I drop a couple of ice cubes in it, fill it to the brim and throw back the entire glass before making another.

"I was thinking coffee, but vodka will work too, I guess." I find Regg propped up against the small table in the center of the room. He is giving me that damn smirk and from his finger dangles a pair of black, basketball shorts. I move the glass away from my lips long enough to look down and see I'm only wearing one of his shirts. Throwing back the remaining vodka, I snatch the shorts off of Regg's fingers and pull them up my legs. When I reach back for my drink, it's gone. My eyes swarm the kitchen, looking for the small, empty glass that is ready for a refill. "You've had two, Red. I think that's enough." Immediately, my vision fogs.

"Regg," I start, pulling my bottom lip into my mouth and biting to try and contain my temper. I squeeze my eyes shut and ball my fists. I try to count to ten, but I'm too pissed to remember what comes after three. I try to think of the leaky faucet, but the clear water only reminds me of what I'm being refused. I open my eyes, locking them on Regg and mutter one word that packs so much meaning; I know for sure he will get the message. "Don't." He stares back at me for a moment before taking the bottle in his hand and walking out. Because there is nothing in here to throw, I turn to follow him into the only room in this fucking house containing shit I can destroy. I scan the room, figuring I could start with that big ass wild boar hanging on the wall.

"Let's compromise." I spin around to find him standing behind me, my glass in one hand and a bottle of vodka in the other. "I'll let you have another drink now if you'll drink something that doesn't contain alcohol while everyone is here. When they leave, if you want, I'll let you have another."

"I'm not a fuckin' kid, Regg," I snap, feeling my hands fist as I curl my toes into the rug.

"No, Red. You're an addict. And I'm not gonna let you swap one addiction for another. I'm not trying to sound like a dick, it's just the facts. The vodka will never be enough. It doesn't matter how much you drink. You'll wipe out every bottle in here and start drinking mouthwash trying to get that high you're craving right now. So, that's the deal. Take it or leave it." Everything he says is matter of fact. No humor, and no fucking compromise. It's his way or no way. And as much as I don't want to give in to his offer, I have no choice. I need something right now. It's either that or me and the pig is fixing to have a pissing contest.

I walk over and snatch the glass from his hand. He pours the drink and I have an urge to take the bottle and hit him over the head with it. The only thing that stops me is the scent of the alcohol and the water that builds in my mouth. I knock the glass back, being sure to drain every drop before handing it back to him and wiping my mouth with the back of my hand in a very unladylike way. Who the fuck am I kidding? I've never been a lady.

"I like my coffee strong and sweet," I snap, hoping like hell he sheds mercy on me and spikes it with a little Kahlua.

"Funny you should say that," he says, that shit eating grin is back on his face.

"Why is how I like my coffee funny to you?"

"Because it's exactly how I like my women." He walks back to the kitchen and I'm glad he gave me a little insight in to his personal preference when it comes to females. It's reassuring to know that there is no chance of a connection between us. Because strong and sweet are the two things that in this moment, I am not.

Chapter Nine
Families of Leather Stick Together

"Damn, I've missed my sexy bitch." My face is buried in Brooklyn's neck and has been for the last five minutes while she tells me she misses me over and over. "It's been too damn long since I've seen you. I just hate it has to be like this." Brooklyn is the wife of Ronnie, Devil's Renegades President, Lake Charles chapter. She stands nose to nose with me at about five foot seven, is covered in tattoos and has lips that are always painted some shade of red.

Brooklyn is the mother I never had. She is the friend I can call anytime to confide in. And she is the MC sister that has my back-always. I've done a pretty good job of making a mess out of life over the years and she has always been there to pick me back up when I fell. Today is no different. But, not only is Brooklyn my confidant, she is the one who has no problem telling me to get my life together. She has a way of making me feel like shit when she lectures me, but she is the one who gets through to me when no one else can. And it might take me days or weeks, but I always call her to thank her for the advice, which is always exactly what I need.

I pat her on the back to keep my hands busy. She still has me held tight to her as if she's afraid I might run away. Which is exactly what I want to do. I want to claw at my skin. Pull out my teeth. Chew the paint off the walls-anything to give me just a hint of relief from the shit I'm feeling right now. My need for a line has never been greater. And I know it's fixing to get worse.

"I'll make you some coffee," I tell Brooklyn, pulling from her embrace so I can try something else in hopes of scratching this itch I have.

I wander off to the kitchen that is, thankfully, empty. Pacing back and forth, I wait for the coffee to brew. I wipe down the counters, rearrange the glasses in the cabinet, clean out the sink and then pace again. Nothing seems to be working.

The wooden door swings open and Ronnie walks in, beaming at me as if I'm the reason the sun shines every morning. Or why Vance and Hines pipes sound better than any other on Harleys. Or why sliced bread is now an option. But in reality, he is part of my family. And today, regardless of my short comings, my family is very happy to see me.

"Hey sugar," he drawls, leaning his long frame down to give me a peck on the lips. The chains of his wallet jingle as he makes his way across the kitchen to the coffee. The scent of leather and man invades the kitchen and it doesn't take me long to realize that Ronnie isn't the only biker in the room. The whole damn space is now filled with leather cuts, filled with brothers, filled with the desire to tell me hello.

Possum is here. His incredible laugh has always brought a smile to my face, but in this moment, I can't appreciate it. I find the strength to say hello and even ask about Punkin, his ol' lady. She is still doing time for killing her ex-husband, but he assures me she will be out soon.

Big Al, aka the 'gangsta' of the club, always has some joke about me dancing for him. But this time, he tells me the same shit they all will-'I'm here if you need me.' The words make me want to take that chain that dangles from his neck and choke him with it. I can actually see myself doing it, but thankfully Mary interrupts.

She's a little thing. Not even five feet tall and her head hits me right in the chest. I feel like I'm smothering her with my tits, but she swears they are a lot smaller than they once were. I want to say, 'no shit, Mary. It's because I'm a heroin addict and I like it better than food.' But, somehow I find the willpower to not say anything.

And they just keep coming. Kyle and Katina-the quiet one and the goofy one. Bryce-the massive one that hardly says anything, other than today of course. More and more keep finding me. And the more they talk, the more fidgety I get. The more I want to scream or pull my hair out. I don't even associate them with who they are and what they mean to me. Only what I hate about them in this moment. And I hate all of them. I want them to leave. Everything they say is heroin. Everything they wear is heroin. Everything I desire is heroin, and heroin is the only thing in this moment that I don't have.

Everyone has a breaking point, and I've already snapped before I realize that I've reached mine.

Throwing shit feels good. It's only a coffee cup, but when the shattered pieces silence the room, I feel like I can think a little clearer. Too bad it did nothing to calm me down.

"I can't do this shit!" I scream, to whoever in the hell is listening. Which is probably the whole damn house considering they are all in the kitchen. In my space. Aggravating the hell outta me. When I reach the front door, I hear Regg coming to my defense against someone. I hear him tell them to just give me some time. I also hear him say that there is nowhere I can go. But, that is a lie. I know exactly where to go. The hell away from here.

With my county issued slippers and my trusty cigarettes, I hit the road. Or driveway. Or fucking field. Whatever you want to call it. And when I get to the end of it, I have the option to go left or right. So, I 'eenie meenie miney mo' it and go right. The only thing around me is trees. Lots and lots of never ending tress. Then, I come to an open field with round hay bales sitting sparingly across it. It's beautiful, but I can't really appreciate it because I only have one thought on my brain.

Heroin. A fine, white line of powder that would take me less than two seconds to snort and less than twenty seconds to feel normal again.

I chew on the inside of my mouth for a while, grind my teeth for a while, pull my hair for a while and then I start to dance. And for the first time today, I feel slightly in control of my life. I'm at a crossroad with no signs. There are no houses, no sounds and no traffic. It's just me, four roads, a few cows, a couple hundred trees and the sky. I play the music in my head, one song leading into another until I collapse and lay face down in the road. Doing this gives me an idea.

I place my ear to the rough asphalt and listen for vibrations that might lead me to a highway. When I hear nothing, I crawl over to another road and do the same thing. And then another, and another. When I stand up, I realize how bad I've fucked up.

"Son-of-a-BITCH!" I scream to the cows across from me, drawing the attention of one for about three seconds before she gets back to her grazing. While I was lost in the moment of dancing and listening for traffic, I got turned around. Now, I don't know which road is what. They all look the same. Just fields, a few trees on a fence line and cows. I take a deep breath, lie back down on my stomach and try to listen once again.

I hold my breath, placing my ear to the ground once more and close my eyes. *Concentrate, Red. Concentrate.* Then, I hear it. Something. Whatever it is has me so excited I'm pressing my face so hard into the road that I know the rocks are going to leave indentions in my cheek. The sound grows louder and I get lost in it. It's comforting, almost like a lullaby. And then it's gone.

"What the hell are you doin'?" My eyes shoot open and I find myself face to face with a boot. I follow it up to a jean clad leg, over to a thigh, pausing for a moment on a wallet chain and then to the biggest damn forearms I've ever seen.

"Regg?" I ask, knowing already that it's him. He says a string of curse words under his breath before getting off the bike and lying next to me on the ground so that we are eye to eye.

"Red, what the fuck are you doin'?"

"I'm listening for traffic."

"What?"

"I'm listening for traffic. I'm trying to get to the highway." Suddenly, I feel sad. My body aches, my feelings are hurt and I just want to cry. "I can't do this, Regg. I can't. Please don't make me do this. Just let me go," I beg, wishing like hell a car would find its way down this road and just put me out of my misery.

"Just a few more days, babe. Then it will get better. I promise. I'd rather see you mad than crying, though. So whenever you need to vent, just vent. But, don't let yourself get depressed like this." I feel him rubbing my back and even that hurts. I squeeze my eyes shut, not wanting to look at him.

"I can't help it. I get so mad and then when my adrenaline wears off, I just get upset. My body starts to feel the results of my fighting and it hurts so ba-." My words break on a sob as I tuck my head into my elbow and let the ground catch my tears. "The only time I feel even half ass in control is when I'm dancing. I miss the stage so much. It's my home. It's my therapy." My rambling is incoherent to my own ears, but Regg assures me he understands.

We lay there a few minutes longer before I feel myself being lifted from the road. I wipe my face on my shirt once I'm on my feet, and finally take a look up into his eyes. The corner of his mouth is turned up in a sad smile, and he looks like he is contemplating something.

"Let's go back to the house. If you can make it through telling everyone goodbye, I'll convince them to leave. When they do, I want to take you somewhere. But first, you have to see Luke and you have to eat." Shit. I'd forgotten about Luke. He had yet to show his face. He was probably on his way back from getting my stuff, or using the excuse to come see me to get everyone together for a meeting. Either way, I'd avoided him but now I would have to look him in the eye. It wasn't something I was looking forward to.

I nod my head at Regg whose eyes have fallen to my legs. His frown has me looking down to find my kneecaps busted and bloody. While I'm surveying the damage, Regg takes my hands in his and turns them over to look at my palms. They too are scraped and bleeding.

"Were you crawling around on all fours or something?" The incredulous look he gives me has me not wanting to tell him the truth. But, the evidence makes it quite clear that's exactly what I was doing. I shrug my shoulders and he releases my hands on a sigh. I hear him mutter something about me not being concerned about my own well being or some shit while he climbs on his bike and extends his arm to help me on.

Because there is no sissy bar, I'm forced to wrap my arms around his waist as he speeds us back in the direction towards his house. My fingers are constantly busy, as are my toes. On top of that, I'm chewing on the inside of my cheek and tightening all the muscles in my body. By the time we make it back to the house, I'm over my sad spell and back to worrying myself sick over what my body is missing.

I don't know how he did it, but Luke manages to have everyone ready to leave as soon as we arrive. I don't even have to hug all of them. I sit on the porch swing and wave goodbye in the general direction of where they are all standing. The only words spoken are by Brooklyn who promises me that she will be back tomorrow, or sooner if I need her. I wish she would wait another week, but there is no point in asking. Brooklyn is going to come whether I want her to or not. That is the kind of sister she is-a loyal one. Despite how I might act or how much they get on my nerves, I need them. And good thing too, because just like Regg said, they aren't going anywhere. Through good times and bad, the Devil's Renegades MC stands behind their motto. Love, Loyalty and Respect.

Chapter Ten
Crow Eaters, Four Wheelers and Sunsets with Regg

After everyone leaves, Regg goes inside and I'm left on the porch with Luke. Alone. I sit on the swing, pulling my knees up and resting my chin on them. This position makes my injury from earlier quite visible to Luke's eyes.

"What happened?" He lights a cigarette and hands it to me before lighting one for himself. I'm hoping he will sit next to me so I can avoid looking at him, but he pulls a chair up so he is directly in my line of sight.

"I thought crawling around on the ground was a good idea." There is no point in lying. I was never good at it where Luke was concerned anyway. He raises his eyebrows but doesn't say anything. I flash him my palms and I can see the question on his face. My hands itch to pick at the dried blood on my knees, so I clasp my fingers together in an attempt to keep them still.

"I think that one still has some gravel in it," Luke says, pointing to my left kneecap. My fingers fly to it and I begin picking at the sore. "Don't pick at it," he admonishes, slapping my hand away from my knee causing my cigarette to fall to the floor.

"Well, why the hell did you even mention it then? That would be like saying 'hey Red, you got a booger in your nose' and then not expecting me to dig it out." This makes him smile as he hands me my cigarette. We avoid each other's gazes for a while. He concentrates on a rip in his jeans while I watch the slow, one sided burn of paper on my Marlboro.

When the silence becomes too much, I decide to break the ice and say what should have been said weeks ago. I suck at eating crow, but it looks like it's on the menu tonight.

"I'm sorry." My words are said in unison with Luke's. 'Sorry' is not something that we usually say we are. We apologize for things that we've done wrong, but in my case, sorry describes exactly how I've treated him. I guess he feels the same way. I pick at the nail polish on my toes, using it as a distraction and a form of coping now that my fingernails are free of color.

"I never should have said those things to you." I don't look at him when I say this, because I don't want to see the hurt in his eyes at the reminder of what I said. "I'm messed up, Luke."

"Tell me what happened, Red." His voice pulls me in and I stare at him through blurry, tear filled eyes. I can't lie to him anymore. Hell, I don't want to. But I'm not ready to talk just yet.

"I need some time. I'm bad today, but I'll be worse tomorrow. We've been through this. You know how I get, but this time it's worse. I've been on it heavy." I wipe my eyes, and turn my head to look out at Regg's massive yard. It's well kept, without a single thing out of place. When he said he lived on a secluded farm, I expected a double wide just outside of town with a yard full of chickens and lawn mower parts. Not all this.

"You take all the time you need." I hear him stand and then close my eyes as he puts his hand on the back of my neck and kisses my head, leaving his lips there for a long time. "I love you, Red." I stay like that until I hear his bike crank up. I open my eyes just in time to see the reaper on the back of his cut, before he disappears from view. And how I'm feeling right now makes me wish the real reaper would come for me.

***

Regg has cooked. I'm not hungry, but when I tell him this his reply is simple.

"Humor me."

Whatever. I take a seat at the table with him and nibble on one of the many biscuits that are stacked up before us. He has fried deer meat, biscuits and macaroni and cheese. The smell of the oil turns my stomach and I don't even attempt to try it. I get up from the table, feeling better the moment I step out of the kitchen. With my biscuit in hand and the lingering odor of fried meat no longer in the air, I curl up on the couch and force myself to eat the whole thing. Regg doesn't come looking for me and it's nice to know I can have a little space when I need it.

I move from the couch, to the floor, to the loveseat until I give up and start pacing the room. Back and forth. From one end to the other and occasionally around the couch to shake things up a bit. I chew my nails until I've managed to remove all the acrylic and my real nails are down to the quick. When I can't chew on them anymore, I start working on the inside of my cheek. My teeth clamp down on tiny bits of flesh and when I feel the skin tear, I get that small sense of pleasure. If I don't stop soon, there won't be any skin left. So, I start picking at the sores on my palms.

"We need to clean and bandage those," Regg announces. He's standing with his arms crossed over his chest, watching me pace back and forth.

"How long you been standing there?" I ask, never slowing my stride.

"Long enough to see that you are gonna wear a hole in the floor if you keep it up." He offers me a smile, and I stop for all of four seconds before my restless feet start again.

"I'm tired. I just want to sleep but I can't sit still." I haven't slept in days. A couple hours here and there have done nothing for me. It's a wonder I can still function. "Do you have any NyQuil?" I ask, pausing long enough to get excited at the possibility of sleeping my way through the next several days. He shakes his head and his news has me pacing again.

"Come on. Let's wrap those knees and hands up. I want to show you something." I follow him out of the den and up the stairs to the bathroom. "Sit," he says, pointing to the toilet while he rummages through an old medicine cabinet above the sink. I fidget nervously, trying like hell to sit still while he wipes the tiny pieces of gravel from my knees before pouring peroxide on them. "Hurt?" The slight sting is actually comforting, but I don't tell him that. I just shake my head. He moves to my hands before wrapping all four injuries in gauze and bandages. It's a little overkill. "I know it's extreme," he says, reading my mind. "But, if I don't wrap it up, you are just gonna pick at it and make it worse. Don't." He emphasizes his demand with a look that tells me he ain't messing around.

"Where are we going?" I'm ready to get the hell outta here. Maybe we will go to town so I can learn my way back to the city.

"You'll see. Luke brought your stuff. You wanna change?" I shake my head and he cocks an eyebrow but says nothing. He leads me back downstairs and out the back door. The yard is large, just as wide as the front, but surrounded by trees just a hundred yards out. We walk to a huge red barn that sits off to the left of the house. The scent of hay and manure invades my nostrils and my nose scrunches in protest. "Here," Regg says, handing me a pair of black, rubber boots. "These should fit. They're Sara's." I feel something spark inside of me. Anger maybe? Jealousy? I don't know why I feel the need to find out who this mysterious woman is, but my ability to filter what comes out of my mouth is forgotten.

"Who's Sara?" My tone isn't right. I sound bitchy. I meant it to sound more curious and less accusing. But I can't help it. First Taylor, now Sara? How many women has he been with?

"My cousin." Oh.

Thankfully, Regg is too distracted with putting on his own boots to notice my sudden bout of rage. I look down at the boots and frown. How old is his cousin? Ten?

"I can't fit these. They're like a size five." I hand the small boots back to Regg and he reaches on a shelf to grab another pair.

"Try these." I slip them on easily. They're a little big, but I can manage. "Better?" he asks, fighting a smile as he checks me out. I know I look hideous in his black t-shirt that hits me mid thigh, his basketball shorts that have been tied and rolled up to just above my knees which are covered in bandages along with my hands. And now, we can add rubber boots to my funky getup. I give him the finger and my 'you're an asshole' look. Flipping my hair over my head, I secure it into a knot that stands straight up in the air. Perfect.

I nearly choke to death when he first sprays himself with some kind of mosquito repellant, and then me.

"Damn, that's enough." I'm coughing, fighting to keep the shit outta my mouth and eyes and failing miserably.

"You'll thank me later." Not a chance.

"So, you really are a farmer." I look around the barn, taking in the stacks of hay bales, feed, tractors and random piles of manure.

"I am. Mostly chickens, but I do have some cows too." I look around, waiting for a chicken to strut by. "The chickens are in houses. They're not free range. Too many of them for that." He opens a door on the side wall and pulls out a rifle. Slinging it over his shoulder, he holds his hand out to me. "You ready?" I cross my arms and stare at him, not wanting to touch him after those feelings of jealousy woke up inside of me. I didn't need to give myself anymore reason to try and stake a claim on him. "Okay then." He drops his hand and starts walking. And I play right into my role of puppet by following him.

We walk to the tree line at the back of the yard and enter a small area of woods. A few minutes later, we emerge on the other side where eight long, white chicken houses take up a flat piece of land that is also bordered by tall pine trees.

"There's a road that leads to these over there," he says, pointing to the left. "But, this is a shortcut." Shortcut, my ass. I feel like we've walked for miles.

"You're not gonna make me work in the chicken houses are you?" I ask, stopping as the realization hits me.

He looks at me over his shoulder, never slowing his pace, and shoots me a wink.

"Not today, babe."

"Not ever, *babe*," I mumble, not loud enough for him to hear.

"I heard that." I roll my eyes and stomp after him, fighting the gnats out of my face with my hands. They don't even seem to bother him. "I just gotta check the computers. I won't be but a sec," he calls out, disappearing into one of the houses. The sun is just starting to set in the sky, and I can't believe everything that has happened today. Jail, court, rehab, family, talking to Luke, checking fucking chicken houses. I haven't accomplished this much in weeks, much less in twelve hours.

I start to pace, kicking gravel rocks until that gets old to me, then I start fidgeting with the bandage on my hand.

"Stop that," Regg says, emerging from the house and jerking his head in the direction of another. "Come on, we're gonna miss it if we don't hurry."

"Miss what?" I ask, confused as to not only what we're missing but why in the hell I keep following him like a puppy on a leash.

"You'll see." I round the corner and find Regg climbing up on an ATV. He throws the gun in the front rack and leans up, waiting for me to climb on. I clamber up, and soon we are speeding between the houses and towards the tree line behind them. We approach a mud puddle filled with water, and to my surprise, he doesn't slow down or look like he has any intentions of avoiding it.

"Hole!" I yell over the roar of the engine. I lean into him and point, knowing good and damn well he can see my extended finger and what it's pointing to. He slows down and I relax, but it's short lived. Just before we hit the wide span of water, he guns it. The impact causes the four-wheeler to slow, just as a spray of muddy, orange water drenches us both. I can hear his laughter echoing off the walls of the houses and I find myself, for the first time in a long time, laughing too.

There is a path through the thick woods just wide enough for us to maneuver through. Regg operates the four-wheeler with the same precision he drives his bike; moving perfectly through the tight space lined on both sides with trees and cut-over. It's darker in the woods but I can see the sunlight filtering in through the trees and I know we are near another clearing. When we break from the trees, we come out on a gravel driveway that leads to a small boat house. And then I gasp at what I see. A massive lake looms before us and I'm awestruck at the view.

Regg kills the engine and steps off. This time when he offers his hand, I take it. He leads us to the end of a pier that stretches out into the water and takes a seat, pulling me down with him. Our legs dangle over the side as we watch the last of the sun set over the trees.

I'm breathless as I struggle to take in the magnificence that surrounds me. The sunset reflects off of the water creating a perfect mirror image. It's overwhelming, mesmerizing and so serene that I can physically feel the peace as it engulfs me like a blanket. "I've never seen anything so beautiful," I whisper, not wanting the sound of my voice to take away from the tranquility of the moment. Fingers graze my cheek before tucking an errant strand of hair behind my ear. I feel him lean in closer, his lips only a breath away from my face.

"I have." And now I'm thinking it's not just the scene that has me breathless, but Devil's Renegades Regg too.

Chapter Eleven
Midnight Mayhem vs. Morning Madness

I'm shown to my room that I'm sure is lovely. But, my only focus is the bed that calls to me. When we got back, I immediately took a shower without any thoughts on what in the hell I would wear when I got out. Regg, who is on top of things, called to me and asked if I wanted him to get me something to sleep in. I asked for another t-shirt and when I opened the bathroom door, it was lying on the floor waiting for me. I've decided he's not a terrible host.

I collapse in the bed, not bothering to even turn a light on and take a good look at my surroundings. The smell of clean linen is comforting. The bed is soft, the covers thick and the air down low-just how I like it. Regg had told me that his room adjoins mine, but the door is locked from both sides. He would be leaving his unlocked in case I needed him. I seriously doubted I would. Right now, there was nothing he could do for me. I just needed to sleep. I toss and turn for almost an hour before my mind finally shuts off and gives in to the darkness.

***

Nightmares are something I'm familiar with. I've had them all of my life. Usually, I sleep until they wake me, then I find something to help erase the images in my brain. But tonight, they are different. They're real. Even when I open my eyes, the images are still there. Shadows dance across the room, their ghostly figures dark in contrast to the white walls. The moon is bright tonight, making the scene even scarier. I pull the covers over my head, but it doesn't protect me. The misty creatures float through the fabric of the comforter and into my hiding place.

I don't know who they are, but they want me. They want to possess me and steal my soul. These are the demons Luke warned me about.

Luke.

I need him. He would make them go away.

"Luke!" I yell his name, hoping that he can hear me. I know he can't because he isn't here. He is fifty miles away. I could drive to him. Even if they followed me, he wouldn't allow them to come inside. He would protect me like he always has. I call out for him again, hoping that the demons will get scared when they hear his name. The sound of heavy footsteps and the door opening has my hopes skyrocketing. Maybe he came to Biloxi tonight and decided to crash at my place.

"Hey," he says, his comforting voice thick with sleep and slightly different than normal. He must have had a long night. His arm comes around my waist and his body molds to mine, pulling me to him and making me feel small and safe-like he's done for years. The cover separates us, but I can still feel the heat of his skin against me. His presence has the demons disappearing one by one until the only people left in the room are the two of us. Just me and my best friend.

Luke's snoring in my ear wakes me and I elbow him in his side. He stops and pulls me tighter to him.

"Hmm?" he mumbles, burying his face in the back of my hair.

"Stop snoring." He freezes and I hear him clear his throat before getting up and leaving me. Luke is an early bird and I sleep till' noon. With my face buried under the covers, there's no way of telling what time it is, but my best guess is it's not even daylight. I drift back off and am just falling into a good sleep when the need for something has my eyes shooting open. It's like an itch I can't scratch. A toothache I can't cure. I can't quite put my finger on it, but I need something to make it better. I poke my head out from under the covers and blink my eyes several times. The white wall stares back at me, the craving in my brain and the clean smell of a home that I know is not mine, reminds me of where I am.

I slowly make my way outta bed, the muscles in my body so tired and worn that it takes every ounce of energy I have to make it to the bathroom. I feel like I have the flu, only it's worse. My body aches so bad that the pain throbs in places I've never felt pain before. Even my hair hurts. My hands shake and I'm covered in a sheen of sweat, yet I'm freezing. A hot shower does little to ease the torture, and I crawl back into bed praying that sleep finds me again.

But it doesn't. So, I lay here and survey the room. It consists of a bed, a dresser, two night stands and three doors. Everything is white except for the brown wooden floors and my lime green luggage. The windows are floor to ceiling and are only covered with a white, sheer curtain; allowing the early morning sunlight to pour in.

Dragging myself back out of bed, I flip open my suitcase in search of something to wear. But the scent of the clothes, the scent of home, turns my stomach, and I'm gagging all the way to the bathroom. I vomit until I dry heave and after several minutes of that, I take another hot shower. When I step out, I feel marginally better. Brushing my teeth, I throw on the shirt I wore last night and head downstairs.

I find Regg in the kitchen, talking to someone on the phone. He watches me as I walk around opening cabinets, the refrigerator, the oven and anything else I can get my hands on. I'm looking for something, but I don't know what. When he is off the phone, he allows me to make several more trips around the kitchen before addressing me.

"What you lookin' for?"

"Something. Anything," I say, while my head is buried in the refrigerator.

"I got you some cereal." His tone is soft, understanding and I wonder if Luke has talked to him about my past. I grab the jug of milk, a bowl and spoon and sit at the table. He turns his head to the side and observes me. It makes me feel like I'm some kind of science experiment and it pisses me off.

"What? What the fuck are you looking at?" I run my hands through my hair, pulling slightly on the ends to feel some kind of relief. It's like having an earache. There is nothing you can do for it, but if you pull on it, the pain is almost a relief. I put my hands on the table for a second before hiding them under it. When I look up to see if Regg noticed their shaking, I can tell he did. "I don't know what you expected to happen, but this is part of it. I can't control them. Just like I can't control my thoughts, my actions or anything else. So, either quit staring at me and show me where the fucking cereal is or be prepared to watch me start throwing shit." I snap my mouth closed, wishing I could contain my temper. The more worked up I get, the worse I feel.

Regg stands and opens a cabinet I know I've opened at least five times and pulls down a box of Fruity Pebbles. He starts to open it when I snap at him again.

"I got it. I'm not an idiot." He sets the box down before pouring a cup of coffee and returning to sit with me at the table. Fucking shit. Ugh. Doesn't he have something to do? Couldn't him and Luke find something to get into? "Where's Luke?" I ask, working like hell to open the box. I don't know why they made this shit child proof.

"He's at home. He'll be here later." I stop long enough to give him a confused look.

"What time did he leave?" It couldn't be later than seven in the morning. My mind goes back to the box in my hand. I get so frustrated, that I bang it on the table a few times before trying again. My hands are shaking so bad that I can't get my fingers to slow down long enough to pull the tab and open it.

"He left yesterday, Red. He hasn't been back." When I look up, his brows are furrowed and he's staring at my hands. He takes a sip of his coffee before finally meeting my eyes. "I was the one who slept with you last night. I didn't know what to do. Luke said sometimes you have bad dreams. You seemed better when I was there so I stayed." Well, that makes sense. I don't concentrate on the fact that sleeping in Regg's arms was comforting or how he held me and made me feel safe. I have too much other shit to worry about in this moment. Like this fucking cereal box.

I finally give up and begin banging it on the corner of the table until I make a hole in the side. I rip the cardboard away and come face to face with another problem. The damn plastic package inside of it. Regg grabs the bag from my hands, cuts the corner of it with a knife and hands it back to me. I bet he is one of those people that rush you to open presents too.

    I pour the cereal in the bowl, and on the floor, and the table before eyeing the jug of milk. Without a word, Regg grabs the jug and pours it for me, then fills up his own bowl. Well, at least eating will give him something to do other than stare at me.

    "I'm going to be gone for most of the morning. Brooklyn will be here." I don't know why, but the news of Regg leaving saddens me. I like that he seems to get me and all of my crazy ass ways. Brooklyn knows me better than he does, but there is something comforting about his presence that I've never found in anyone else. Not even Luke.

    Because I'm sad, I become angry.

    "I don't need a babysitter," I snap, already feeling nauseated from the three bites of cereal I have eaten. "And what's the matter? Bit off more than you could chew?" My goal is to hurt him. Just like he is hurting me, but he is undeterred.

    "No, I just have some stuff I need to handle. I'll be back this afternoon." I push away from the table, knocking my chair over and listening to the cereal crunch underneath my bare feet as I make my way to the den. My eyes scan the mini bar, looking for my other guilty pleasure. But, it's gone. Water bottles line the cabinet that held liquor bottles just yesterday. It feels like a slap in the face. I spin on my heels, ready to unleash on Regg, but a cramp in my stomach sends me to my knees. It feels like someone has stuck a knife soaked in gasoline inside of me. It's a burning agony, and each time my heart beats it feels like I'm being kicked in the ribs.

    "Red?" I hear Regg call from the kitchen, but I can't answer him. I curl into a fetal position on the cold, hard floor and wait for the excruciating pain to subside. It starts to ease just as he opens the door. "Shit," he says, running to my side. His first reaction is to pick me up, but I moan in protest.

"Don't touch me," I manage, trying to take small, shallow breaths. Breathing deep only causes the pain to worsen. In my awkward position, the pain slowly fades away, but I stay there in fear of it coming back. I shiver from the cold, and try to control the involuntary jerk of my arms and legs. This shit isn't worth getting clean. I would have rather died from an overdose than have to endure this.

A blanket is thrown over me and then Regg comes into my line of sight. He is lying on the floor beside me, just like he did on the road yesterday.

"Can I do anything?" This is what I like about Regg. He doesn't ask if I'm okay because he knows I'm not. He doesn't tell me 'I'm here' because it's obvious that he already is. He just does what he thinks needs to be done which is usually the right thing.

"Cramps." My one word is the only explanation he needs. He nods his head in understanding, propping it in his hand while he lies on his side.

"I watched my mom go through this. It was a long time ago, but I still remember. There was no one else to help her, so I had to. My brother was too little to even know what was goin' on." I listen to his story, watching as his eyes grow distant at the memory. "I've never told him about that. Lucky for him, he got out before he could even remember who she was."

"But you didn't get out?" Knowing that he was forced to take care of his mother when he was just a kid has me seeing Regg in a different light.

"I did, just not soon enough." I feel my insides twist from his confession and it has nothing to do with my body's reaction to the lack of drugs. It's because I feel pain for Regg. Familiar pain that I myself have felt when it came to being brought up in a shitty home.

I hear the front door open and Brooklyn announcing her presence. This sends Regg back to the present and he shoots me a wink and an encouraging smile. I give him what I can manage of one just before Brooklyn busts into the room. She is silent as she walks slowly through the den until she is right up on us. Without warning, Regg throws his hands up and yells something, scaring the piss outta her and me. Brooklyn screams and clutches her chest before hitting him with her purse, which he blocks easily with his arm.

"Holy shit! I thought y'all were dead," she confesses, giving a now standing Regg a hug. She puts her hand on her hip and looks down at me. "What you doin', baby girl?" Regg comes to my rescue and informs her of the sudden approach of a stomach cramp and the comfort I'm finding on the floor. "God love you. Have you had breakfast?" I nod up at her just as Regg says,

"About that." He grabs her elbow and steers her into the kitchen where I hear her gasp at the mess I made. Then she laughs and I smile knowing that even if Regg takes the day off, I'll be in good hands.

Chapter Twelve
Out of Sight and on My Mind

Regg leaves without even telling me goodbye. Brooklyn tells me it's because he didn't want to wake me, but since I wasn't asleep, I'm not buying it. Just because I was lying on the floor with my eyes closed doesn't mean shit. So, now my mood is worse than its been since I got here yesterday. I'm snapping about every little thing until eventually Brooklyn has to walk outside so I can keep my teeth. Or at least that's the reason she gave me. The last thing I want to do is piss her off, so after I walk through the house a hundred times, I decide I'm calm enough to join her.

"I apologize. I don't know what's wrong with me," I say, falling down into the swing. Brooklyn looks up from the book she is reading and peers at me over the top of her glasses. She is sitting in the same seat Luke sat in yesterday and I wonder if she did it knowing I would have to sit and face her. Sneaky little shit.

"You don't have to apologize to me, baby. I get it." Brooklyn has been in this life long enough that nothing surprises her. This isn't her first round with an addict either. The club firmly believes in taking care of their own, and I am not the first one she has helped get through this shit.

"It's hard knowing that I can make this all go away with something I use to have at my disposal for years." I rub my hands down my arms and legs, trying to relieve the irritation of my skin. It feels like tiny little bugs are crawling all over me.

"That's no kind of life for you, Red. I know you love to dance and none of us have ever looked down on you because of it. But, if the cause of your problems stem from your career, then maybe it's time to find something else to do with your life." Her words are wise and ones I need to hear, but I don't want to. I keep my mouth shut, afraid of saying something that I might regret. I want to scream at her, but I know it's only because of my situation, not because she is wrong.

"I think I'm gonna go take a shower," I say, ready to leave this uncomfortable situation and do something to relieve this fucking itching. I pause at the door, then go back to where Brooklyn is sitting and lean down to give her a hug. It doesn't last long, but it's full of meaning and the smile on her face shows me that she understands.

I spend the next several hours pacing the floors and looking outside every few minutes for any sign of Regg. Brooklyn cleaned the kitchen and offered to re-wash all of my clothes so they smell like here instead of home. If it weren't for the shaking and fidgeting and the nausea, I wouldn't even remember the fact that I'm going through withdrawals because my mind is focused on something else.

Regg.

I need him here. I know that it could possibly be that today is worse than yesterday and would have been no matter if he were here or not. But, I feel like I'm even more fucked up since he's gone.

By two o'clock, I can't stand it any longer. I stomp into the den where Brooklyn is watching T.V. and start shouting my demands. I don't want to take it out on her, but no one else is here.

"Regg hasn't come back yet and I need him here." Brooklyn starts to say something but I cut her off. "I don't give a shit how you do it, but you find out where he is and tell him to come home. I can't do this without him. I can't." My confession wasn't intended to sound so desperate and needy, but my lack of a filter doesn't allow me to say it any other way. Like all the other times, I've let myself get worked up for too long and my mood nosedives, sending me spiraling down into a depressing crash. I start to cry, right here in the living room, in front of Brooklyn, for no reason at all. I sob into my bandaged hands and allow her to lead me to the couch where she leaves me, but returns a few minutes later and lets me lay my head in her lap. I cry into her leg while she scratches my scalp with her long nails. It feels good and I'm debating what I want more. I don't know if I want to tell her to go find Regg like I asked, or for her to continue scratching my head. The dilemma has me crying harder.

"I can't do it, Brooklyn. I can't do it. Please, help me," I beg, wanting her to take me from this place and back to my life. "I'm an addict. It's what I'll always be. If it's not drugs, it's gonna be something else. I'd rather die than live like this." I shake and cry and scream in her lap, while she keeps a steady rhythm of running her fingers over my head.

"It's okay to want to some things, baby. And what you're craving now, isn't a bad addiction to have." I know she's not talking about the drugs. She's talking about Regg. But, it's the change that I didn't like. It's the fact that we started this journey together and only two days in, I need things to remain as they are. I don't need anything distracting me, like the lack of his presence. Because there is no way I could ever be addicted to a man I hardly even knew.

Could I?

Sometime during my breakdown, I fall asleep. When I wake up, I'm still lying on the couch, but Brooklyn has repositioned us so that I'm lying against her arm instead of her leg. She is behind me, and her hand is no longer scratching my head, but rubbing my hair. I close my eyes and concentrate on the movement of her hand that starts at my forehead and stops halfway down my back.

"I'm sorry I lost it. Again," I mumble, knowing that she will understand.

"You're not sorry. And it's my fault." The voice that speaks to me is not Brooklyn's. It belongs to Regg. My cheeks flush with embarrassment as I remember the things I said. Brooklyn must have called him at some point and told him to come home. He keeps rubbing my hair and I keep letting him do it. No point in trying to have any dignity now.

"I shouldn't have left. I wasn't expecting to stay gone so long. It won't happen again." And I believe him. If I didn't know anything else about Regg, I know he was a man of his word.

"I'm hungry," I say, more to change the subject than anything. I know I need to try and eat something. Food is the last thing on my mind, but I'm sure I've burned a thousand calories by pacing all morning. I can't afford to lose any more weight. I've avoided a mirror like the plague, afraid of what I might find.

"What you feel like eating?"

"Anything, just as long as it ain't fried." I feel him shake with laughter before he kisses my head and moves out from behind me. The intimate gesture has butterflies floating in my belly. When Luke does it, it just feels natural...brotherly. With Regg, it's so much more.

Without his hands on my hair or his body next to mine, I find myself becoming anxious and lonely. I yell out that I'm going to take a shower as I make my way upstairs for my fourth bath of the day. It is the only time, other than when I am asleep, that I don't feel like my skin is crawling.

Brooklyn has washed, dried and put away all of my clothes. Luke must have cleaned out my entire closet and when I walk in the bathroom, I find that he cleaned out my vanity too. Brooklyn has also unpacked my cosmetics and lined the basket in the tub with my favorite body wash and shampoo. I pull the curtain around the tub and turn the water on as hot as I can stand it. By the time I'm finished, I smell like pomegranate and my skin is red and steaming.

I brush back my hair and wipe the steam from the full length mirror that hangs on the back of the door. I feel my eyes brim with tears at the sight of the woman staring back at me. My breasts are smaller, at least two full cup sizes smaller. My once curvy body is now a straight line of hip bones and ribs. My collar bone juts out of my chest and my eyes look dull and sunken. My knees are starting to scab over, as are my hands, and they are a reminder of the extreme measures I've taken to get back to the life that made me this way.

"Red? You okay?" Regg asks from the outside of the bathroom. I grab my towel and wrap it around me before opening the door to show him I'm okay. I would have answered, but I didn't in fear of my voice cracking and sending into another sobbing hysteria.

He doesn't pay attention to my body, only my face as I stand there shifting from one foot to the other.

"What's wrong?" What isn't wrong? But instead of telling him, I show him. I let the tears fall from my eyes as I open my towel up to reveal my body. He's already seen it, of course, and he is well aware of the transition. He's seen my body at its best over a year ago, and at its worst just yesterday. He turns his head for a moment and I fear it's out of disgust. "Red," he says, meeting my eyes with his that are full of compassion. "I don't care what you think about yourself. You're still beautiful to me, babe." His words are sincere, but they do nothing to make me feel better.

"Look at me. Look at what I've done to myself." Instead of looking at me, he pulls me into his arms. I'm not expecting the gesture, and I'm not expecting to enjoy it this much either.

"All that matters now is that you get better. Nobody is going to be looking at your body but me. And what I see is a beautiful woman that even at what she thinks is her worst, outshines most women's best." I hug him tighter as I let his words warm my heart. Nobody will see me but him. And he thinks I'm beautiful.

He holds me until I can't stand still a moment longer without losing it. And my mood swings are so crazy that I don't know what losing it entails. I might start crying, biting or laughing at any moment. So I pull away and move to my room. I take one look at the clothes in my closet, and then back over at the bathroom where Regg is still standing. He smirks knowingly and disappears for a moment before returning with another one of his t-shirts.

"I just like wearing it, ya know?" I ask, hoping he understands. He smiles and slips the shirt over my head. Leaning in, he kisses my cheek then pauses to say something that leaves me with a fluttering feeling in the pit of my stomach.

"I know, 'cause I like you wearing it too."

Chapter Thirteen
Chicken House Sleepover

Later that night, I can't sit still. My mind is racing, my body is restless and nothing seems to be working anymore. I've taken showers, danced in the yard, repainted my nails just to pick off the polish–I've tried everything. Now, I'm back to pacing. My path starts in my room, around the upstairs den, down the stairs, through the kitchen, around the downstairs den, up the stairs and back to my room. Then, I start all over again. It's after midnight and I'm pacing my room to avoid the stairs. I've almost fallen twice because my legs have become like jelly.

Regg eyed me every now and then when I would pass wherever he was, but he never said anything. He went to bed hours ago and I find myself putting my ear to the adjoining door of our rooms listening for him. I've made my circle and am pressing my ear next to his door before starting another round when it opens and I nearly fall on my face.

"What were you doin'?" he asks, looking at me like I'm the crazy one. I am, but that's beside the point. I start to answer him, but my eyes are drawn to the half naked man standing before me.

Regg's arms are muscular, as is his chest. He doesn't have rippling abs or the infamous V leading down into his blue boxer briefs, and that's fine by me. Because Regg is hot as hell, just like this. He is all man with calloused hands, strong arms, a powerful chest, a smooth stomach and a bulge in his underwear. It's the first thing I've been able to concentrate on today.

Before I can stop myself, my hand flies out to rub the soft, smooth skin of his flat stomach. I move my fingers up to his chest and through the small patch of light brown hair in the center. He grabs my wrist, pulling it from his body then kisses my fingers before releasing my hand at my side.

"I have to go to the farm. One of my computers is down and my fans aren't running. I have about an hour before I lose over twenty thousand birds. Get dressed." Desperate for a distraction, I agree- not that he gave me an option. I watch as he goes back into his room and starts getting dressed. He's on the bed pulling his boots over his jeans when he looks at me.

"Red. Today." Right. I throw on a pair of pajama pants, swap out Regg's shirt for a tank top of my own and put on a bra for the first time in two days. I sort through the endless pairs of shoes at the bottom of my closet. If they're not heels, they're flip flops and I only own a couple pairs of tennis shoes that I refuse to have covered in chicken shit. I'm still debating when Regg grabs my hand and starts pulling me through the house.

"I don't have shoes," I say in protest, but he just keeps walking. Well, jogging really.

"I got some boots in the truck." Regg never lets go of my hand as he pulls me from room to room to get a gun, keys, his hat and my cigarettes. How thoughtful of him.

Instead of taking me to the passenger side, or letting go of my hand so I can walk over there on my own, he opens the driver's door of the big truck, picks me up and all but throws me inside of it.

"Damn, Regg. Calm down," I say, trying like hell to right myself in the seat. It's a battle considering he is driving like a maniac. Who would have ever thought that I would be the one with the level head?

His bulky cell phone falls to the floorboard on a turn and he looks at me pleadingly. I roll my eyes before searching for the damn thing while trying to prevent a broken neck. My shaky fingers grab it and just as I'm passing it to him, we hit a bump in the road and I drop it again.

"Shit!" I yell in frustration. Now it's in the floor on his side of the truck. I scramble between his legs, feeling around for it when another pothole sends my head flying into the dash. "Ouch! You asshole!"

"Damn, you okay?" His laughter overpowers the concern in his voice and I want to bite the calf I have my head pressed up against. I grab the phone, clutching it as if my life depends on it, then like an idiot, I hoist myself up using the steering wheel. The truck swerves hard to the right, then the left. I'm screaming on the floor, my body folded up like a pretzel while Regg fights to keep it between the ditches. When I hear him say, 'hold on,' I know we are about to crash. I feel the truck tilt forward as we barrel down a rough hill and the only thought going through my head is what in the hell am I supposed to hold on to? The truck spins in a complete three-sixty before it finally comes to a stop. I hear the door open and feel Regg get out, leaving me lying there with my head next to the gas pedal, one leg extended over my head near the steering wheel, and the other curled under my ass. My tits are in my neck and for the life of me I don't know how in the hell I'm gonna get out.

"Red?" His voice is cautious and I start to pretend I'm dead just to freak him out. Instead, I stick my arm up and in my shaky hand, I hold the cause of our dilemma.

"Take this motherfucker and staple it to your head. Cause if it ever gets in my possession again, I'm gonna eat it." Fighting to control his laughter, Regg takes the phone from my hand before helping me untangle myself from the truck. "I don't like you," I tell him, even though I can't help but find the humor in this awkward situation myself.

"Well, allow me to redeem myself. Your boots, my lady." Regg pulls a pair of zebra striped rubber boots from the back seat of the truck and slips them on my feet. It might not mean a lot to some people, but the act has my heart swelling in my chest. He bought me boots. My very own pair. And they're cute too. So what if he bought them so I could slave on his farm? It's the thought that counts.

Regg managed to not total the truck by taking us through another one of his shortcuts. We end up only a few feet from our final destination. He leads us into one of the chicken houses where the ammonia almost takes my breath.

"What is that smell?" I ask, dramatically holding my nose and fanning my face.

"Chicken shit. You get used to it." I doubt anyone other than him could get used to something like this. "Red, I need your help." Great.

I walk over to where he is standing in front of a wall filled with some kind of digital boxes that look like big calculators. He writes some numbers down and hands me the piece of paper.

"Now, I'm fixing to open this door. Inside are a whole lot of chickens. They won't hurt you so don't freak out. But, don't do anything to scare them because if they start piling up, they'll start dying." I shake my head, not ready to be responsible for the death of all these innocent chickens.

"I can't. I'll freak out. I know it." I start fidgeting with my hands and shuffling my feet, feeling the anxiety building inside of me.

"I know you can do this. If I didn't think so, I wouldn't ask you. Have a little faith in yourself, Red." He gives me a reassuring smile and opens the door without waiting for a reply. Shit, shit, shit.

I wipe my hands on my pants and follow him through the door. Inside the stinky, hot house, thousands of chickens stare back at me. Regg walks slowly through them and they get out of his way without him even having to shoo them. They must know him. I have a feeling that when I walk in, they're gonna lose their shit.

"Come on, Red. Just follow behind me." I take a deep breath, draw a cross across my chest and step into the house. The soft mulch gives under my feet as I follow the cleared path Regg has made. We walk all the way to the end where four big fans sit on either side of the house. "Call out that first set of numbers to me." I unfold the paper in my hand that is now damp with sweat. I call out the number to Regg, and watch as the fan comes to life. "Okay, give me the next." We repeat this process until all the numbers are called out and the fans are up and running.

"Can we go home now?" I ask, feeling as if the chickens are starting to close in on me.

Regg shakes his head, as he joins me in the middle of the house. "I can't. Looks like I'll be staying here tonight. My computers are down and if these fans go out, I have to manually reset them. I had to disconnect the alarm, so there's no way for me to know unless I'm here." We walk back through the house and to the small office space away from the chickens. My mind races with what to do. Do I go back to the house by myself? Or stay here in this place with Regg? "Stay with me. Look, I even have this amazingly uncomfortable cot for us to sleep on." He rolls a twin size cot from a corner of the room and unfolds it. I scratch my head, unable to find the exact spot it's itching.

"Will you rub my hair?" I don't know why I ask him that, but now that I have, I hope he says yes. He gives me a smile and nods.

"Yeah, babe. I can do that." I take off my boots and curl up on the cot, using my arm as a pillow. I feel Regg slip in behind me and grab my waist, tucking me into him. I like how he does that. He doesn't make me ask for it, he just does it like he knows what I want. The moment he starts rubbing my hair, I feel myself relax. And with his hands in my hair, his body next to mine and his arms shielding me from harm, I drift off to sleep.

"You cold?" Regg asks, sometime during the early hours of the morning. I don't know if it was my shaking or moaning that woke him. But, I do know that I don't want him to let go of me. Every muscle in my body is cramping and all I can do is lie here. My bladder feels like it's gonna bust, but I don't think I have the strength to get up.

"I'm hurting," I say, hoping like hell he can hear me. I feel him shift and I find the energy to beg him to stay. "Don't let go of me." He stops and pulls me back to him.

"I need ten minutes. I'll be right back." He doesn't wait for me to say anything; he just kisses my head and leaves me. The absence of his body hurts worse than the cramps. I'm cold one minute and hot the next. The cot I'm lying on is wet from my sweat and my breaths are coming in short bursts that are barely enough to fill my lungs with oxygen.

The urge to go to the bathroom is so intense that I know if I don't get up now, I'll piss all over myself. I prop myself up on my elbow, letting my vision focus before standing. I've taken one step when I fall to my knees in pain. The charley horse in my leg hurts so bad I become nauseous. I sit on my ass, pulling my leg to me in an attempt to rub out the cramp. My hands are too weak to apply enough pressure for relief, and just before I scream, Regg comes into view.

He seems to know what's wrong, and takes my leg into his hands, massaging the muscle. It hurts so good and I cry out in relief. I lay there, allowing him to continue to rub me until the ache is gone. If only it were that easy for the rest of me.

"I need something," I tell him. Begging that he understands. "Just a little bit. Just one hit."

"You know I can't let you do that, Red." He sounds helpless, looks worried and is torn between doing what's right and giving me relief. He sits on the floor next to me then pulls me onto his lap. His phone is in his hand and I watch as he dials a number I know so well.

"Brooklyn, I need some help."

Regg carries me to the truck, holding me close to him even when we are inside. Back at the house, he carries me up the stairs and deposits me just outside the bathroom door. I sigh in relief at not only finally draining my bladder, but at actually making it without peeing all over myself and Regg. I curl up on the floor of the bathroom, finding that same fetal position that offered me relief the last time. But it doesn't work. My insides feel knotted and every beat of my heart causes another pain to shoot through some part of my body.

"What is it with you and the floor?" Brooklyn asks, squatting down to look at me.

"Nothing is working. Please tell me you have something."

She opens her palm, revealing a small baggie and smiles. "I have pot." Fuck, I love her.

Regg looks nervous as we make our way to my bedroom. I know this isn't what he wants. I know Luke would disagree too, but nobody is gonna argue with Brooklyn. She knows what she's doing. I watch her roll a joint from my position on the bed. My eyes drift between her and Regg. The look in his eyes tells me that he thinks he is a failure. The purpose of the marijuana is to help relax my muscles. It isn't for any kind of recreational use, and will be the same as taking a narcotic. The problem is, I'm an addict.

When Brooklyn fires up the joint and passes it to me, I hesitate. Now, I'm torn. I know that in a matter of minutes my body will start to relax. I know that the pain I feel will soon disappear. But, the look on Regg's face isn't worth it. I will make it through this. And I will do it without the help of another drug.

"I can't." I look at Regg when I say this, but his face gives nothing away. I turn back to Brooklyn who is looking at me like I'm crazy. "I'll be fine. It will go away soon enough. I just want to be alone." My eyes shut in pain as another cramp hits right under my left breast. I concentrate on not breathing too deep, but the aroma of another potential guilty pleasure still haunts me. With more determination than I thought I had, I push myself out of bed. "I said I want to be alone. Now." I hold my side and limp my way to the adjoining door in my room. On the other side, I'm greeted with the scent of Regg and fresh linen. I slam the door, blocking the smell of my only saving grace. I just closed the door on the one thing I craved, the one thing I thought I needed and the thing that can bring me instant relief. But even through the thick wood, I can feel the pride radiating off of Brooklyn and Regg. And that makes it worth it.

Chapter Fourteen
The Light at the End of the Tunnel

    It's been a few hours, but it only took me half that time to realize the mistake I made. Right now, I don't give a shit about Regg, Brooklyn, Luke or anyone else. I don't care what they think of me or how proud of me they are. I should have taken the pot. I would eat cat shit if I thought it could cure the pain. The only thing comforting is the huge quilt I'm wrapped in that smells just like Regg. His scent is masculine and clean with the faintest hint of cologne. He's checked on me a few times, but I don't answer him when he speaks. I just lay here and shake, sweat and occasionally groan.

    Brooklyn tried to get me to drink some water, but I refused. When she came in with a juice box containing one of those little straws that bend, I accepted. Since then, I've drank five. I pray for sleep to take me, but just when I start to doze, another cramp hits me, and each time it's in a different place. I would love a hot shower, but just the thought of the amount of energy it would take has me staying in bed.

I hear heavy footsteps on the stairs and am more than surprised when Luke walks into the room. That damn smirk is on his face and I'm sure he's gonna say something that will result in him getting throat punched.

"You look like shit," he says, sitting down on the edge of the bed.

"You can't see it, but I have my middle finger up." He laughs, and it makes me want to smile.

"Good to see you haven't lost your touch. You gonna make it?" His smirk fades and he looks at me with concern. But, I show him no pity. What kind of question is that anyway?

"Probably not. Shed some mercy on us all and just kill me. I think I'd be a lot better off." His smile is back and I don't know why. I wasn't kidding.

"You're too fucking mean to die. Want me to lay with you?" The question is innocent. It's one that I've heard many times. Only this time, it isn't him that I want. Because Luke knows me so well, he gets it before I have time to say anything. I watch his face morph into understanding before he smiles. "Ah. You know my rules, Red." Fuck his rules. He's always told me that his brothers are off limits. He claims it is because he doesn't want me to break their hearts and leave him with the shit to clean up. I know the real reason is because he doesn't want me to get my heart broken.

"It's not like that. I just like having him around. He gets me."

"Bullshit."

"I'm serious." There was nothing about Regg I liked other than the way he made me feel, the things he did for me, the way he took care of me, the time he devoted to me, his arms, his smell and his smile. That was it.

"Whatever you say, gorgeous. I gotta go. I'll come check on you later this week." I know he doesn't believe a word I said, but I can't be angry with him about it. Because, truthfully? I don't believe a damn word I said either.

"No! I don't want to go!" They can't make me. Not this time. This time, I was staying in the only place I was sure nothing bad would happen to me. It always smelled funny. The bathroom was shared with six other girls, but it was better than the unknown.

"Denny, we've been through this. They're good people, now. Stop being a pain in my side, and get your skinny little butt in the car." Ms. Hart, the counselor at the group home, has been through this more than once with me.

The big man appears in the doorway and just his presence has me cowering away from him. His name was Mr. Baggett, or Winston or daddy. He told me I could call him either one. I didn't want to call him anything. I just wanted him to stay the hell away from me.

"Denny, I won't tell you twice. Come on." My feet betray me and out of fear, they follow him to the old, beat up van that waits outside. His wife, Pat, sits in the driver's seat, waiting with a fake smile. I have nothing but a backpack with a few changes of clothes and Mr. Bear, my best friend.

When the door closes on the van, I look up, hoping to find someone on the front steps of the orphanage. I pictured them standing there with sad faces, wiping tears from their eyes as they watch me leave. But, the only thing occupying the concrete steps is an old plant that hasn't been watered in days.

"How much for this one?" I hear my new mama ask. She lights a cigarette, not even bothering to crack a window.

"Twelve hundred. And she's a pain in the ass." Winston turns in his seat so that he is facing me. On the floor at my feet, he lays a long, thick switch that seems fresh picked from the bush just outside the group home. *"But, we ain't gonna have any problems with you, are we, Denny?"* I feel my heart beat harder and my eyes widen in fear as puts his fat, dirty hand on my knee. When I don't answer, he squeezes it, forcing the unshed tears to fall down my cheeks. *"Are we?"*

"No, sir."

I sit up in bed, gasping to catch my breath. Fucking dreams. Why couldn't I have just been born normal? Why couldn't I have had a mother who constantly worried over me and a father who cleaned his shot guns when boys came over? Why did I have to be born to a woman that didn't want me? Why did I have to have a father who couldn't give two shits less about me? Why was I being punished?

To add to my torture, Regg walks in with a determined look on his face that says, 'I'm here to save the fucking day.' I'm through with being saved. I'm through with asking for help. I just want to do my time so I can please the judge and go back to doing what I do best. Being a junkie and a pathetic waste of space. I want to dance my problems away, on the stage, in front of a bunch of people who only care about what color panties I'm wearing. I want to snort until my demons are my best friends and my endorphins are back to fully functioning. I miss being happy.

Regg doesn't talk to me, he just hands me a juice box, then proceeds to start taking off his clothes. The scene is surreal and I contemplate pinching myself to make sure I'm not still dreaming. He pulls his shirt over his head, leaving him naked from the waist up. I can see his tan line peeking out from under the waistband of his gray underwear. He still says nothing, leaving the constant slurping of my juice box as the only noise in the room. His eyes stay trained on mine as he lets his jeans fall to the floor.

"What are you doing?" I ask, feeling a desperate need to say something. Or maybe I'm feeling a desperate need for something else.

"I'm getting ready for bed." I watch him walk across the room, his body moving with confidence and oozing with sexiness. He sets the alarm then crawls in under the covers behind me. Without question, he pulls my body to his and plants a kiss on the back of my head. "Goodnight, Red." What? That's it?

"Who said you could sleep with me?" I ask, knowing good and damn well that I won't be asking him to leave.

"I think I should be asking that question. This is my bed, after all." He has me there. I set my empty box on the nightstand and I let myself snuggle in closer to him. My body is sore and tired, but the cramps have subsided. It feels good to have Regg here, and it doesn't take long at all to find myself asleep in his arms.

***

The next morning, when Regg leaves to walk the chicken houses, I join him. Today is the first day that itch I've had since I've been here is gone. Do I still want drugs?

Yeah. If they were offered to me right now, would I take them? Hell yeah. But, the urge isn't as strong as it was yesterday. I should feel better. I had the best sleep I've had in years last night. I don't want to claw my eyes out or peel the skin from my body. My body feels better than it has in days. But, instead of being happy about this, I feel depressed.

It's hard saying goodbye to a life you've lived for years. Letting go is difficult, but not knowing what's ahead is worse. The future scares the shit outta me. When I danced, I knew that's all I was going to do. Sure, the drugs were a problem, but those three minutes I spent on stage made it all worth it. I miss my life. I miss the spotlight. I miss how I felt when I let the lyrics of a song take me away.

I've tried to stay busy today, hoping to keep my mind off of dancing. But I can't. It's who I am and what I was made to do. I let drugs ruin my life. I let them destroy everything I worked so hard for. And I'd do it all again, if I could just get rid of this feeling inside of me. The feeling of losing the only thing I've ever loved. Dance.

I have a problem. A big one. I could stand here and beat around the bush about it, or I could face it and deal with it right now. Before this moment, I couldn't concentrate on my personal feelings because I was too busy dealing with my addiction. I was so absorbed in what I once was, that I never once thought about what would happen when the pain subsided and the drugs were not at the forefront of my thoughts. Now that I am thinking with a clearer head, it is all becoming obvious and just slightly overwhelming.

From day one, Regg had my interest. From the very first moment I laid eyes on him, there was an instant connection. Many nights, I laid awake thinking about him. I thought about the way he looked at me. How he made me feel. What his lips had felt like on mine.

Then, I hit rock bottom. By that time, he had become only a distant memory. But, then he appeared and rescued me from the deepest, darkest hell of my life. Now, less than a week into my sentence, I've found myself dependent on him. I need him in my life. I claimed it was because I needed his help, but in reality, I want him because he's made me feel something no one else ever has. I'm drawn to him. I delight in just his presence. I want him in my life. I need him with me. And he is the one thing I don't deserve.

"You sure are quiet today," Regg says, interrupting my thoughts.

"Yeah, just got a lot on my mind."

"Wanna talk about it?" Yes.

"No, I'm good. I just want to be alone a while. I'll catch up with you later?" I try to form some sort of smile, but my lips refuse. He gives me a worried look but nods his head.

I walk back to the house with a heavy heart. When I cross through the woods and into the backyard, my prison looms big before me. Almost three months I have to spend here. If my feelings are this strong now, what will they be by the time I leave? As I make my way up the stairs, I realize what I have to do. To keep Regg safe, I have to keep my distance. I won't allow myself to fall for him. I can't. He doesn't need a poison like me in his life. I can get through this with no emotional connection. Can't I? I only have eighty-six days left, but with how I'm feeling, it might as well be an eternity.

Chapter Fifteen
Depression's Cure

I'm six weeks in, twenty pounds heavier and moments away from setting fire to my bedroom when someone bangs on my door. I roll out of bed, kicking clothes, shoes and other random objects out of my way to clear a path. Regg stands on the other side, exhaustion evident on his face.

"Take a shower and get dressed. We're going out tonight." It's not a request, but a demand.

"I'm pretty tired. I'm gonna call it a day." That was a lie. I was going to sit here and read magazines, watch trash T.V. and eat junk food until I passed out. But, he doesn't have to know that.

"You've been holed up in this room for weeks. You've barely spoken twenty words to me. You never come downstairs. You avoid the club and your room smells like something died in here." This is true. All of it, but mostly the 'your room stinks' part. I was gonna clean it up today, I just haven't gotten around to it.

"Regg, look. We've been over this."

"No, we haven't. All you said was 'I don't wanna talk about it.' That doesn't tell me shit. I've asked you to talk to me. You said you didn't want to, so I gave you your space. That shit ends now. You've got thirty minutes. If you ain't downstairs, I promise you'll regret it. Now, get a shower, put on some jeans, and brush your hair. I think rats are livin' in it." He leaves, forcing me to talk to his back.

"Will you at least tell me where we're going?"
"Nope." Asshole.

I'm showered, dressed and even wearing makeup when I trudge down the stairs just as he's coming up them. He looks good, really good. He's wearing his cut, jeans and an orange and black bandana. Farmer Regg is hot, but biker Regg has you thinking nasty, dirty thoughts. When he scans my body with his eyes, they are possessive and daring. And I want someone to fuck with me just so I can see how far his limits can be pushed.

"Here," he says, shoving an envelope at me. "It's a card for Punkin. She's out. Club's giving her money to help on her fines. This is from me and you." I pull the card from the envelope, and find a simple 'thinking of you' Hallmark message inscribed on the front. Regg pulls a pen from his cut and I add something personal to the card that I know Punkin will love.

Don't thank em' just shank em'
-Red

It's words of wisdom that she once told me years ago. I've never taken her advice, but I've never forgotten it either.

Regg takes the card from my hand, sliding a thick envelope inside of it before tucking it into his cut.

"You remember how to ride?" he asks, that sexy smirk of his playing on his face.

I cock my eyebrow at him. "Do you?"

"Oh, baby. If you only knew." He walks away smoothly, full of confidence. I, on the other hand, have to hold onto the banister to keep from falling.

***

The ride to Luke's is liberating. It's been a while since I've been on the back of a bike for such a long trip. I let the sound of the pipes drown out my thoughts and let the wind carry away my problems. It's the first time I've been back to Hattiesburg since my court appearance. The only day I've even left the farm was to take a piss test, and that was in Collins-the town Regg lives in. Brooklyn has taken me and even paid to have my nails done. Since I butchered them during the first few days of my withdrawal, a new acrylic set was much needed. Afterward, she admitted that it was Regg's idea and Regg's money that paid for it. Two of the twenty words that I'd spoken to him in the past few weeks were 'thank you.' But, words couldn't describe how much the gesture meant to me.

The clubhouse at Luke's is filled with people. Knowing how skittish Punkin was likely to be, I was sure it was only our club that was here. And sure enough, every Devil's Renegades patch-holder from Lake Charles and Hattiesburg were here. All except for Pops who was unable to make it due to an illness.

I've seen them all several times at Regg's over the past few weeks. I am always cordial, but I mostly avoided them. So, much like Punkin, I was a nervous wreck to see all of them too.

I follow in behind Regg, staying close to him even though many of these people I've known a lot longer than he has. He never leaves my side as I take turns hugging all of the men and women that are here in support of Punkin, just like they supported me. No one mentions anything about drugs, or my previous career. There is only an encouraging smile on all of their faces.

I see Punkin across the room, sitting in a corner by herself. She watches the room cautiously, rubbing her hands back and forth together in a nervous gesture. I make my way to her, leaving Regg in a crowd of people.

"Hey Punk," I say, smiling at her. I keep my distance, not wanted her to get uncomfortable at my sudden approach.

"Red?" she asks, squinting her eyes to get a better view of me.

"Yep." She stands and I close the distance, allowing her to take me in her arms.

"You look good. Real good." She holds me at arm's length, taking me in. I wipe the tears from my eyes with the backs of my hands. I've missed her.

"Me? Look at you!" She's lost weight, but other than that nothing has changed. Her dark hair is pulled into a tight bun at the back of her neck, and her eye makeup is heavy-just like I wear mine. Her lips are painted Brooklyn style in a deep red, and she's proudly sporting a Property patch on her back.

"Can you believe all these motherfuckers are here? They've gotten some fine ones since I've been gone." I laugh at her words, surveying the crowd of bikers. But only one draws my attention. Regg. He gives me a chin lift and I offer him a smile, earning myself a wink. I flush and look away. Shit. I've missed him. I hadn't realized it until this moment, but damn. Why have I wasted the past three weeks avoiding him? Oh, that's right. Because I'm an idiot.

"Uh oh," Punkin says, pulling me from my thoughts.

"What?" She's staring at me, shaking her head and I start to wonder if there is something on my face. "What, Punkin?"

"You're in love with Regg."

I gasp at her words. "What? No, I'm not. We're just friends." I roll my eyes at her ridiculous assumption and start to fidget for the first time in days.

"Honey, I've seen that look before. You love him." She lights a cigarette and I pull it from her mouth, feeling like I need it more than she does right now. She glares at me a moment, seems to remember where she is, then lights another one.

"I don't even really know him. I mean, I know him, but not really."

"That don't even make sense. You've been living with him for weeks. And I know you knew him before that." She places her cigarette in the corner of her mouth, drawing off of it without taking the time to remove it from her lips.

"I'd only met him a few times before that. When he showed up in court, it'd been five months since I'd even talked to him." This causes Punkin to snatch the smoke from her mouth and narrow her eyes on me.

"What?" Oh for fuck's sake.

"You heard me right, Punkin. Like I said, I barely even know him." Her shocked expression has me thinking that maybe prison did something to her mentally.

"You mean to tell me that motherfucker paid off a judge for twenty thousand dollars, for someone he barely even knew?" Now, it's my turn to be shocked.

"What?"

"You heard me right, Red," she says, throwing the line back at me.

"Tell me everything you know, and Punkin, you better not leave anything out." Apparently, this was a well kept secret since this is the first I was hearing of it. Whoever told Punkin was a fool. She couldn't hold water when it came to her sisters. And in this moment, I was never more proud to have a sister like Punkin.

It takes her a few tries, a couple of cigarettes and a few times of me saying 'stick to the subject' for her to get it out. But, I finally get the truth.

The judge refused to give me rehab when Luke first asked him. He said it was out of his hands, and that I deserved the time because we'd tried rehab and it didn't work. When Luke told Regg, he said he'd handle it. After giving the judge twenty grand and his word that he'd make sure I was taken care of, the judge gave in to Regg's offer. The story he gave in the courtroom was complete bullshit. It was just a show for the DA and everyone else there.

Finding out the truth has me looking at Regg in a whole new light. Why would he do that for me? Punkin was right. Twenty grand was a lot of money to spend on someone he barely knew. Was it for Luke? Did he do it because he didn't want to see Luke hurt? Or did he do it because he didn't want to see me hurt? I don't know what to say to him, but I'll have to ask eventually. I need answers. And more than that, I need to thank him.

"What do I say to him, Punkin?" I ask, pleading to her for advice.

"Say? You better do more than say. That's twenty thousand dollars worth of something. And I don't think talking is worth that much money."

"I'm not a prostitute, Punkin. I'm not gonna fuck him just because he bailed me out of a bind." Although I wouldn't mind fucking him for just the sheer pleasure of it.

Punkin lights a cigarette, looks at me, looks at Regg and with a hopeful look asks me the question burning in her mind. "Well, do you mind if I do?"

I'm sitting with the ladies, in a circle of chairs we've formed so we can see everyone at the same time. The conversation is light, mostly consisting of stories from

Punkin about her time in jail. A pretty girl comes around, offering everyone drinks and without hesitation, I order vodka on the rocks. At my request, the women become silent and the situation becomes uncomfortable. I'm just about to cancel the drink and ask for a water instead when Regg walks up.

"Make it a double, babe. She's gonna need it." The conversation picks right back up and I give Regg a grateful smile before diving back into the topic at hand.

The moment is forgotten temporarily, until the waitress returns and hands me my drink. I know what they're all waiting on. But, I surprise even myself when I only take a sip before setting my glass on the table to light a cigarette. I've always been known for my ability to chug liquor like water, but I have sense enough now to know I need to take it slow. It's a milestone for me. And it doesn't go unnoticed by my sisters who all look at me with pride. Except for Punkin, who doesn't even know what the hell is going on. God love her, and her scatter brained ways.

"Come with me." Regg holds out his hand and I take it, letting him lead me to one of the rooms in the back of the clubhouse. They're set up for the guys to have a place to sleep after long rides or when guests are in town. Judging by the clothes strewn across the room and the unmade bed, this one is already occupied. Leaving me to wonder what in the hell we're doing in here.

"I know you miss dancing. I know the absence of it from your life is what has you so depressed. So, I wanted to do something for you." He grabs a bag from the floor and hands it to me. Inside are beautiful pieces of lingerie that are classy, but extremely sexy. "I want you to dance tonight, Red. Everyone here loves you, and we all want to see you happy. And I think this is the cure you've been searching for." I'm speechless. What is this man not capable of doing? Does his compassion not know any limits?

"Why are you doing all this for me?" I ask, my voice barely a whisper. Without hesitation, Regg gives me the answer to my question.

"Something happened that first night I met you, and it's been happening ever since. There isn't a day that went by after that first night that I didn't think about you. I know that girl is still in you somewhere, and I'll do everything in my power to find her again." I let his words sink in, and I'm still processing them long after he's gone. I may not be in love with Devil's Renegades Regg, but I'm sure as hell falling.

Chapter Sixteen
A New Side of Regg

Everyone was in on the secret of my dancing except for me. Even Punkin knew what was going down. And Luke, wanting to make sure I really got my chance to shine in the spotlight, invited some outsiders to the show, just to pack the house. I wasn't nervous about performing in front of them. Strangers would be easier to make eye contact with than any of the brothers.

All the ladies were crammed into the small room that belonged to Ronnie and Brooklyn for the night. After a heated debate and a few rounds of paper-rock-scissors, I thought my outfit was finally chosen. But, Punkin, who had the final say in the matter, chose the one thing none of us had even considered. A neon orange bikini. Everyone disagreed, but since it was her night, I agreed to wear whatever she wanted me to wear.

I would only be dancing for three songs. There wasn't really a time limit, but I didn't want to steal the glory from Punkin. This night was about her, not me. My song choice was easily agreed on. I would open with *Cherry Pie* by Warrant, the first song Regg saw me dance to. My second song, *Living Dead Girl* by Rob Zombie was the first song Luke saw me dance to the night I made my debut. My third and final song was a dedication to all my sisters- *It's a Man's World* by James Brown.

As I prepared to take the stage, I didn't need the rest of my drink. I didn't need a line of coke or heroin. All I needed was the support of my family. And that's exactly what I had.

Luke and Regg had gone all out. A ten foot by ten foot stage had been built out of wood and covered with a sheet of thick, polished acrylic. An eight foot, silver pole stood mounted in the center. The stage stood about three feet tall and chairs were lined up around it. I don't know if it was a joke, or just an extreme measure to make me feel like I was back at Pete's, but several burly men stood around wearing t-shirts that labeled them as 'security.'

The lighting in the club house was dim, which wasn't unusual, but the black lights lining the stage were clearly bought for this moment. If I wasn't so anxious to dance, I probably would have cried. I just hoped like hell I still had it in me.

Catcalls ring out across the room as I make my way onstage. Regg had somehow managed to sneak a pair of my shoes out of my closet, and the heels clicked loudly against the floor as I rub the pole to find it smooth and already prepared for me. I offer the crowd a smile, noticing the foreign cuts and citizens that weren't here earlier. The seats at the stage are occupied by only the ladies and I scan the room until I find Regg sitting next to Luke on a stool at the bar. I shoot them a wink when the introduction to *Cherry Pie* begins. Regg shakes his head, his smile wide as he recognizes the song. He wanted that girl he met a year ago, and I was going to show him she was still around. Only this time, I'd be keeping what little clothing I had, on.

I test my strength, bracing my hands on the pole and lifting my feet off the floor in a slow spin. I climb a little higher, then wrap my knee around the pole, let go and smile as my body remembers exactly what to do. It's effortless and nothing is forgotten. I don't pay attention to the lyrics or the crowd. I tune out everything until the only sound I hear is the beat of my heart, as it comes back to life.

I feel free. No drugs or alcohol, only me and the stage. The song ends, and I'm so lost in the moment, I don't even give it the dynamic ending it deserved. But, when Living Dead Girl begins to play, I transform into the role and include the crowd in my performance. I find Luke first. He's smiling, nodding his head in tune with the music and singing along. I point to him and he points back, giving me the same encouraging wink he gave me that first night years ago.

The moment is shattered when some guy screams at me over the music.

"Let's see some titties!" He is obviously drunk, but just having a good time. I laugh at his demand, and look over to find Regg shaking his head and laughing too. He yells a few more times, and I shoot him a sad face, letting him know I'm sorry, but he won't be getting what he asks for. "You fucking tease, take that shit off!" I'm too happy to let him ruin my moment, plus I'm used to it. But, Regg isn't so forgiving.

Chairs start flying, the women are screaming, fake security is everywhere. I am still dancing, but Regg is making his presence known. I watch him from the stage, loving the way his body exudes power and dominance as he walks across the room. This new side of him has me so turned on; I have to tighten my hold on the pole to keep from throwing myself at him.

There is no holding him back when he reaches the man who'd been yelling at me. His fist makes contact with the man's jaw, and I swear I can hear the sound over the loud music. When the man tries to fight back, Regg welcomes it. He avoids the man easily, then head butts him in the nose, causing blood to gush down the front of his shirt. The club begins breaking up the fight; pulling Regg out of reaching distance of the man takes damn near all of them. Even through all the chaos, I can't keep the smile off my face. Only one thought races through my head as I watch them hold Regg back. That motherfucker was fighting for me.

When the man is gone, Regg shakes free of the arms that restrain him and makes his way to me. He climbs the stage, walking directly up to the pole I'm still tightly clinging to.
"You okay?" His voice is calm, his eyes searching me for a sign that will tell him if I'm not. But, his body still radiates anger. This makes my pussy wetter, my desire for him stronger and my breathing heavier.
"I want you to kiss me," I tell him, as my eyes fall to his lips. He licks them and I can tell he is struggling with his desire to give me what I want, and the effort to not make a scene. On second thought, I don't want him to kiss me. Because I know once he does, there will be no stopping us.
He leans into me, placing his lips right next to my ear. To everyone else, it appears he's whispering to me. But, what he's doing is so much more.
"Dance for me, Red. And then I promise to give you want you want." He pulls my earlobe between his teeth before pulling away and reassuring me of his promise with his eyes. I'm so worked up, I don't know if I can dance, but the ladies at the stage are demanding I do. I hear them, but I'm only listening to Regg's words as they replay in my head.
I stare at his back until he reaches the bar and takes his seat. When he faces me, that possessive look in his eyes is back. He wants me to dance for him, and I will. At

this point, I'll do anything he asks. Because telling him no, is the only thing I don't want to do.

The ladies go nuts when my third song starts, and they all sing along. I'm sure James Brown would be proud if he were standing here today, because I gave it all I have on this one. I wasn't intentionally holding back, but my moves prove that clearly, I was. By the time I'm finished, there isn't a spot on the stage that isn't covered with money.

I'm smoking a cigarette, chatting with the ladies who are doing their best to re-enact my moves, when a PROSPECT hands me a huge wad of bills. I don't know how much is there, but I do know that it's a lot.

Without a second thought, I hand the bills to Punkin, who declines on my first attempt, but has no choice but to accept it when I shove the money down her shirt. She thanks me, but there is no need to. She would have done the same for me.

"You're crazy. I wouldn't give it to you." Well, maybe she wouldn't. But, Punkin needs the money more than I do right now. It isn't like I have shit to spend it on. Brooklyn is taking care of my smoking habit, and Regg is supplying me with food and a place to stay. I have a pretty good feeling he would be getting his money's worth tonight.

It seems like hours pass before we finally say our goodbyes, and the ride home takes twice as long as the ride there did. When we finally make it, I walk hand in hand with Regg into the house, anticipating every second to be the one where he makes good on his promise.

I don't know if he was crawfishin' or just fucking with me, but he insists on cooking me something to eat. It is after midnight, but we haven't had dinner and my growling stomach betrays me when I tell him I'm not hungry.

"What you want?" he asks, rummaging through the cabinets for something.

"Pizza." It was simple enough. And it only took three minutes to preheat the oven, ten for it to cook and less than five for me to eat it. Not that I am counting.

"Pizza it is."

While it cooks, we watch late night T.V. with him on one side of the couch, and me on the other. I look over at him every few seconds, noticing how relaxed he is and wondering why I can't be that calm. I wasn't a nun, but it's been a while since I've been intimate with anyone. In my profession, you didn't just sleep with random people, because chances were they had something. Even at my lowest, I hadn't succumbed to sleeping with just anybody. I'd come close, but never went all the way. Thinking of this reminds me of how much I don't know about Regg.

"Do you have a girlfriend?" It was an honest question. One I already knew the answer to. I hoped.

He smiles at me, mutes the T.V. and repositions himself so that we're facing one another.

"No, Red. I don't have a girlfriend. Do you have a boyfriend?" His tone is mocking, almost like our conversation is too juvenile for his ears.

"No. Have you ever had a girlfriend?"

"What is this? Twenty questions?"

"Just answer the damn question, Regg. Have you ever had a girlfriend?" He looks at me like I'm crazy before shaking his head.

"Yes, I've had girlfriends." Girlfriendssss. As in more than one. What a whore. "I was engaged for three years. She was my world. She broke my heart and it's the best thing that's ever happened to me." There is no sadness in his words, no remorse over the loss of his fiancée. It's actually a little sad.

"What about you?" I'm saved by the bell when the timer goes off on the oven. I start to get up, but his words halt me.

"That's the five minute warning. Talk." Five minute warning? Ovens have that?

"I dated a few guys on and off through high school. Met a few at the club. But, I've been dancing since I was eighteen. It pretty much consumed my life. I've never made the time for a relationship. I've never really found anybody I wanted to give up my career for." As I say this, I realize how pathetic my life actually sounds.

"So you've never been in a serious relationship?"

"I mean, yeah. They were serious just not... that serious." What the hell was the definition of serious? Proposing? Starting a family? Moving in together? "I cared about them, hell I may have even loved a few, but I'm only twenty-three. It's not like I've had time to find someone to settle down with." My excuse is weak, but in my defense, I've only been an adult for five years. That wasn't very long. Was it?

"How old are you?" I ask, feeling stupid for not even knowing his age.

"Twenty-six." Old fart.

"I didn't realize you were older than Luke."

"I didn't realize Luke was so young." That playful, sexy smile is on his face and I feel a big, goofy grin crawl across mine. We sit there a few minutes longer, neither one of us really knowing what to say.

"Shit! The pizza," Regg says, jumping up.

"I thought it had a five minute warning?" I ask, running behind him into the smoky kitchen.

"I lied." Of course he did.

Red

Chapter Seventeen
Them
@!#$%^%$#^&*@
Chicken Houses

"Best pizza ever." I'm lying. He knows I'm lying. The truth is, I'm too excited to eat anything. I just want him to kiss me. I want him to grab me with one strong arm, clear the table with the other, throw me down on top of it and fuck me into oblivion.

Okay, so maybe that's a little dramatic. But I know what I want-the man sitting next to me, dressed in leather who has a face that would look great between my legs. And I'm pretty sure by the way he is looking at me, he is thinking about how great his face would look there too.

"Shit." Regg's eyes roll to the back of his head as he pulls his phone from inside his cut. I watch anxiously, praying like hell that it's not the club needing him to go somewhere. What in the hell would I do? How would I make it? I'm a huge ball of sexual tension and I need Regg to massage my knots of need.

"Knots of need?" Motherfuck me.

"Hmm?" Please tell me he didn't really ask that.

"You just said, 'I have knots of need.'" He looks amused. I'm humiliated. We make such a great couple.

"Who was on the phone?" I'll change the subject; he'll go back to rolling his eyes at the reminder of the nuisance on the phone. All will be good.

"What is a knot of need?" Maybe I should just vomit. That would be a nice distraction. Or, I could just pretend to pass out.

"Red?" Or I could just answer the question.

"What I said was, 'I've got to pee.'" I watch him to see if he buys it. He doesn't. But, he does shed some mercy on me.

"Well go pee, and hurry up. We gotta go to the farm."

"What?" My knots of need have vanished. My sexual tension is nonexistent and now I'm just a big pool of disappointment. Regg raises an eyebrow at me, giving me that 'you alright' look.

"They should have it all sorted out this week. I'll meet you at the truck." He shoots me a wink and disappears through the swinging door. The past few weeks, I've been keeping my distance from him. But even if I hadn't I wouldn't have been able to see him a lot. I'd heard bits and pieces of conversation about Regg having to replace all the computer systems in the houses. That's why he's been so tired and absent.

Even still, I'm a little pissed that those damn chicken houses are getting in the way of him making good on his promise to kiss me. I just need to suck it up, and deal with the fact that tonight I will go to sleep without him.

I trudge my ass upstairs in a not so nice mood. I'm let down, disappointed and maybe a little pissed. And if you were being deprived of that sexy beast that is one Devil's Renegades Regg, then you would be pissed too.

I meet Regg at the truck wearing my rattiest pajamas. My face is makeup free, my hair is piled on my head and I look hideous in my knee high rubber boots. But, I don't give a shit. I light a smoke, ignoring him and his amused stare.

"Somebody's in a great mood." Somebody needs an orgasm. I make sure I only think my words this time.

"How long is this gonna take?"

"We pullin' an all-nighter, babe. Hopefully, this will be the last one. I don't even remember what my bed feels like." Poor Regg. Here I am being a bitch after all the sacrifices he's made on my behalf. I am sure Regg needed to be home more than he needed to be with the club tonight, but he went. And something in the back of my head tells me it was more for me than it was for anyone else.

We barrel down the gravel road and stop just in front of the houses. I walk with him through one, wait for him to start the fans and then follow him back to the small office. Kicking my boots off, I curl up on the cot. Regg tells me he will be back shortly and leaves me alone. I don't want to go to sleep, but I'm so tired that I find myself fighting to keep my eyes open.

I keep my eyes closed when I hear him come in, and I feel that tingle in my belly at his presence. He lies down next to me and without hesitation, pulls me to his chest. His mouth is dangerously close to my ear and his warm breath sends chills through me.

"Are you asleep?" I'm debating on answering him. He knows I'm not. Or maybe he just thinks I'm having a dream that makes my heart race and my breathing a little erratic. I decide to stay silent and I can feel him smile against my ear. I let out a squeal when he grabs my waist and flips me so that we are facing one another.

"I'm a man who makes good on his promises." I start to say something, but his mouth closes in on mine. Our first kiss months ago is nothing compared to this one.

Instantly, I give into him, knotting my fingers in his hair and pulling him closer to me. I want this. I want him. I've never wanted anything more in my life. I've gone too long without feeling the heat of passion from someone who genuinely wants it. And I know by the way Regg kisses me, he wants it.

He moans into my mouth and a fire ignites. Raw need blazes into an inferno, desperate for more fuel to add to its flame. I grind my hips into him, begging him for more. He gives into my demands and slips his hand beneath my shirt. His calloused thumb grazes my nipple and I moan in response.

"Please," I beg. My plea for more is lost in our mouths, silenced by the invasion of his tongue dancing with mine. He squeezes my breast in his hand, letting the weight of it fill his palm. I grind harder into him, finding his cock hard and ready for me even through the thickness of his jeans. His hand slides down my stomach, leaving a trail of goosebumps and a wave of chills in its wake. He finds the waist band of my pajama shorts and easily guides his hand beneath them.

He teases me through my panties until the satin material is wet with my arousal. His fingers follow along the seam, tracing a path over my hip bone and to my ass. His large hand covers a cheek, squeezing it hard before moaning in appreciation. I throw my leg over his hip, allowing him access to my pussy that begging for his touch. Roughly, my panties are pulled to the side before his long finger gently rubs between my wet lips. He pushes a finger inside of me and stars burst behind my eyelids.

"Damn," he mutters, breaking from my mouth to trail kisses along my jaw and neck. His nibbles the tender flesh, smoothing the sting with his tongue before kissing it reverently and moving on to another spot. His finger works in and out of me as he teases my neck with the heat of his mouth. I've never been this turned on by a man and the wetness between my legs proves it. As if I need further confirmation, Regg tells me again.

"You're so. Fucking. Wet." The appreciation in his tone and the enunciation of each word, says one thing. He likes me this wet. And he should since he is the cause of it.

He finds my ear with his mouth and my clit with his finger. He applies just the right amount of pressure as he rubs it in a circular motion, demanding the one thing I want most. Release. His demand is not only with his movements, but with his words.

"Come for me, beautiful." The way he says 'beautiful,' makes me feel like the definition of the word only applies to me. Like it's my given name-one so rare that there is no mistaking who he's referring to. My whole body stills once I finally make it to the top of my climax. And then on the free fall, my body jerks in pleasure, while my moans echo off the walls of the room. By the guttural sound that rips through Regg's chest, it's as if feeling me come apart beneath him is better than his own release.

I delight in the aftershocks of my orgasm long after it's over. Regg's hand is on my neck, his thumb grazing my jaw. My eyes flutter open to find brown pools of lust and desire staring back at me. I want to feel him inside me. I want him to make love to me all night until we collapse in exhaustion. I want to wake up with him buried inside of me; starting my day with the same pleasure he ended my night with. Then, he tells me something I never thought he'd say in this moment.

"I just want to hold you." There's something about the way he says it that makes me feel loved. He doesn't want to fuck me. He isn't expecting me to give him anything in return for what he just gave me. He just wants to hold me.

So, I let him hold me. And I drift off to sleep in the arms of the man that I'm pretty sure I love.

Chapter Eighteen
Falling... Literally

"Wake up, sleepy head," Regg says, rubbing my back. I'm not a morning person, but the previous night's events have me wide awake, anticipating the movement of his hands. Maybe he woke me up to give me another dose of what he gave me last night. I turn over, trying like hell to look sultry and sexy.

"I'm awake," I say, batting my eyelashes. I was hoping my voice would come out as a purr, but I sound like I ate gravel for breakfast. Figures.

"Good. Let's go shoot some nannies." He gets up and I notice he's dressed head to toe in camouflage.

"Shoot some what?" It's too early for this shit. If he ain't gonna kiss me, then he needs to let me go back to sleep.

"Deer, babe. Come on, we're late." Late? It isn't even five in the morning.

"I think I'm gonna sleep in," I say, already rolling back to my stomach.

"Oh, you must have misunderstood me. I didn't ask." He grabs my ankles, dragging me until my knees hit the floor.

"What the fuck is your problem?" I yell, holding onto the cot for dear life.

"Watch your mouth. Come on." I'm left staring at his back, knowing that if I don't get up now, he will just come back and forcefully take me with him. It's not a bad idea.

Huffing, I pull my boots on and step out into the blue morning. It's freezing outside, and just the short walk to the truck has me shivering.

"Put these on." He hands me a pair of camouflage overalls, an orange vest and some gloves. I easily slip the overalls over my pajamas, zipping them up to my neck. I secure the hood over my head, tying it tight around my neck before putting on the vest and gloves. Regg looks at me from the other side of the truck and smirks.

"Well, ain't you cute." Asshole. The sun isn't even up. Nobody is cute at this time of day. Except for him, of course. He's all bright eyed and bushy tailed, looking like a model for Mossy Oak wear.

I light a cigarette, letting the nicotine fill my lungs, reminding me that I'm alive and adding to the morning stench of my breath. Ugh.

"Can we at least get some coffee?" I ask, ready to unleash the beast if he denies me morning caffeine.

"Here." He hands me a thermos and I frown. Did he expect me to drink it black? "It's fixed just how you like it." I smile at him, wondering how I can hate him one moment and want to smother him in kisses the next. The coffee is perfect and a wonderful addition to my cigarette. We ride in silence along a dirt road until Regg pulls the truck into the edge of the woods.

"If you have anything to say, now is the time to say it. When I open this door, don't talk. I'm serious about my huntin'." And his expression shows it. I shake my head, not having anything to say. The moment the door is closed and we begin our descent into the woods, I'm overloaded with shit to tell him. I want to tell him that I've never been hunting. I want to tell him I've never shot a rifle. I want to talk to him about last night, and make him promise to kiss me again. My cheeks heat at the reminder and suddenly it isn't that cold anymore.

We come to a stop a couple hundred yards into the woods and Regg points up. Way up. In the very top of the biggest damn oak tree I've ever seen, are three white boards. While I'm still trying to figure out what in the hell it is, Regg is already halfway up the tree. Not to be outdone, I follow. The steps consist of old wood that is rotting away in some places, and some boards are even missing. I have the urge to yell out and cuss at him, but I keep my mouth shut to keep from hurting his feelings. And because I'm too winded to say anything.

Ten minutes later, I make it to the top and take a seat next to him on a wooden bench. To my left is about a fifty foot drop to the ground. I find myself edging closer to him in fear of falling.

"My uncle built this years ago. I'm impressed. I never thought you'd make it up here," he whispers, smirking at me.

"You're an ass," I whisper back, still trying to catch my breath. Regg on the other hand isn't the least bit winded.

"Shh." I look up at him in shock. So, he can whisper but I can't? I start to come back with something, but his hand covering my mouth silences me. He points and I follow his finger to see nothing but a bunch of trees. "Thought I saw something," he says, keeping his hand over my mouth. I remove it, and instantly miss the warmth as his body pulls away from mine.

"I'm cold," I whisper, but Regg ignores me. Not even bothering to look my way. I wait a few minutes before trying to strike up another conversation. "So, you come here often?" Silence. What an asshole. "Are you ignoring me?"

"Yes." Finally. Now that I have his attention, I continue.

"I'm hungry. Are we gonna have breakfast when we leave?" He turns to look at me, I can see the aggravation in his face and it makes me smile. "Am I bothering you, Mr. Rawls?"

"You know, I can make you shut up," he whispers, the corner of his mouth turning up in a smirk.

"What you gonna do? Push me outta the tree? You drug me up here. The least you could do is talk to me." I stuff my hands in the pockets of my overalls, wishing the sun would hurry up and make its way over the trees before I freeze to death.

"That's a good idea, but no. If I did that, you might scream on the way down and I don't want you to scare off the deer."

"I think I have to sneeze," I say, wiggling my eyebrows at him. He narrows his eyes on me, trying to show just how mean he is, but the affect is lost because he is still smiling.

"Last warning. Stop talking." The dare in his eyes is too inviting. Now, I want to talk just to see what he will do. He wouldn't really push me outta the tree. Would he?

"And what if I," my voice carries over the trees but it's short lived. His hand comes back over my lips silencing me, as he pulls my hood down to whisper in my ear.

"If you promise to keep your mouth shut, Red, then I promise to give you something that I know you want." His breath is hot against my skin and I shiver in response. Regg always makes good on his promises and just as sure as I'm sitting here, I'll make good on mine. Nothing could make me talk in this moment. Hell, I'll stay silent for the rest of the day as long as he puts his hands on me tonight. I nod, my breath is panting in anticipation while my insides pulse with need.

He pulls away from me, winking before motioning for me to replace the hood on my head. I'm so caught up in my daydream of what's to come that I forget what we're doing here in the first place. So, when I see a deer, I act like an idiot.

"Look!" I say. Or yell. Or scream at the top of my lungs. You get it. I act a complete fool and in response, the deer disappears from view and back into the cut over. I'm scared to look at Regg. I feel fear building inside of me. I've never pissed him off, but I bet if I could, this was a good way to start.

I stare straight ahead, squinting my eyes closed in hopes that maybe I will just disappear. How could I be so stupid? Not only have I scared the deer, but now, I won't be getting what I wanted more than anything. Him.

"POW!"

The sound of the gun going off is so startling that I take to my instinct to run. Too bad I didn't think it through. Before I can realize my mistake, I'm already falling. Panic surges through me as I try to regain my balance, but gravity takes over and soon the ground is coming up to meet my face. I close my eyes, not wanting to remember the moment just in case I actually survive it. A tree limb catches my ankle, and I'm left dangling in the air.

"Red! Calm down! I've got you!" I don't know why Regg is screaming at me at first, and then I realize it's to be heard over my own screams. I open my eyes to find myself lying on my stomach, in the floor of the tree stand. The only thing hanging over the side is my head. I didn't fall, I tripped. And I don't know what's worse-tripping or not falling at all. I think I would have rather plunged to my death. At least that would have made a better headline.

'Local stripper trips in tree stand but is unharmed' doesn't seem like it would sell. "Damn, girl. What the hell is wrong with you?"

"What's wrong with me? What in the hell is wrong with you. You almost let me die!"

"Um, hardly. I missed the deer if that makes you happy." Regg seems aggravated when he should be falling to his knees, kissing the life back into me.

"No, Regg. That doesn't make me happy."

"You're such a drama queen." Wrong words, buddy. Wrong fucking words.

"Drama queen? You wanna see drama queen?" I scramble to my feet, finding the exit to the horrifying contraption before moving down the ladder like a damn monkey.

"You're fucking crazy. You know that? Bat shit fucking crazy," Regg calls down the ladder. I pause, looking up long enough to give him the finger and yell at him one more time.

"And you're an asshole!" When I take a step down the rotten wood beneath my foot snaps, allowing all of my weight to fall on the board my hands are currently on. "Regg!" I scream, feeling the panic rise inside of me. Again.

"This is me ignoring you again," he says, I look up but he's turned the other way.

"Help! Help me!" The desperation in my voice has him turning and I watch as the horror registers on his face.

"Shit," he says, moving rapidly down the tree towards me.

"My fingers are slipping!" I scream, looking down to see that the drop is about twenty feet. I watch as my grip loosens, keeping my eyes trained on my fingers at they slip from the board one by one. Then, I'm falling. For real this time.

I land in a pile of brush which cushions my fall. I wiggle my toes, my fingers and move my neck to make sure nothing is broken. I'm fine, and other than my pride, nothing is hurt. Regg comes into view, his eyes scanning me, surveying my body for damage.

"I'm telling everyone that you pushed me," I say, reaching my hand up for a little assistance. He pulls me to my feet, turning me so that he can brush off the leaves from my back. He turns me back to face him, taking my chin in his hand and looking over my face. I can see the concern and regret in his eyes. He's worried. "I'm fine. Really." I half expect him to come back with some smartass comment, but he pulls me into his arms and holds me close.

"You scared the shit outta me." I pat his back, unsure of what to do or how to answer him. Then, I get a very selfish idea.

"Since I fell and almost died, will you still make good on your promise?" He takes my face in his hands, smirking down at me as he lowers his lips to mine. We're so close I can feel the heat of his mouth against my lips. I close my eyes in anticipation of his kiss. This time, I know it's gonna be better than the last. Our adrenaline is pumping and the passion is motivated by fear-fear that he almost lost me.

"I told you, Red. I always make good on my promises." He backs away from me, leaving me standing cold, alone and un-kissed.

"Where are you going?" I ask, refusing to follow him until he gives me what I'm owed.

"To give you something I know you want. Breakfast." Did I mention he was an asshole?

Chapter Nineteen
Jealousy and Its Reward

"Let's go out tonight," Regg says from across the table. He's taken me to a diner that serves the best damn fried eggs and bacon I've ever eaten. It's a small, local country store with a tractor suspended in the air as advertisement. I've never been to a place that sells tractors, toilet paper *and* breakfast before now. You can smoke in here too.

"What you got in mind?" I ask, shoveling a piece of toast smothered in grape jelly into my mouth.

"I have some business to handle in Jackson. The meeting is set for a nightclub up there. The whole club is coming, thought we could make a date out of it." A date?

"Yeah, okay." Regg seems pleased with my answer, but there is tension in the air. I have a feeling that there is more to this 'date night' than he's telling me. "Is there anything else I need to know?"

"The night club is a strip club." Suddenly, I've lost my appetite. How dare he even mention taking me on a date to a fucking strip joint. "It's cool if you don't want to go, but I have to." I have two options here. Either I stay home and pout, or I suck it up and tag along. If the other girls weren't going, I would just tell him to leave me with them. But, he'd already said they were which makes me wonder how long this has been set in motion. And how long they've kept it from me.

"It's fine. I'll go. We taking the bike?" I ask, trying to keep cool even though I want to flip the fucking table over and throw shit.

"You already know the answer to that question. Quit trying to act like this doesn't bother you. Talk to me, Red. Don't shut me out." Can I be honest with him? It's obvious that I'm conflicted, but can I trust him with the real reason?

"I've done really good these past couple of weeks. I just don't want to get caught up in the atmosphere. Withdrawal was bad, but knowing that the dancing part of my life is over, is pretty depressing. Imagine not being able to ride anymore. It's hard to say goodbye to the only thing you've ever known." I've just poured my heart out to him. Now, he knows my struggle. But even still, his faith in me is unshakeable.

"Trust me when I tell you that you'll be fine. You're a lot stronger than you give yourself credit for." I smile at his answer. He gives me a wink before pulling his phone out and excusing himself from the table.

I pick at the rest of my food, contemplating what he said. He's right. I am strong, or a hell of a lot stronger than I once was. I can do this. I will do this. With a newfound energy and confidence in myself, I go in search of Regg. Tonight will be the start to the rest of my life, and for the first time, I am looking forward to it.

"I lied. I can't do this," I say, once we are standing outside of Rick's Lounge. It's located in the heart of downtown Jackson, Mississippi-about an hour ride for us. Even though the temperature is in the forties, I feel sweat break out across my lip and on the back of my neck.

"Yes, you can. And I want you to wear this tonight." I look down to see that Regg holds a black and orange bandana in his hand. It's embroidered with 'PROPERTY OF DEVIL'S RENEGADES.' I place it in my back pocket, allowing everyone in the bar to know that I'm spoken for. The only problem is, it doesn't have Regg's name on it. Not that I want to be his property, but I wouldn't mind all these bitches knowing that he isn't available. Just the thought of some girl trying to stake a claim on him has fury flowing through my veins.

"You okay?" Brooklyn asks, coming to stand beside me.

"I'm fine. I just need a drink." Tonight, the only people here are Luke, Ronnie, Brooklyn, Possum, Punkin, Regg and me. I don't know what the business is, but when the doors open, I find several patches sitting around a booth near the stage. The room is dark, the only light coming from the one illuminating the stage and the beer signs above the bar. At one time, it was comfortable. Now, I felt the need to watch my back.

"Goose on the rocks," I tell the bartender. My eyes scan the room, noticing the half naked women parading around in hopes of getting a private. They look strung out and desperate and I wonder if I ever looked like that.

When the bartender informs me that I owe her eighteen dollars, I start to ask if she's out of her fucking mind. Then, I remember I don't have any money.

"Um,"

"Here," Regg says, slipping some money in my hand as he walks past me. I look down to see three, one hundred dollars bills, and wonder how much he thinks I plan on drinking tonight. I pay for mine, Brooklyn and Punkin's drinks and order a round of beer for the guys. Including the three men from the other club. Maybe then, I can keep the blood sucking female wolves from interrupting their meeting, and the hell away from Regg.

I link the bottles between my fingers and pass them out to the men, flashing them my best smile. I feel the tension dissipate a little and Luke shoots me a thankful smirk. Punkin insists that we sit at a table in the far corner of the room. She chooses the seat that has her back to the wall and I'm forced to sit in a chair that has my back facing the room.

"What's the meeting about?" I ask, sipping my drink and enjoying the slow burn of the vodka a little too much.

"Same ol' shit. Luke's tryin' to take the club in a different direction. Wants to work something out with the Freebirds MC. Give them a piece of the business." Brooklyn's words are spoken with pride. I know a lot of the MC doesn't stand behind Luke in his decision to incorporate the club in something that isn't illegal. The money is too good for them to take such a risk. But, the ones who want a better future for their families and the club, are definitely on board.

"I feel like I've been so caught up in my own shit that I'm behind on what's going on." Even though I wasn't an ol' lady, I still had deep ties with the club. There wasn't much Luke didn't share with me, and he knew no matter what he said, he could trust me with the information. I was a vault.

"Well, I'm glad you're better. Club needs you around. It's hard enough finding good men for soldiers, much less the women. And Lord knows we're the glue that holds it all together."

"Truth," I say, lifting my glass to Brooklyn's. She's right. The men might do the dirty work, but we are the ones there when shit falls to pieces.

"Can we get a table dance?" Punkin asks, oblivious to our conversation. As if she could hear her say it, a beautiful brunette walks up to the table, offering us a dance. I sit back in my chair, silently critiquing the girl on every move she makes. Most dancers make the mistake of underestimating women. They spend all of their time and energy on the men, but it's the ladies that are usually the best tippers. The fact that she never made eye contact and never took off her top, showed me that either she was inexperienced, or was just trying to pass the time.

I excuse myself during the middle of the dance, hoping it pisses her off. Maybe next time, she will be a little more accommodating. I don't particularly find joy in watching women take off their clothes, but I do believe that if you're gonna represent this business, then you need to do it to the best of your ability.

The bathroom smells like baby powder, vomit and liquor…home. I take a minute to stare at the woman looking back at me in the mirror. I've gained almost all of my weight back, allowing my black, leather pants to fit tight on my hips. My black shirt clings to my skin and the knee high boots and leather jacket not only kept me warm on the ride here, but they compliment my outfit. My red hair has gotten long, hanging freely down my back in soft waves. It seems strange being here with all of my clothes on.

After I've stayed gone long enough for the dancer to leave our table, I walk back into the smoke filled room, stopping at the bar for another drink. While I'm waiting, my eyes wander over to the booth lined with leather cuts and I feel the hair on the back of my neck stand up. In the lap of Regg, sits the brunette that was just dancing at our table. Her tits are pressed against his chest as she runs her fingers through his hair. The sexy smile he's giving her has my blood at a boiling point. When I notice his hands on her ass, I can't stop my feet from moving towards them.

I know I have no right to claim Regg as mine. I know I shouldn't feel this jealous rage inside of me. But, the only tits on his chest should be mine. The only hands in his hair should belong to me. And the only ass he needs to be squeezing is on its way over to him right now.

Ignoring the men around me, I walk up behind the girl who's grinding in the lap of a man that doesn't belong to her. I hear Luke say something, but the only sound registering in my brain is the ringing in my ears. Without a second thought, I grab the bitch's hair in my hand and pull, dragging her and her ratchet-ass body off of my man. While she's too busy fighting with my left hand that is in her hair, I connect with the tip of her nose with my right. Blood gushes everywhere, but I don't stop. I manage to get a few more quick licks in before someone grabs me around my waist. My hand is still tangled in her hair, and I refuse to let go.

"Enough!" Regg yells, grabbing my chin and forcing me to look into his eyes. They are burning with power, and instantly my fingers release their death grip. Dominance radiates off of Regg in waves that hit me straight in the chest and fall straight to my pussy. This is angry Regg. I've seen him once, but this time it's different. The authority in his voice has me longing to drop to my knees and submit to him. Or take him in my mouth. Or turn around so he can take me from behind.

"Outside. Now." His command is not one to be argued with. I step over the crying girl on the floor, fighting like hell to control the urge to kick the shit outta her. I push through the glass doors that lead outside, fumbling for my cigarettes. I light one up, keeping my back turned to Regg who I know is standing behind me. I don't have to look and see if he is there, I can feel his presence.

"We are not gonna talk about this. All I'm gonna say is that if it ain't already obvious, I didn't like that girl sitting in your lap." My voice is controlled, even though I am anything but.

"Red," Regg starts, but I cut him off.

"Just shut up, Regg." He mumbles something under his breath and tries again.

"Look I-,"

"I don't want to hear it."

"Will you just look at me?" Without waiting for me to reject him, he grabs my elbow and turns me around, pushing me against the brick wall and pressing his body against mine.

"I said, I don't want to hear it," I snap, not in the mood for a lecture.

"And who the fuck said I wanted to talk?" His mouth closes in on mine, and I immediately give into him. My hands fist in his hair as his knee separates my legs, pressing against my pussy and igniting a fire in my groin. I moan in his mouth, loving the way his hands feel on my neck. He pushes my jacket off my shoulders roughly, causing it to bunch at my elbows-limiting my mobility.
"Tell me this is what you want," he demands, pulling my earlobe into his mouth and sucking.

"You know this is what I want." It's all I've wanted. I've waited months for this to happen, and now, outside of a strip club, in the open for anyone to see, it's going to happen.

"Say it. I want to hear you say it." His eyes burn bright with lust, exuding power that has enough force to make me give him anything he wants in this moment.

"I want you to fuck me," I say, wishing my words were stronger. But, his body demands all of me, making me feel submissive and lacking control.

"After I'm finished with you, babe, you'll have every fuckin' reason in the world to be jealous." Just his words have me whimpering with need. With skilled precision, he unbuttons my pants, sliding his hand around to my ass and beneath my panties. "Damn, I want this," he says, pulling my bottom lip between his teeth, and I don't know if he's talking about my lips or my ass, but he can have either or both. He deepens the kiss, pushing my pants to my knees before pulling his mouth away from mine.

"Turn around, Red," he commands, making my belly swarm with anticipation. I face the wall, placing my palms on the brick while his hand moves over my hip bone to my throbbing clit.

"Oh fuck." My knees go weak when he begins the slow, torturous movement of his fingers across my pussy. I hear the tear of a condom wrapper moments before I feel his cock, thick and hard against my ass, causing my breath to leave me.

"Pretty little ass," he says as he guides himself to my wet and begging entrance. He pushes inside me slowly, filling me completely before stopping. It's everything I've never had and more. I want to walk around with him strapped to my back, buried deep inside of me because I can't imagine not having him there. "Damn girl. You're so fuckin' tight. Why is your pussy so wet, Red?" he asks, and when I take too long to answer, he thrusts his hips, sending a jolt of electrifying ecstasy through me. "Answer me."

"It's wet for you. Only you," I pant, wanting him to move, but wanting him to stay still in fear that this might be over too soon if he does. He moves inside of me, long slow strokes until I've adjusted completely to him and I'm begging for more. He backs up a step, pulling me with him then places his hand in the center of my back, urging me to bend over. He wraps my hair around his hand, holding my head back as he continues to slowly fuck me.

"Tell me you want it harder," he says, his grip on my hip tightening.

"Please, Regg. Fuck me harder." I need him to. If he doesn't, I'm almost positive I will die. I've never needed him as much as I do in this moment.

"You have no idea how long I've waited to hear you beg for my cock." Before my mind has time to process his words, he's moving. He's fucking me hard, working his cock in and out of me at a pace that I didn't think was humanly possible. His strokes are deep, fast-never letting me recover from the elation I feel every time he hits that sweet spot deep inside my pussy. My back arches further, intensifying his movements, and causing that feeling of release to build rapidly inside of me. Unable to hold out any longer, I come around him, my walls pulsating, squeezing him tight inside of me. I cry out, and he releases my hair to smother my screams with his hand. His movements slow, and then on one final thrust, he groans as he comes deep inside of me.

We stay like this a few moments longer as we both fight to catch our breath. The music from inside is dull in comparison to our heavy breathing. All too soon, he pulls out of me, leaving me feeling empty and in need of him again. He pulls me back to his chest, letting me rest my weight on him while he rights my clothes. His fingers graze my neck, pulling my hair away from it to kiss just below my ear.

"Anger looks good on you, Miss Deen," he whispers, causing chills to run down my body. "Next time, let's try to avoid the bloodshed."

"There better not be a next time," I say, feeling that familiar sense of jealousy forming again.

"Well, if there is, I promise to make sure there is a parking lot around to fuck you in." I smile to myself, still reeling in the aftershocks of my mind-blowing orgasm that only he is capable of giving me. I let him lead me back in the bar, thoroughly fucked, utterly sated and completely open to the idea of him making me jealous anytime he wants.

Chapter Twenty
No More Loneliness

Nobody said anything when we walked back inside the club. The bouncer had tried to prevent me from coming inside, but Regg stuffed a few bills in his hand to keep him quiet. If Brooklyn and Punkin were aware of what Regg and I had just done, they kept it to themselves. Regg kept me close by his side for the remainder of our time there, which wasn't but about thirty minutes. He looked totally put together, not in the least effected by what had just taken place. I was beginning to think that he'd completely forgotten what happened until I saw him put the same finger he'd had in my pussy in his mouth.

The ride home is unbelievably cold. When we stop at the halfway point to smoke, I can't even light my cigarette. My leather pants look amazing, and were enough to keep me warm on the way down, but the ride back is a different story. I don't complain though, that's something that is highly frowned upon in the MC. If the bitch can't hang, then she don't deserve to ride. I know that all too well. I've seen too many women left in parking lots for bitching.

"I know your ass is cold," Luke says, fighting hard to keep from laughing his ass off. I'd give him the finger, but I can't get it to function. If I was gonna go back to riding, I would definitely have to buy some new leathers. "Say it, Red. Come on, bitch about the cold. I'm beggin' you." Luke's smartass mouth has me thinking of riding home naked just to prove I can.

"You can't look good and ride, sugar," Ronnie chimes in, leaning back on his heels to give me that raspy laugh I love so much.

"K-keep talking shit," I stutter, standing close to the motor on Regg's bike to try and thaw out.

"Leave her alone, Ronnie. Nobody knew it was gonna get this cold." I smile at Brooklyn, thankful for her coming to my defense. "I'll give you twenty bucks if you bitch, Red." The club erupts in laughter, and I can't help but laugh myself.

"Hell, that ain't even enough for a taxi to get me home."

"You could always pit and pat. You'll have blisters the size of golf balls wearing them damn heels," Possum laughs, confirming that I'm on my own here. I look to Punkin, seeing if I have at least one on my team.

"Don't look at me, I ain't carryin' your ass." Great. Even though I'm the butt of the joke, it's comforting being in the presence of this greatness-my family. I never realized how much I missed this until now.

"You gonna make it?" Regg asks, coming up behind me and placing his body dangerously close to mine.

"I thought you had faith in me, Regg." I turn to him, allowing him to light the cigarette that's been dangling from my mouth since we stopped.

"I do have faith in you, Red. I have a jacket too. You want it?" That slimy bastard. This whole time, he'd had a jacket and had not offered it to me. Because I'm a stubborn bitch, I refuse.

"I'd rather ride home naked," I say, narrowing my eyes at him.

"Suit yourself."

Ronnie announces that break time is over and we mount the bikes. Only thirty more minutes. I can totally do this.

For the second time tonight, I lied to myself. I totally cannot do this. We're running well over a hundred. My back has yet to feel the sissy bar because I'm pressed as close as possible to Regg-nearly up under him. I can no longer feel my legs, snot is frozen to my face and we're only fifteen minutes in. When the red light for Collins comes into view, I nearly pee from the excitement.

Breaking off from the pack, Regg steers us down the winding road that leads to his house. From the highway, he lives down a gravel road, up a hill, through a pasture, across a creek and deep in the woods-somewhere. By the time we finally turn down the drive, I'm sure my blood has slivers of ice in it.

He pulls the bike into the barn, and even long after he's cut off the engine, I can't move.

"You gonna get off?" Those words have so many meanings, that it takes me a second to realize what he's saying.

"I don't think I can," I say, keeping my hands that are under his cut, wrapped tightly around his waist. He grabs my arms, easily removing them and I start to protest, but he wraps them around his neck. He then grabs my legs, wrapping each one around his waist before getting off the bike and piggy-backing me inside. Well, that worked.

He carries me up the stairs, pausing in the den for a moment before taking me into his room. Prying my limbs from around him, he deposits me on the bed where I land with a soft thud. He pulls off my boots and pants, then pulls me to a sitting position before removing my jacket. My nipples are pressed hard against the fabric of my shirt, drawing his eyes to my breasts.

"Did you leave your headlights on, or are you just happy to see me?" he jokes, ridding me of my shirt, but leaving me in my bra.

"I'm just cold," I say, unable to find a cool comeback. His smirk fades, replaced with an understanding smile.

"I know, babe." He pulls one of his shirts from the dresser then slips it over my head. Pushing me to my back, he pulls the covers up to my chin and kisses me chastely on the lips. "Night, Red." I watch him walk away, turning off the light before walking back into the upstairs den.

"That's it?" I call, as he's shutting the door. I was hoping for another late night love scene. Or at least for him to sleep with me. I didn't want him to put me to bed like a child, and then disappear to do whatever in the hell it is he does.

"My chickens need me," he says with a smirk. I need him too, but I don't say that.

"If you were planning to leave, why didn't you just put me in my own damn bed?" I huff, acting like a moody teenager instead of a grown woman.

"I just did." He shuts the door before I can answer, leaving me with the knowledge that his bed and my bed, are now one in the same.

***

I've often wondered what Regg's mouth on my pussy would feel like, and by the way he's sliding my panties down my legs, I have a feeling I'm fixing to find out.

"What are you doing?" I ask, fully awake now that he is back in the room. I know what he's doing, but I want to hear him say it. He's between my legs, the covers forgotten as he replaces the warmth of them with the heat of his body.

"I've wanted to taste this sweet pussy all night." He doesn't bother kissing his way up my legs or teasing me.

When Regg wants something, he goes in for the kill. Pushing my knees as far apart as they will go, he buries his face between my legs, running his nose up my pussy, then dragging his tongue back down my slit. The act has my back arching off the bed, and I grip the sheets beneath me to keep from pulling his hair out. He moans against my clit, letting the vibrations from the sound add to the pleasure his tongue gives me. Placing his hands beneath my ass, his thumbs lay on either side of my swollen lips, opening me up completely to him.

"You taste just like you smell. The sweetest kind of sin." I assume that's a good thing. I mean, he could have said I taste like diet Pepsi. Nobody likes that shit. And by the way he's devouring me, he likes his sin sweet. His tongue moves in the motion of an eight, never giving me enough to come, just enough to make me writhe and beg beneath him. He shows no mercy as minutes pass and he continues his slow, circuitous movement. When I can stand it no longer, when my body is on the brink of combustion and my ache for release becomes almost painful, he gives me what I want. Focusing the attention of his tongue on my clit, he pulls the small, sensitive bud into his mouth and sucks. I come hard, my orgasm hitting me in waves that intensify with every beat of my heart, causing my body to jerk in response. I scream, my voice echoing off the walls so loud that I bite down on my lip to contain it.

"Scream for me, beautiful. Nobody here to listen but me." I whimper at his words. Every time he says something to me, another wave of ecstasy ripples through me at the sound of his voice. Nobody's words have ever made me feel as special and wanted as his do.

I'm still blinking away the stars from my vision when he slides up my body. Running his hands up my sides, he removes my shirt and bra in one swift determined motion. Cupping my breasts in his hands, he takes a moment to feel the weight of them against his palms before lowering his mouth to my nipple, pulling it between his teeth before soothing it with his tongue. He pulls a condom out of thin air, ripping it open and sliding it over his cock. I take him in my hand, feeling him for the first time. He's long and thick, and I can feel him growing as I stroke him harder.

Grabbing my hand, he pins it behind my head before covering his body with mine. He kisses me deep, guiding himself inside of me.

"Fuck, that feels good," I say, breaking from his mouth because the need to tell him how much I like this is too much to contain. His hips roll in a slow and steady pace, giving me exactly what my body craves. He kisses my neck, my mouth, down my chest-everywhere, but never slows his stride. This is not fucking. This is making love, but just like fucking, Regg is good at it.

He tells me I'm beautiful. He tells me how perfect I feel, and how he wants to stay buried inside of me all the time. He tells me things that make me feel loved, and it takes everything I have, not to utter the three words that could possibly send him running away from me.

We come together, our bodies seeming to know when the other is near its climax. I long to feel him without a condom. I want to feel the hot bursts of cum as he explodes inside of me. But, even wrapped in latex, the feeling is amazing. He pulls out of me slowly, never letting his mouth leave my face or his hands leave my body. I curl into him, letting him fold me into his arms and hold me tight to his chest. It's just too perfect. My whole life I've been alone. I've never felt what I feel when I'm with him. It's not just safety and warmth. It's so much more. It's a need that can't be filled by any other. And the feeling doesn't just come from me. I can sense that he needs this just like I do.

"I'm tired of being lonely," I say to the darkness. I don't know why I said the words out loud, but his response has me glad that I did.

"You don't have to be lonely anymore." If I didn't think I loved him before, now I'm absolutely, positively sure of it.

Chapter Twenty-One
Small Places, Tiny Spaces and Little Brothers

I'm eight weeks into my sentence. I only have four to go before I'm released back into the real world. It's bittersweet. Part of me doesn't want to leave in fear of what will happen to Regg and I when I do. The other part of me can't wait to get the hell outta this place, so I can start making my own decisions and my own mistakes again.

Even though being with Regg is great, something is still missing. I can feel my passion to dance dying, and it scares the shit outta me. I don't want to give it up, but I know that it's the right thing to do. Brooklyn was right. I would never be able to have a career in dancing because it was that path that led me to the drugs. I will not allow myself to go back down that road again. Ever.

Dancing is a part of me, though. It helps make sense of a world full of shit that I don't understand. Regg's house has to be at least three thousand square feet, but every day I feel like it shrinks a little more. Now, the huge upstairs den where I do cardio every afternoon isn't so huge. The massive downstairs den where Regg and I watch movies isn't so massive. The kitchen that is small in comparison to the rest of the house, now feels like a closet.

The only time I've been out of the house has been when I went for my scheduled drug screenings, twice with Regg on the bike and once on a late night trip to get ice cream with Brooklyn. I find myself going to the farm to work with Regg, just for a change in scenery-not that I actually work. The problem has me on the verge of a mental breakdown, and I find myself torn with what to do.

I've been like this for a few days, and told Regg I just needed some space. He never questioned me, just gave me what I asked for. Now, it's after three in the morning, I'm lying awake in bed, in my own room. Sleeping by myself presented more of a problem than what I had anticipated. The first night, I stayed awake for hours until I finally passed out from exhaustion. The next night, I fell asleep on the couch with Regg, but woke up in my room. Tonight, nothing is working and I'm on my feet, making my way to the adjoining door of our rooms before I know it.

"You awake?" I whisper to the darkness, my mind battling between hoping he is and hoping he isn't.

"Yeah, babe. I'm awake." His voice is alert, making me wonder if he's been lying in bed thinking like I have. I tiptoe across the cold floor to his bed, crawling under the covers that he holds up for me, and turning into his side. His body is warm and inviting. His hard chest presses against me as he grabs my waist, pulling me tighter to him.

"I miss dancing," I say into his neck. He kisses my head while his hand slips under my shirt to rub my back.

"I noticed that at Punkin's party. You seemed pretty lost in the moment." I think back to that night, how free I felt. It was the first time in years that I danced without being under the influence of something. "I don't want to hold you back from doing something you love, Red," he says, tilting my chin up so that I'm looking at him. The moonlight filters in through the windows, allowing me to see the compassion and understanding in his eyes.

"I can't dance, Regg. I know it will only lead me back to the drugs. I'm not strong enough to refuse them." My eyes drift to his lips. I want him to kiss me. As if he can read my mind, he lowers his mouth to mine, giving me a deep, passionate kiss that I wasn't aware I needed until now. He pulls away all too soon, and when his body moves over mine, I'm sure it's to give me more of him. But he stands and pulls on his jeans and his boots.

"What are you doing?" I ask, sitting up in bed to look at him.

"Stay in bed. This bed. I have to go to the farm." I look over at the clock, which reads twenty-five minutes after three in the morning.

"I didn't hear your alarm," I say, confused by his sudden energy and quick departure.

"Farmer's intuition. I'll be back later." He leans down, giving me one last long slow kiss before he stands to leave.

"Want me to come with you?" I ask, already pulling the covers off to get up.

"Stay. Get some sleep. I'll be back in a little while." He leaves, and I listen to his heavy footsteps as he walks down the stairs.

"Well, that was weird," I say to the darkness, grabbing his pillow to curl up with. Even though he's gone, the scent of him fills my head, and like a lullaby, it puts me to sleep.

***

"I'm Todd," the young guy at the door says. It's just before noon and Regg still hasn't returned. When I heard a knock downstairs, I figured he'd left his keys and needed me to let him in. I was surprised to find a younger, brown haired, tanned version of him instead. The boy stands as tall as Regg, with bright blue eyes, wearing a ball cap with a backpack slung over his shoulder.

"Hey, Todd," I say, becoming nervous at his sudden presence.

"Regg is still working. He sent me over here with lunch." From the front pocket of his backpack, Todd presents me something shaped like a hotdog wrapped in foil. "It's a smoked sausage dog. It's really good." His cheeks redden and I have to fight the urge to pinch them. I smile, motioning for him to come inside and letting him lead me to the kitchen. I sit at the table, watching in amusement as he makes his way around the kitchen getting glasses, napkins and the jug of sweet tea from the fridge.

"So, Todd," I start, feeling like I should strike up some kind of conversation. "You're Regg's brother?"

"Yes ma'am. Sorry, Reggie doesn't usually have company." He calls him Reggie. How sweet. And he says ma'am. How respectful. He looks a little nervous now that his hands aren't busy. I take the sausage dog from him, noticing that he's brought one for himself too, and I don't hesitate taking a huge bite.

"Shit, this is good," I say through a mouthful of food. I grab the mustard from the fridge, squirting a generous amount on my sausage before offering it to him. He declines with a wave of his hand, and I shrug, placing it between us in case he changes his mind. All dogs, no matter what kind, are better with mustard. "How old are you?" I watch his cheeks redden again, and know that he may be Regg's brother, but looks are all they have in common.

"Sixteen." He meets my eyes when he speaks, but quickly looks down when he's finished talking. That shy, cute boy act might not work in high school, but if he held on to it, he'd kill the ladies when he gets a little older.

"You play football?" I remember Luke and Regg's conversation months back about Regg saying he was going to his little brother's game. He was referring to Todd, unless he has another brother, which I doubt.

"Yes ma'am." Okay, he was going to have to stop with the ma'am shit.

"Just call me Red. I'm not that damn old, you know." He laughs and I feel the ice between us crack.

I learn that Todd lives with his aunt and uncle not too far from here. Regg offered to let him move in with him, but he's lived with his aunt and uncle for most of his life and that is his home. Not only is he a football player, but he takes honors classes and has endless knowledge about guns and American History. When he starts to tell me about some German made rifle, I can see the passion in his eyes as he speaks.

He doesn't ask what I do or who I am. He doesn't make me feel uncomfortable or uneasy while he is here. He is very respectful, smart and loves his brother very much. There is no sign of him being brought up in anything other than a loving home. If Regg hadn't already given me a hint of his past life weeks ago, I never would have guessed it.

Todd and I have yet to find anything in common with one another until he mentions something about a 007 video game.

"Goldeneye?" I ask, through a mouthful of food.
"You know it?"
"Know it? I'm a beast at it." I'm not lying. Many people have tried to beat me, and they have all failed.

"Is that a challenge?" I match Todd's smile with my own. "I mean, I got the game. I can bring it over right now." Todd's smile is gone and so is mine. Shit was fixing to get serious, and my excitement was through the roof at the thought.

"Well, what the hell you waitin' for?"

"Shit!" Todd says when I find the golden gun before he does. "Don't tell Regg I cussed. Shit!" I laugh at him as I chase his character down a hall and into a corner before taking his life with one shot.

"I won't tell him," I promise, pausing the game to get a refill of sweet tea. "You want something?"

"I'm good." Todd is a great kid. We've been at it for most of the evening and he refuses to give up. I let him win one in hopes that he wouldn't quit. It wasn't necessary. The little shit is not a quitter.

Since I had Todd to entertain me, it allowed Regg's absence to go unnoticed. He'd been gone since he left me this morning, but having his brother here is almost like having him around. Almost. I doubt Regg would play video games with me for endless hours.

I return to the living room where we have taken over Regg's man cave with candy wrappers and game controllers.

"I can't play but one more game. I have to be home by six. I have tests tomorrow and a pretty big game. We're playing the Bulldogs for the district championship. Y'all comin'?"

I'm caught off guard by this question and totally unsure of what to say. "Um," I start, trying like hell to come up with something that won't be the wrong thing. If Regg hadn't planned on going, I knew it was likely because of me. But, I didn't have the right to confirm something that would ultimately let Todd down if Regg didn't want to go. "I don't know," I say truthfully, offering him a smile. He gives me a smirk and I have to remind myself that he's not Regg. And that he's only sixteen. Thank God Regg doesn't have any older brothers.

"I hope y'all do. It's the last game of regular season." Todd plays with the remote, using my distraction to choose the one setting in the game I suck at.

"Has he made any of your games this year?" I ask innocently, thinking back to every Friday night I've been here.

"Most of them. He missed a couple, but I know he's busy with the club and all. He works a lot too. I help him during the summer and when I'm out on break. Next week is Thanksgiving so I'll work the whole week I'm out."

"That sucks." I know all too well. My evenings and holidays were always spent working when I was in school. Unfortunately for me, I didn't have parents that bought me shit like cars and clothes. I guess Todd's aunt and uncle are a lot like that too. Although, I'm sure they are that way because they wanted him to appreciate the finer things in life, not because they didn't give a shit. I could never imagine Regg making Todd miss out on his childhood just to shovel chicken shit.

We focus our attention on the game, both of us fighting like hell to get to the golden gun before the other one does. I contemplate letting Todd win again. I want him to come back and play video games with me all the time. But, as I pass the room with the golden gun, I can't resist. Thirty seconds later, he's dead.

"Dammit!" he yells. I fall back, laughing my ass off as I program my name in the number three spot, completely knocking him out of the top ten. He mutters a string of cuss words through his smile, making me laugh harder. Some of them don't even make sense.

"Hey, boy." The room grows silent as I peek over the back of the couch to see a very tired, very dirty Regg standing just outside the kitchen door. "Watch your mouth." Todd flushes with embarrassment and I shoot him a wink, letting him know that he has no reason to feel humiliated around me.

"He tells me to watch my mouth too," I whisper, earning myself a smile from little brother. I help him pack up his game before walking him to the door. "Maybe we can play again soon?" I give him a hopeful look.

"Definitely. See ya later." Regg follows him outside while I clean up our mess in the living room. Something about being around Todd made me feel like a teenager again. It was nice to laugh after three days of feeling sorry for myself.

"So, I see you and my brother are getting along," Regg says, a smile forming on his tired face as he enters the room. Dark bags hang under his eyes, and his body moves slow with exhaustion. He throws his cap on the pool table as he walks up to me. Wrapping his arm around my waist, he takes me with him to the couch. Positioning us so that we're on our sides, he tucks me under him. He smells like sawdust, sweat and Regg. It's delicious. I love the smell of a working man.

"He has a ball game tomorrow. Did you know that?" I ask, feeling him bury his face in my hair. He inhales and the gesture gives me goosebumps.

"I did." His answer is short, and I dig deep to find the courage to ask him to go. I don't know why I'm so nervous. Fear of rejection comes to mind. What if he doesn't want me to meet his family? I'm sure they will all be there.

"Um, are you gonna go?" 'You.' Not 'we.' Maybe he will invite me to go with him.

"Do you wanna go?"

"Yes." That was too fast, Red. Dammit. Why did I have to sound so desperate? I feel his body shake with laughter.

"Okay, then. We'll go. But right now, I need some sleep." I smile, thinking of surprising him with supper while he sleeps. I move to get up, but he holds me tighter. "You stay with me. Watch T.V., sleep, read...whatever. But, I want you in my arms. It's been too long." It has been too long. I haven't slept in Regg's arms in three nights. I am overdue for some much needed body to body with him. Too bad we have on clothes. I start to ask him to take off his shirt, but he's already snoring in my ears.

I turn on the T.V., finding an old rerun of Saved by the Bell. By the time the first commercial break is over, I'm snoring too.

Chapter Twenty-Two
Friday Night Strobe Lights

It takes me three hours to find something to wear to Todd's football game. Regg's aunt and uncle will be there, as will his cousin and some of his old high school friends. Girlfriends too, I'm sure. I finally decide on dark wash skinny jeans, knee high brown riding boots, a cream-colored, turtleneck sweater and my brown leather jacket. I leave my hair down, teasing it slightly at the scalp before positioning it over my left shoulder. By the time I run my hands through it a hundred times, it will look messy-just how I like it. I don't go overboard on the makeup, but I make sure I have enough eyeliner and mascara to make my hazel eyes pop.

I meet Regg downstairs, who's dressed in jeans and a multi-colored button down shirt consisting of brown and orange hues. We match perfectly and I demand we take a picture together. Since I don't have a camera, we use his. It's a deer camera and it takes us a few tries before we're sure the picture is taken, but the flash finally comes on.

I smoke light a freight train on the way to the game. I'm a huge bundle of excitement and nerves by the time we arrive. Not wanting to smell like an ashtray, I soak myself in body spray, causing Regg to choke, before popping a piece of spearmint gum in my mouth. We walk hand in hand to the gate, and the huge lights illuminating the field have me nearly dragging Regg to the stands so I can get the full effect.

"Do you want some nachos or something?" he asks, tightening his grip on my hand to slow me down. I shake my head, too excited to eat. "You that happy?" I've been smiling since we got out of the truck, and I guess he's just now noticing.

"I am. It's nice to get out of the house." It is, but that isn't the reason for my happiness. As a teenager, I went to all of Luke's football games. Sometimes, I went as far as painting myself blue and white or wearing a shirt with his name spray painted on it. Some people thought it was stupid, but Luke always looked for me in the stands before he took to the field. Dressing in something crazy made me easier to locate. He liked it, so what other people thought didn't matter.

We stop to talk to a few people. Regg just introduces me as 'Red.' He never says 'this is my friend,' or 'this is my girlfriend.' I guess he just lets people assume whatever in the hell they want to. We finally make it to the stands and I let Regg pull me across the metal bleachers as I take in the fresh cut grass, bright lights and people on the sidelines.

"Red," he says, pulling on my hand until I turn to him. "This is my Aunt Kathy and my Uncle Roland." I smile down at the couple, who refuse my hand and instead stand to give me a hug. Even though I just met them, like Regg, I feel like I've known them for years. We take a seat next to them, Regg positioning me between him and his aunt.

"It's cold out here, sista," she says, pulling her blanket tighter around her.

"Ahh. Quit your fussin'," Uncle Roland jokes, but I watch as he pushes his body closer to hers to keep her warm. They're the epitome of a happy couple and it gives me a sense of peace knowing that Todd lives in a home with such a loving family.

The announcer comes over the loud speaker, and I watch as the Tigers storm through the paper banner. Everyone is on their feet cheering, including me. Once the ball is kicked off, we spend more time standing than we do sitting.

Todd plays an exceptional game, not allowing a single quarter-back sack. According to Aunt Kathy, it says a lot. Apparently, the Bulldog defense is rated number one in the state. Pride swells in my chest each time Todd makes a block, and my smile widens each time Regg yells out something encouraging to him. Before I know it, halftime is here and the band takes the field as the players run off. Todd chances a look in the stands, giving us all a confident smirk. But, when he points a finger gun and shoots, I know it's meant for me.

"Who the hell is he shootin' at? I know he ain't shootin' at me." I laugh at Aunt Kathy, taking time to tell her about the video game and the motive for Todd's actions. Uncle Roland chimes in, letting me know that he's a gamer too and another challenge is offered and accepted. I have a feeling I won't be *letting* him win.

I feel hot air on my fingers and turn to Regg, finding my hand cupped in his as he warms it. "How 'bout them nachos?" I ask, thinking a coke, some peanuts and a pickle wasn't a bad idea either. He leads me down the bleachers and towards the concession stand. The night has been perfect. Then, I see a familiar face making her way towards us. Taylor-Regg's date from a few months ago. I feel my body stiffen, but if Regg notices, he doesn't say anything.

"Regg!" she calls, all smiles, sunshine and fucking rainbows. The bitch looks great, better than I remember.

"Hey, Taylor." Regg's words are cautious, and I wonder if he's trying to hide something. "You remember Red?"

She gives me a quick once over before forcing a smile. "Of course. Good to see you again. You look great." I smile, not sure how to respond to that. If she was expecting me to say the same, we'll grow old and die right here before I would. "I'll see you around?" She asks, looking back at Regg. I almost laugh at how desperate she looks. Not that I can blame her.

"Yeah, babe." Babe. Not darlin'. And definitely not beautiful. I'd set the whole damn stadium on fire if he called her beautiful. That was my name. He'd be better off calling her 'Red.'

We walk away, and I decide to keep my mouth shut about the whole scene. It wouldn't do any good anyway, and I wasn't going to let one girl spoil my night.

"Regg!" I look up to see a heavy-set blonde approaching. She's beautiful. Like breathtakingly beautiful. I imagine she is some sort of model. I'm too awestruck by her beauty to take in the fact that she is wrapping her arms around Regg's neck.

"Sabrina, this is Red," Regg says, explaining who I am and what we've been doing with a hint of a marriage proposal and the possibility of fifteen kids in only four words. If she didn't get the picture, she was nothing more than a stunningly gorgeous face.

"Oh," her face falls, but she recovers quickly. "Nice to meet you, Red." I smile, not offering her my hand. Judging by the look in her eye, she would likely jerk it from my wrist. "Great seeing you again." The dreamy look in her eyes doesn't go unnoticed by me. I raise my eyebrow, and watch Regg's face turn red. His embarrassment is almost worth the interruption.

Again, I choose to not say anything. We almost make it to the concession stand when I hear his name being called from behind us by another female voice.

"Oh, for fuck's sake. Are you shitting me?" I turn to him, having had my fill of ex-lovers for the evening. I'm just about to smack the shit outta whoever is behind us when I look down to see a cute, blonde haired girl who couldn't be over ten. This time, Regg lets go of my hand to pick the girl up in his arms.

I stand there for a good minute feeling like an idiot for almost hitting a ten year old before Regg sheds mercy on me. "Red, this is Sara. My cousin." He draws out the last words and I shoot him the finger. I realize my actions and immediately try to play it off, by throwing up my index finger to give him the peace sign. Sara, returns my warm welcome by giving me the middle finger too. Before Regg can say anything, she completes the peace sign with an innocent smile.

"Sara. That's my favorite name. Did you know that?" Forgetting that a ten year old is ten and not three is a mistake. So, when Sara throws her hand on her hip and says 'I do now,' the remark is well-deserved on my behalf. She joins us at the concession stand, and I'm thankful that the kid is here to potentially stop anymore advancing women. For all they know, Regg and I are happily married and Sara is our child. If we run into another ex, I'll be sure to tell them that. Considering little Sara is a smart ass like me, I'm sure she'll be on board.

Nachos, two hamburgers, four cokes, one dill pickle, two bags of peanuts and a pack of sour straws later, we finally head back to our seats. No sooner than we're seated, we're back on our feet, cheering for the boys as they take the field for the second half. Through time-outs and a few injuries on the field, I learn that Sara is the daughter of Regg's mother's sister who'd died during childbirth. Aunt Kathy and Uncle Roland have had her since she was born. Regg, Todd and Sara were all like children to their aunt and uncle who were never able to have kids of their own. I guess God had a plan for everyone.

The Tiger's take home a victory that night, with a score of 36-6. They are now the district champs and playoffs begin next week. I've already decided that even if Regg doesn't want to go, I am. We meet Todd outside the locker room before saying bye to the family. Somehow, I feel like they are my family too.

The ride home is silent. I curl up next to Regg, taking advantage of the middle seat. He rides home with one arm around me and one on the wheel, making me feel like a teenager who's just left her own high school football game. We don't turn down the driveway, instead, Regg takes the road that leads to the farm. I don't care. I'd gather chicken shit in my hands tonight if he asked me to, just to repay him for such an amazing night out.

It was things like this that I'd missed out on in life. My boyfriends were all a bunch of guys who thought it was cool to hate their family. I'd never been around anyone who had a normal life. It made me feel better about my own, I guess. Regg's family didn't make me feel like an outsider. They made me feel like I was part of the team.

Shit.

I was turning into a love struck, Susie-homemaker pussy. Before long, I'd be up at dawn cookin' up some breakfast for auntie and uncle. I'd be doing math homework with Sara and helping Todd with girl problems. Hell, I might start knitting and watching soap operas. The thought is sobering. I am losing who I was and becoming someone I don't want to be. How was Regg able to be a biker and a big brother? How was he able to be such a badass at times, yet have the patience to teach a ten year old how to tie her shoes? He was amazing. That's how. Me? I wasn't amazing. I was a stripper stuck in rural hell. Yet, I liked it.

I'm lost in my thoughts. I don't know who I am. I've forgotten who I am and who I'm destined to become scares the shit outta me. I light a cigarette, but when I try to roll down the window, I can't. I look up to find that we have stopped. We're not at the farm, but at the lake. I can see the moon reflecting off the water, and the only thought that comes to mind is fishing for supper and running around barefoot. I have to get the hell outta here. I reach for the door handle, but Regg grabs my arm, stopping me.

"Do you realize how transparent you are?" He's smiling. I'm shaking my head, contemplating jumping into the freezing lake to snap some sense back into me. "You're scared to death of a family. This," he says, motioning between the two of us. "It feels right to you. Being with my family, that feels right too. But, you're so scared of losing who you think you are, that you're ready to run from something good out of fear." Was I that transparent? No fucking way. I must have said all the shit I was thinking out loud.

"I have no idea what you're talking about," I say, laughing nervously. It's the only defense I have in this moment. I'll just laugh it off.

"Red, you don't have to change who you are for people to love you. They love you because of who you are." I've heard that line. He stole it from someone famous. I am sure of it. "Come on, I want to show you something." He gets out of the truck, and it takes me three deep breaths before I can find the courage to follow. I take a pull from my cigarette, letting him lead me near the boathouse at the edge of the lake. We stop just outside the door and he takes the cigarette from my hand, throwing it down before placing his hands on either side of my neck.

"I fell for you, Red. You. I told you that I'd do everything in my power to find that girl again. I have a feeling that tonight, I'll get her back." He rubs his thumbs over my jaw before releasing me to open the door to the boathouse. It's warm when we walk inside, not at all what I was expecting. I push the door closed behind me, staring into the dark. Regg flips a switch and a strobe light illuminates the room. Within seconds, I know Regg's words to be true. Tonight, he would get that girl back, and I would find myself once again.

Chapter Twenty-Three
Finding Red, Losing Battles

The boat house has been completely transformed into a dance studio. Thick, acrylic floors cover the space that was once used for boat docking. A tall, shiny pole centers the floor, reaching all the way up into the second story of the house. A massive strobe light hangs above my head, just off the front of the stage. Speakers are placed in the corners of the room, and a stereo has been built into one of the walls. One chair is positioned in front of the stage, next to a mini bar offering an array of vodkas. Ropes of black lights line the room, making everything glow brighter.

"You did this for me?" I ask, still unable to take it all in. Was this where he'd been all day yesterday? How did he manage to pull this off?

"I might have done it for me too." I turn to look at him, watching as his eyes go half mast. He slowly unzips my jacket, his eyes following the path of my zipper. "I want you to dance, Red," he says, his voice low and husky. "But, I only want you to dance for me." I nod, unsure of how to answer him. I can't think of anyone else I want to dance for. His eyes are the only ones I want to see me, and from now on, they are the only ones that will.

I strip in front of him until I'm wearing nothing but a white lace bra and matching panties. The black lights illuminating the stage make my underwear glow and my skin look darker than what it really is. Regg backs away, pouring himself a drink before taking the only seat at the stage. Nervously, I cross the floor to where the entertainment center is set up.

"Hit play on the first CD," I hear him tell me. I locate the power button, bringing the stereo to life before hitting play. *Blue on Black* by the Kenny Wayne Sheppard Band booms through the speakers, and I feel like it's a perfect fit.

It doesn't matter how much I try to change who I am. I'll always be me- Red. Trying to change that would be like trying to cover black with blue. It's pointless. I let the lyrics and the moment take me away, finding myself again on the tall, shiny pole centering the room. I don't stop when the song ends and another begins, I just keep dancing. The CD is filled with music ranging from country to pop, and I tell the story of each one with my movements.

I've forgotten Regg. I can feel his presence, but I don't look at him. I know he's watching me. I can feel his eyes on me, possessing what belongs to him. When *Closer* by Nine Inch Nails sounds around me, the sexual tension in the room rises. I chance a look at Regg, noticing that his shirt has been unbuttoned at the collar and his sleeves are rolled up. His hat is turned backwards, displaying DFFD stitched in orange. Devil's Forever Forever Devil's. Even dressed like this, without a stitch of leather in sight, he still makes it known where his loyalties lie.

He takes a sip of his drink, peering over the top of his glass at me with eyes full of feral need. They pull me to him. When I'm straddling his legs, he drops the glass, not at all bothered by its shattering. His hands grab my ass, squeezing hard as he pulls his bottom lip between his teeth. Moving my hips, I give Regg the show I'm famous for. I feel him harden between my legs as I role my body against him, working him in all the right spots.

I reach behind my back, unclasping my bra and letting it fall to the floor. Leaning back, I let him hold me by my waist as I bend, my hair dragging across the broken glass as I massage my breasts, letting him watch me pleasure myself. I sit up, wrapping my arms around his neck. His hands slide down to grip the back of my thighs before standing with me in his arms. Pushing me against the wall, I fumble with his jeans as he claims my mouth, kissing me hard. Freeing him, I moan at the long, heavy cock in my hand, desperate for it to be inside me. Pulling a condom from his pocket, he sucks the sensitive flesh of my neck, distracting me while he rolls it on.

Pushing my panties out of his way, he powers into me, showing no mercy as he fucks me hard against the wall. The music screams loud in my ears, drowning out the sound of my own screams as I cry out with pleasure. His fingers dig into the cheeks of my ass while my nails claw at the skin of his back. The moment is powerful, earth shattering and we're savage beasts, fucking the hell out of one another.

The back of my head hums with a mild pain from being repeatedly slammed into the wall behind me. My throat hurts from the cries of pleasure he pulls from me. But, I'll endure it forever, as long as he keeps fucking me like this. I squeeze my eyes shut, feeling my climax build. When I come, my whole body explodes in rapture, heating me with a fiery storm of bliss that's felt deep within the walls of my pussy and everywhere else his body touches me.

Regg stills inside of me. Burying his face in my neck, I feel his lips on me, making sparks ignite inside me once again. Slowly, he pulls out of me. Unwrapping my legs from around him, I stand.

"Ouch! Shit!" I yell, picking my foot back up. Regg follows my eyes down to the floor where I'm standing on one foot. Picking me back up, he carries me to the bar. The music has stopped and the only sound in the room is the crushing of glass beneath his boots. "Don't touch it!" I scream like a baby. He raises an eyebrow at me, in a silent dare to yell at him one more time.

Gently, he takes my foot in his hand, rubbing his thumb over the bottom of it until I flinch. I watch as he pulls his knife from his pocket. The sight of it has my head spinning and I hold tighter to the edge of the bar. I close my eyes, trusting him not to cut my toes off. A small pinch later, he tells me I'm good. Having to see for myself, I pull my foot up to my face to examine it. I have all five toes and nothing seems to be missing. I'm not even bleeding. It's embarrassing. A huge gash would have made me feel better about being such a tit.

"Better?" he asks, his expression amused.

"I might survive." I look around the room again, feeling my heart melt a little more when I remember that he did this for me. "Thank you." I look down at my hands, suddenly shy. Nobody has ever done anything so nice for me before. It's like my very own private paradise. "Life's hard ya know? I'm not one to ask for pity, but sometimes it sucks getting dealt a shitty hand in life. This," I say, motioning with my hand around the room. "Is something I've only ever dreamed about. I can never thank you enough." He comes to stand between my legs, resting his arms on either side of me so that we're face to face.

"I'll build you a million more if that's what you want. I'll spend every dime I have making you happy. I know you've had a shitty life. But, the hard part's over, Red. All you have to do now is just let me love you." Tears swell in my eyes at his words. He loves me. I mean, he didn't say it in those words, but the look in his eyes tells me he does. I want to tell him I love him. I want to tell him how much he means to me and how I can't imagine living another day without being with him. But, I can't find the courage to say the words.

"You know I'd never tell you to do anything that you didn't want to do." I nod my head, unsure of where in the hell he's going with this. "And I'd never tell you to say something that I know you don't want to say." Oh shit. Now, I know where it's going. I start shaking my head. He can't force me to tell him I love him.

"Tell me you love me, Red." I laugh nervously, looking around the room for an escape. If I told him, it would make this, what we have, official. There would be no going back. That is a huge step. I can't do it. I just can't.

"No, I can't," I say, shaking my head unable to meet his eyes. He pulls my chin up, but I squeeze my eyes closed, refusing to look at him.

"Red." It's a warning. One so powerful that I feel my eyes open, but I bite my lips so I can't speak.

"Tell me you love me." He needs this. He's given me everything I've asked for and so much more. Now, I need to give him something in return. They are just words. He knows I love him-how could I not?

His eyes stare intently into mine-trying to read what's going through my head. The moment he notices my resolve, his lip curls up into his infamous, sexy smile.

"Don't be so sure of yourself there, Regg. I'm only telling you because I'm scared not to." I joke, feeling the tension leave my shoulders.

"I don't care what your reason is. I just want to hear you say it." He narrows his eyes at me, daring me to back out like the chicken shit I am. But today, I found myself again, and the girl he met a year ago, wasn't scared of anything.

"I love you, Regg. More than heroin, vodka and dancing." My confession earns me a laugh.

"That's a lot." I smile, waiting on him to say the words back to me. I feel like a kid who's just asked the cute boy on the playground if he likes me. We're so stupid.

I'm still waiting and he's still staring, trying to read my mind. Maybe he didn't hear me. Since I've already said it once, it wouldn't kill me to say it again. I clear my throat and give him an expectant look.

Nothing.

He pulls away from me, grabbing my boots and slipping them on my feet before helping me down from the bar. Wrapping me in his jacket, he takes my hand and leads us outside to the truck. Ushering me in, he folds me into his side, acting as if the silence isn't at all unusual. Unable to keep my mouth shut any longer, I turn to him.

"Do you love me, Regg?" I ask, feeling my heart beat heavy in my chest in anticipation of his answer.

"Yes." There is no hesitation.

"Then tell me."

"Tell you what?" I want to claw his fucking eyeballs out. He is so infuriating!

"Tell me you love me," I demand, having the sudden urge to kick something.

"Make me tell you." The challenge in his eyes and the smirk on his face is enough to have me yelling in frustration.

"You are such an asshole!"

"Why am I the asshole? I had to force it out of you. What makes you so much better than me? Why do you deserve to hear it when I didn't?" He has a point, and it pisses me off. I get what he's playing at.

"How about I beat the shit outta you? Set your house on fire? Key your truck? Turn all your chickens loose? Would that be enough?" He laughs and it makes me want to punch him in the nuts.

"You can try. Don't worry, Red. If I know you, you'll come up with something." He had no idea. I'd make him tell me, and I knew exactly what I possessed that would have him saying anything I wanted him to.

Chapter Twenty-Four
Operation 'Tell Me You Love Me' Is a Go

It's been seven days since I first told Regg I love him. Every time I promise myself I won't say it to him until he tells me first, I wind up caving. I'm such a pushover when it comes to him. He has me right where he wants me, and he knows it. Just a look from him has me confessing my love over and over.

I've tried everything.

*Monday-*No Sex.

"Damn, baby. You look sexy as fuck," Regg said, coming up behind me in the kitchen. I was wearing a corset, heals and nothing else. Shaking my ass against him, I could feel him hardening. I let him lay me across the table, eat me like I was the turkey at Thanksgiving dinner, get completely naked, then I made my first attempt.

"Tell me you love me," I whimpered, rocking my hips against his fingers that were buried inside of me.

"You know I do." His voice was low and rough; another sign that told me Regg was completely turned on and at my mercy.

"Say the words," I demanded, trying to keep my mind focused on the prize. It was hard considering he had me on the verge of orgasm number two.

"Get on your knees." I was on the floor in the kitchen, on my knees before I realized my mistake. I quickly moved around so that I was sitting on my ass.

"Tell me you love me." This time, my words are said a little harsher. Damn him for making me do this.

"Not gonna work, babe."

"Look, *honey*," I said, digging deep to lace my voice with malice. "I hold the key to your happiness, so you better tell me what I want to hear."

"You're wrong, *honey*. I hold the key to your happiness. And it's a skeleton key, it'll fit any lock."

Regg-1 Red-0

Tuesday-Wreck shit

I practically destroyed his man cave. I'd built a bad-ass fort using his pool table, strewn my clothes from one end of the room to the other and left candy wrappers, glasses, plates and a half-eaten sandwich for him to find when he got home from the farm.

"What the fuck happened to my house?" I feigned a look of fear, but on the inside I was smiling. When he stomped off to his room, I was sure I had him. When he ran back down the stairs less than an hour later, he was in a panic. Seeing him in a panic had me panicking too.

"What's wrong?" I asked, already on my feet.

"Have you seen my granddaddy's watch? It was by the T.V." I moved through the den like a mad woman, picking shit up in hopes of finding the lost watch. After everything was cleaned, I had my head buried under the couch doing my second thorough search when I heard the T.V. come on. I looked up to find Regg completely relaxed, watching the hunting channel.

"Did you find it?" I asked, already forgiving him for not telling me.

"Find what?"
"Your granddaddy's watch."
"My granddaddy never had a watch. But, he would be proud to know I have a woman who keeps a clean house." That motherfucker.
Regg-2 Red-0

Wednesday-Food
I cooked breakfast and served it to him in bed.
Nothing.
Lunch was served to him at the farm.
Nothing.
Dinner was served at the table with candles and a paper menu with me listed as dessert.
Nothing.
Dinner also had a few ex-lax tablets in the meatloaf.
It wasn't a total win, but I'm counting myself a point anyway.
Regg-3 Red-1

Thursday-Classic Country
Old Violin was on the radio when he walked downstairs that morning. He danced with me and we re-enacted the scene from the clubhouse months ago. I made my move as soon as I saw an opening.
"I said, Regg. Tell me you love me." My words are said in unison with the words spoken in the song. When the music began and Regg kissed me, I thought I'd won. Then, when the speaking started again, I knew I'd lost.
"I said, Red. You already know I do. But you need to try a little harder, if you want me to say them to you."
Regg-4 Red-1

Friday-Sticky note hell

It took me three tries to convince Brooklyn to bring them, but finally she arrived with a stack of five hundred sticky notes. I made up some bullshit excuse about why I needed them so bad, but she never pushed the subject. My best guess was that she really didn't give a shit about the reason.

Three hours later, I had all five hundred plastered around the house with the words 'Tell me you love me' handwritten on them.

Regg acted like he didn't notice them, but sometime during the night, he found a way to respond to every, single note.

"No."

Regg-5 Red-1

It's Saturday and I'm out of play. I've never been one to back down from a challenge, but this shit was getting ridiculous. A knock at the door reminds me of my date with Todd and 007. Regg is out with the club, and I'm relieved that I won't have to see that shit eating grin on his face today.

"You okay?" Todd asks, eyeing me warily.

"I'm fine. It's stupid, really. Can I tell you?" I needed him, this sixteen year old boy. After all, this was shit that people his age normally did.

"Um, I guess." Immediately, I tell him everything. It only takes about ten minutes before I'm finished. Looking at me like I'm crazy, he gives me the obvious solution. "Just ignore him."

"I can't. You don't understand. I don't like to lose," I whine, not even getting a little satisfaction when I beat him in our first round.

"No, seriously. Ignore him. Regg can't stand that. He'll cave in a matter of hours." Todd was a fucking genius. I tackle him with a hug, leaving him looking very uncomfortable. I don't care. Regg might have won the battles, but I was fixing to win the war.

Two hours into the silent treatment and sure enough, Regg is about to snap. He's gone from playful, to furious to downright sad since he's gotten home. I manage to keep a sad look on my own face, never once letting him see me smile.

"Babe, please. Talk to me. Tell me what's wrong." I want to say 'you know what's wrong,' but I know I can't. That would be like starting over. "I'm not gonna stay here if you ain't gonna talk to me." Silence.

"What do you want? You want to go for a ride?" He paces in front of the T.V., running his hands under his cap in frustration.

"You want to dance?" Nope, Regg. That ain't it either. He paces a few more minutes before letting out a growl of frustration. "I fucking hate to lose." Coming to kneel in front of me, he puts his hands on my legs, fighting hard to look me in the eye.

"I love you. I love you more than Harleys, Chevys and pussy." I smile in victory, leaning in to give him a kiss before speaking to him for the first time today.

"That's a lot."

Chapter Twenty-Five
Freedom, Threats and Maddie

Ninety days. I was only forced to spend ninety days with Regg. Today, marks the one hundred and second day I've been with him. Time has no meaning to me anymore. There is no place I'd rather be than right here with him.

Yesterday, he asked me to move in permanently. I thought I already had, but I guess this made it official. I only had a few loose ends to tie up like moving, selling my trailer and getting my car. A couple hours ago, Regg dropped me off at my old house to pack while he went to Luke's for a club meeting, or church as they call it.

Now, standing on the threadbare carpet of my old living room, I wonder how in the hell I did it. The place stinks. The odor is a mixture between Doritos and feet. I was fucking disgusting. Wallpaper peeling away at the corners of the old walls. The floor vents are rusty and some were even missing. I've already about broke my ankle twice since I've been here.

I crank up the stereo on the wall, the only good thing about the place. I start packing up a bookshelf, dancing to the music that is so loud I almost miss the knock on the door. Figuring it's a neighbor, I turn down the volume before answering, prepared to offer an apology for the noise to whoever is on the other side.

"Don't you look good." On my steps is not a neighbor. It's Chip. I nearly choke to death, trying to find words to say to him. "May I come in?" Memories of the last time I saw him come flooding back. The asshole drugged me and almost had me raped.

"Fuck no, you can't come in. What in the hell are you even doing here, Chip?" His charming smile spreads across his face as he removes his glasses so I have a clear view of his dilated pupils.

"I hear you're off of lockdown." His smooth talking repulses me.

"Like you care. You left me in a hotel after you almost forced me to have sex with your friend." He frowns, shaking his head like he doesn't quite remember it like that.

"I'm sorry about that, Red. I never would have made you do that. You know me."

"Yeah, that's the fucking problem. I know you. Leave Chip, or I'm gonna call the cops." He doesn't know I don't have a phone. But, his evil smile tells me that he just might.

"No need. I just came to offer you an opportunity of a lifetime. I'm opening a club. I want you to be my featured girl. I guarantee six figures in the first year." He has to be kidding me. No way was I going anywhere with him.

"I'm not into that life anymore. I'm clean, I'm in a relationship and the only dancing I do is at my house." I almost smile as I say the words out loud. Who needs a strip club when you have a studio like mine?

"That's great, Red. I'm happy for you. You look really good. Better than ever. If you change your mind, here's my card." I take the card from his fingers, shoving it in my back pocket without even giving it a second look. Slamming the door in Chip's face, I give him the same courtesy.

"You ready, beautiful?" Regg asks, loading up the last box in the back of his truck.

"Yeah, I'm leaving the other shit. I don't need it." I pull my keys out of my purse, praying like hell that my car will crank after sitting for so long. It purrs to life on the first try. It seems to run smooth, not having the same miss I was used to.

"A present from the club. The guys took it over to the shop a few weeks ago. They fixed it so it runs like new." I melt against the seat at Regg's words. Everyone has been so good to me. There was no need to ask how I could repay them. I knew that in time, the club would demand something from me, and just like them, I wouldn't hesitate to do whatever they asked.

"Think you can keep up?" I ask, pushing my foot against the accelerator, sounding off the pipes.

"In that thing? No." He points to his truck and I laugh. I've never seen Regg do over the speed limit in that truck. The tires are so big, I was sure he'd run off the road if he ever hit eighty. "But, I bet I beat you home."

"What makes you so sure?" I ask, ready for the challenge. No way could he beat me in that big clunker.

"I know the way." Okay, so maybe there was a way for him to beat me.

When we finally arrive home, a few prospects from the club are there to help. Because I have such a soft spot for them, I immediately begin cooking dinner for the poor, overworked souls. Prospecting is a period where they prove themselves. It was a test of endurance and loyalty. But, I didn't always approve. Luke has often told me to stop babying them, but I never listen. What was he gonna do? Spank me?

The rest of the evening, I'm busy cooking, unpacking and setting up home in Regg's house. Just adding my favorite dishes to the kitchen, colored towels to the bathroom and pictures in the upstairs den make the place feel a little more like mine. Not that Regg has ever made me feel like it wasn't. Although, he did tell me that the downstairs den was off limits. It's his sanctuary. Men.

Dinner turns out to be a feast with the whole damn club. Everyone showed up and now there are men, women and children running around the house. But there was one in particular that held my interest more than the others. Maddie.

Maddie is the step daughter of a former club member who had been put out of the club with a bad name. But Maddie stole everyone's hearts years ago and had a permanent home within the club, much like I had at her age. At seventeen, Maddie is beautiful. She is book smart and street smart with looks that have Luke working overtime to keep the boys away. She has been like a little sister to both of us, but I'd lost touch with her a few years back. She is another person in my life that I turned my back on for drugs.

"Hey Red," she says, giving me her impression of Luke's infamous smirk. I put my hand over my mouth, afraid of screaming my emotions. Tears stream down my face as I pull her close, telling her in that one hug how sorry I am for my absence. Her teenage years couldn't have been easy being raised by a bunch of men. I should have been there for her, but at least she had Brooklyn.

"Maddie," it's the only word I can manage through my sobs.

"Stop crying and show me your studio. I wanna see it. I might want to take up a career in stripping," she jokes, but Luke doesn't find it very funny.

"Don't even fucking think about it. You're going to college. You ain't gonna turn into pieces of shit like me and Red. You're better than us."

"Um, thanks Luke. Asshole." I know what he is saying. He doesn't see me as a piece of shit. He doesn't see himself that way either. But, he did see us taking paths in life that we don't want Maddie to ever go down. She *is* better than us.

Maddie and I take the four wheeler down to the boat house. It has become my most used form of transportation. I drive slow, letting Maddie take in all of the magnificence of the yard and lake. And because it's thirty fucking degrees outside and we'll freeze if we go any faster. I can't wait for summer so we can go swimming, and have green grass and I can sunbathe naked in the front yard. Or backyard. Or six roads over. Lord knows it's not like anyone is gonna pass by and see me.

Maddie is awestruck when I open the doors to the boathouse. Even after all this time, I'm still awestruck myself. Sometimes, I spend hours in here. I even get up in the middle of the night to ride down just to dance. Many of those times, I find Regg sitting in the one chair, watching me. He comes in silently, never notifying me that he is here. But, I always know the moment he walks through the door. I don't have to see him. I can feel him.

"This is awesome, Red. Please dance for me," Maddie begs, poking her lip out on a pout. Because I owe it to her, I strip down to my panties and bra and allow her to sit in Regg's seat. I turn on the stereo, letting Eve's *Let Me Blow Ya Mind* sing out through the room. When I'm finished, she gives me a standing ovation.

We spend the next hour filling each other in on our lives. She pretty much knows about mine, but I'm surprised to hear she has a boyfriend that Luke hasn't killed yet. Later in the conversation, I find it's because he isn't aware of him. Luke is like our Superman. Maddie and I both depend on him so much, and he never lets us down.

It's after ten when everyone leaves. On the way back inside, Regg notices a box sitting by the door addressed to me. that the return address says it's from Lucy and I smile. I miss my old friend. Regg goes to take a shower while I curl up on the couch in the den to open the box. Inside, there is a letter along with five hundred dollars and a manila envelope.

Red,
I asked you nicely and you refused. Did you really think I'd let you do that? You have two days to make your decision. If you aren't at Café Du Monde by noon on Wednesday, I'll break the boy's legs.
-Me
P.S. If you tell anyone about this, I'll do more than break his legs. I'll kill him.

My heart pounds in my chest as fear runs through my veins. Chip isn't one to make idol threats. I know he will do what he says, just like I know what is in the envelope. I feel bile rise in my throat at the thought of Regg being hurt. I can't do that to him. Not after everything he's done for me. Holding my breath, I spill the contents of the envelope out on the couch. But, it's not Regg's face I see. It's Todd's.

Chapter Twenty-Six
Decisions, Lies and Contracts

I lie in bed, listening to Regg's soft snoring in my ear. How can I leave him? I can't risk not going. I know that Chip has the connections to follow through on his word. There is no way of escaping this without involving the club or telling Regg. Leaving is the only solution that will keep everyone safe. I can't keep the images of Todd out of my head. Someone took a picture of him during football practice, one standing outside the school and one with who I can only guess is his girlfriend. They were at a movie theatre. The closest one is thirty miles away which tells me that whoever took these pictures has been following him.

If I tell Regg, chances are he would find Chip, eliminate him and possibly go to jail. He would probably tell the club, who would refuse to let him do this on his own. That means that he, Luke and all the others would be facing jail time too. I refuse to allow them to sacrifice their freedom for me. They have already given me so much.

I was poison. Regg and Todd were fine until I showed up. If it weren't for me, Todd wouldn't be in danger and Regg wouldn't have had to deal with the shit he has for the past several months. I will have to concoct a lie to get away, and I will have to find one that will hurt the least. I close my eyes, trying to find sleep, but knowing that it won't come. Because, there is no way I can lie to Regg. At least not in a way that it won't hurt him.

***

"We need to talk," I tell Regg the next morning. I only have one more day and that will be spent trying to get out of town without having anyone tailing me. There is no time to waste.

"What ya wanna talk about, babe?" His eyes are bright this morning as he stands in nothing but pajama pants leaning against the kitchen counter. He looks so beautiful barefoot and sleepy. I feel my heart twist in pain at the thought of not seeing him again. Even if I did come back, he won't want me anymore. If I go through with this, I will be saying goodbye to all of my family.

"I've been doing some thinking." I clear my throat, hoping to strengthen my words. I have to do this. "Now that I don't have to be here, I don't want to stay. I miss my job and I have some things I need to handle. Things I have to do on my own." Regg keeps his face impassive as he processes my words. He walks to the coffee pot, filling another cup before resuming his position.

"Does this have anything to do with that package you got last night?" Panic fills me, but I fight hard to keep it hidden. There is no way he found it. I hid it well.

"Yes, Lucy has me a job down in Miami with her. It's a great opportunity. They have a zero drug tolerance and we're gonna be staying with her sister." My words are rehearsed. I concocted the story this morning before he even woke up.

"You know, Red, if you're in some kind of trouble you can tell me." His words make me want to spill my guts. I trust this man to take care of me. I trust him to handle everything and keep me and his family protected. But, at what cost?

"Sometimes, you just have to follow your heart. And right now, my heart's on a flight to Miami. I'm sorry, Regg." I can't meet his eyes. I don't want to look at him in fear of what I might find.

"You really mean that?" I nod, unable to form words. I fight against the tears burning the backs of my eyes. I stand, unable to stay in a room with him any longer. I have to get out of here. I have to save Todd. Save Regg. My life will be the sacrifice and it will be worth it.

"Wait." I pause in the doorway of the kitchen, keeping my back to him. I feel him walk up behind me; the only sound is our heavy breathing. "Please don't do this, Red. Tell me what it is and I'll fix it. I promise. I can take care of you." Tears stream down my cheeks as I hear the crack in Regg's voice.

"I'm sorry, but I can't stay." My own voice breaks and I snap my mouth shut, afraid of what I might say.

"Look at me, Red." His words are so demanding that I'm turning, unable to stop myself, but I still don't meet his eyes. "Look me in the eye and tell me you don't love me." I shake my head. That is something I could never do. "I can't let you leave. I won't."

"You have to," I say, snapping my head up and finally meeting his eyes. They are determined, and I'm prepared for the fight. "Please, Regg. Just let me walk out of your life. Please," I beg him. If he would just agree, then I could leave without hurting him further.

"Tell me." His body shakes nervously, anticipating my response.

"I can't."

"Tell me and I'll let you go. Just say the words, Red. Break my heart and I'll let you walk away, no questions asked." I picture Todd winning his state championship. I envision him growing older, marrying the girl from the picture. I see Regg with someone like Taylor, smiling happily as he holds his newborn baby in his arms. Images of the club thriving, following Luke into the direction of a better life flash through my head. With this, I find the courage to stop the flow of tears and say the words I never thought I could.

"I don't love you, Regg. I don't think I ever did."

It is the last time I see his face. Having packed a bag last night, I run to my car and speed down the driveway, never looking back. I cry hysterically all the way to the airport in Biloxi. Leaving my car in the garage, I take a cab to the bus station where I buy a one way ticket to New Orleans.

I don't contact anyone-not even Luke. I will write him a letter later, apologizing and assuring him that I'm good and that he doesn't need to worry about me. I doubt I don't need to be worried over, though. I have no idea what Chip has in store for me or even where this business will be. I just hope like hell it isn't in Miami. I am sure someone will be looking for me down there.

The next day, I'm at Café Du Monde by noon sharp. Seated at a table outside, I see Chip sitting alone.

"You know, that big guy two tables down looks pretty fucking obvious," I say as a form of greeting, referring to the man that has to be his bodyguard. What a pussy.

"Red, so nice of you to join me." His face is twisted into an evil smile and I want to throw the steaming cup of coffee in his face.

"Cut the shit, Chip. What do you want?" I'm not here to be nice. I'm here to save a life. He needs to know I'm not in any kind of mood to play his games. Reading the expression on my face, his smile fades and he gets right down to business.

"One year. That's all I'm asking for. After that, you'll be free to go back to your pathetic little life with Regg and the club. You're better than biker trash, Red." Before I can stop myself, I reach over and slap his face. While he's still in shock, I let him have it.

"Don't ever let his name come out of your mouth again. Don't think for a minute that he won't hunt you down and cut your throat. The only reason I'm here alone is because I don't want him doing a life sentence behind bars on my conscience." I lean back in my chair, shooting a murderous glare to the big guy who is now on his feet standing beside Chip. I wish a motherfucker would. I'll take him out too. I'm pretty sure I had the strength to do it in this moment.

"You'll pay for that," he promises, waving off the guy beside him.

"What? You gonna fuck me up? Fine, because this," I say, motioning to my face. "Is gonna make you a lot of money. If you want to damage it, by all means please do so. I'm sure the clients would love a toothless bitch to look at."

"You still got that grit. That's why I love you, Red." He's back to smiling, and I'm ready to vomit at the mention of the word love. "Like I said, one year. Here's your contract with everything I promised." I ignore the paperwork, unable to keep my eyes off of his. I've never wished looks could kill so much.

"Whatever, Chip. Where's the club?" I'm bored with him. I'm sick of small talk. I'm ready to do my time. I getting pretty damn good at being sentenced.

"Look at the contract, Red." Ready to move this along, I reluctantly pull the contract out, skimming it over. Just like he said, I had to promise to work for one year. My salary was for ten thousand a month plus I'd get to keep one hundred percent of my stage tips. Of course it says nothing about Todd. No lawyer would have gone for that shit. But, I'll pull the plug on him if he even so much as mentions Todd's name.

"You're pretty fucking confident, don't you think?"

"More than confident. I've built an empire, Red. And who better to be the face of it than you?" I roll my eyes, almost laughing at the fake license with the name 'Mary West.'

"Really? Was this necessary?" I ask, holding it up for him to see. At least the picture of me is decent.

"I couldn't have your friends trying to track you down." He's thought of it all.

"Why the hell do I even need a fake license?"

"You have to have a picture I.D. to fly, Red."

"Where the hell are we going?" This should have been the first question I asked. His sardonic smile has me thinking that I'm not gonna like his answer.

"Vegas, baby."

Chapter Twenty-Seven
From Bad to Worse

How the hell Chip was able to afford property on the Las Vegas strip, I'll never know. But, just across the street from the Bellagio Fountains, sits a huge building that was once home to over ten department stores. Now, it's a strip club with a name that makes my heart ache every time I read the flashing neon sign-Devil's. If it was only a coincidence, I wasn't buying it.

I hadn't even performed, but the bright screen that sits on top of the building displays my picture, my name and the words 'Performing Nightly.' Once again, I got my wish to be famous. To have my name in the lights. Now, I regret not wishing for a pony instead.

I spend the first week in Vegas doing photo shoots and shopping. I have a security guard with me always. I tell Chip there is no need, but he says I have to earn his trust. I tell him to suck a dick. Everyday I'm here, I'm forced to see his face. The only thing that gets me through is remembering why I'm here. Oh, and vodka. Thank God for vodka.

The second week, I meet all the staff. The girls are beautiful and I wonder why Chip hadn't asked one of them to be the face of Devil's. When I ask, his answer is simple, "They're not you." What the fuck ever. They all hate me. They know why I'm here, and I know that they're jealous. But, what they don't know is that I'd trade places with any of them if I could.

My third week in Vegas brings me to the night of my first performance. There isn't enough vodka in the building to calm my nerves. I promised Regg I would only ever dance for him. In less than five minutes, I will be breaking that promise. Not that it means a whole lot now.

Tonight, my I keep my family at the forefront of my thought. Todd is my family. Regg is my family. The club is my family. They need me to do this. I always knew there would come a time when I could return the favor. When I could repay them for all they have done for me. Now is that time.

"Let's go," the bouncer tells me. I don't know why he's such an ass. I've yet to make any friends and I guess I can mark him off my list too. I walk backstage, drink in hand. I wait for the current song to finish and for the emcee to make the announcement. My outfit is ridiculous, consisting of a pleated skirt and a white top that ties at my breasts. I am supposed to be going for the school girl look. It really isn't my thing. My song is *Catholic School Girls Rule* by The Red Hot Chili Peppers. It is fast paced and not something I chose to open with.

My name is called and I walk out. I can't bring myself to make eye contact or smile. The song is less than three minutes long and I barely make it through. The crowd seems pleased, why, I don't know. I looked like a total amateur. My movements didn't even correspond with the song. Before I have time to put my robe on, I'm grabbed by my arm and ushered to Chip's office- topless.

"You better be glad you got a pretty face," he says, fuming as he stubs his cigarette out in the ashtray. Leaning over, I grab his pack and light one for myself. "I can't have you going out there, half-assing your performance."

"Yeah, well what if that's all I got?" It isn't, but he doesn't know that. He only saw me dance in the last couple of good months before I got so bad on the drugs that I couldn't function.

"I thought you might say that, so I thought of a way to encourage you." He's pissed and I feel my stomach twist with worry. There is no telling what in the hell he's done. Punching the speaker button on his desk phone, he punches in a number before leaning back on his desk with his arms crossed. The other line rings a few times before a very cheerful, very familiar voice comes on the line.

"Hello... Hello?" My heart sinks at the sound of Aunt Kathy's voice echoing in the room. Chip leans over to hang up the phone and I have to sit to avoid passing out.

"The next time, it'll be little Sara, but she won't be talking." I can't even get angry at his words because I'm too busy trying to catch my breath. My heart is in my knees, my head is spinning and I feel like I've just taken a punch to the gut. "You still think that's all you got?" he sneers at me as I continue to freak the fuck out. I put my head between my knees, concentrating on slowing my breathing. When I'm composed, I meet his eyes, pinning him with a glare that I swear causes fear to creep across his face.

"Let me pick my own outfits, my own songs and perform my own way. I'll keep the house packed and keep them coming back, but you leave my family alone." He throws his hands up, looking around the room at the men standing there. "Now, was that so hard? I'm a sensible guy, Red. You give me what I want and I'll give you what you want." I stand to leave, ready to be out of this place and breathe some fresh air. "Oh, and Red?" I stop, but keep my back to him. "I'm gonna need you to strip naked. The guys don't like paying for something they can't see." With what little pride I have left, I walk out on his words.

It's midnight, the house is packed and I'm the performance everyone has been waiting for. Chip has promoted my name on billboards, the sides of buses and even has people on the street handing out vouchers for free drinks, just to come see me dance. This time, I dressed myself and chose my own song. Wearing a fedora, thigh high boots and a trench coat, I make my way out on stage. The audience is quiet, listening to the sound of my heels as I strut across the stage in the darkness. The music is timed perfectly with the lights, and the opening of Britney Spears' *Slave For You* has the crowd going nuts. I keep my head down with my hand on my hat while the introduction plays. When the actual music starts, I throw the fedora into the crowd. Walking around the stage, I make eye contact as I slowly unbutton my trench coat.

I imagine all the faces looking back at me belong to Regg, and soon, I'm nearly naked in front of all of them. I keep my g-string on, giving the crowd a good show, but making them wonder what's hidden beneath the thin piece of material. By the time the song is over, I'm breathless, the crowd is crazy and the stage is littered with monetary tokens of their affection. I am empty.

When I exit the stage, Chip is waiting for me, drink in hand.

"There's my girl." Knocking back the drink, I take the cigarette from between his lips, taking a pull before blowing the smoke back in his face.

"I'm not ya girl." I am his slave.

***

Chip has provided me with a fully furnished apartment under his name in the northern part of the city. It's quiet here away from the noisy, busy streets of downtown.

Under different circumstances, I might have liked it. I have a driver that takes me everywhere I need to go. He even lives in the same building as I do, and is at my every beck and call. But I'm no fool. I know it's not because Chip is a nice guy- it's because he wants to keep an eye on me.

I have everything I need. I have the finest clothes, the finest food and the most expensive fucking bed I've ever seen. But here I am, on the floor, eating Oreos, dressed in one of Regg's old t-shirts that don't even smell like him anymore, crying because I don't have everything I need. I don't have him. I'm reaching my breaking point. If I could just see him, I might be able to get through this. It is like withdrawals all over again.

I head down to the gym with no intention of getting an early morning workout. My eyes zone in on the phone hanging on the wall. I look around, forgetting that it's too damn early for anyone other than me to be up. Picking up the receiver, I block the call before dialing Regg's number. It rings once before I hear his voice.

"Yeah?" Tears fall from my eyes from just the one word. Keeping my hand over my mouth, I listen to his breathing. "Hello?" I'm struggling to stay quiet. I want to tell him I love him. I want to tell him to come get me from this godforsaken place and take me home with him. I hear him moving and picture him sitting up in bed, our bed.

"Red?" My name is my undoing and the hope in his voice has me hanging up the phone. I slide down the wall, crying loudly into my hands. He was the only man who's ever loved me-the only man willing to dedicate his life to me-the only man who's ever made me feel like I was someone. He was the heroin in my veins, the vodka in my blood and the dance in my heart. He was my lifeline. My world. My Regg. And now, he is gone.

Chapter Twenty-Eight
Hitting Rock Bottom Doesn't Keep You From Falling

I've been in Vegas Hell for two months. I hate it here. I hate the lights, the people, the smells, the heat and most of all... I hate Chip. I don't see him a lot. He spends most of his time in the casinos gambling, but not a day passes that I don't get a phone call from him-asking me to come to his place. Not in a million fucking years.

We've compromised over me not getting completely naked on stage. I can keep an article of clothing on, if I agree to strip nude in a VIP private dance. There is no telling the amount of money he is making off of me. My cut is two-fifty, and I'm sure he is making at least three times that. Just the thought of someone paying a grand to see my pussy for fifteen minutes makes me sick. But, I don't want to push Chip too far in fear of what he might do.

The club is always packed. I don't know one day from another. I'm just as busy on Tuesdays as I am on Saturdays. Chip keeps me booked and has me on a tight schedule. Like a puppet, I let him pull my strings and move me in any direction he wants.

It's Monday and my schedule tells me that I have a private in twenty minutes. Perfect. Another fifteen minutes of misery that I'm so not looking forward to. Wearing a simple tube top and mini skirt, I strut to the private rooms in the back to wait for my customer. Even when I worked at Pete's, I always provided my clients with a drink on me-vodka on the rocks. Chip has managed to import Kauffman's just for me, but I don't share that. They usually get house vodka which is still pretty good. At least here it is.

I take a seat on the velvet couch, leaning my head back and getting lost in the music. I dance to whatever is playing over the speakers and right now, it is a popular rap song that has already been played twice tonight.

Minutes before my client arrives, I pour their drink and plaster a smile on my face. Any second they will be walking through the heavy drapes that separate us from the rest of the club. A man wearing a ball cap and a heavy jacket walks in, making me raise my eyebrow in question. Even though it is the end of January, the weather is in the fifties which doesn't warrant a coat of this magnitude. Oh well, who am I to judge?

"Welcome, handsome," I say to the man who keeps his head down. The curtain is closed, and I extend my hand to the shy guy who I am sure has the interest of the bouncers. No doubt in only a few minutes, they will be coming in to check on me. "Vodka?" I offer, handing him his drink.

"I'm more of a Jack and coke kinda man." My body goes into sensory overload and my head spins at his voice. Picking his head up, I come face to face with Regg's soft, brown eyes. I don't know whether to cry, laugh, hug him or push him away. I've longed to see his face for months, and now he was here. "What are you doing here?" I manage to say, my voice nothing but a whisper.

"What do you think I'm doing here, Red?" Shit. Fuck. Dammit. Dammit. DAMMIT. This is not happening. He has to leave. Right now. If Chip finds out he is here...

"You have to leave, Regg. Please." He smiles at me, throwing a piece of my broken heart back in place.

"I don't think so, Red. Tell me what's going on." He hasn't touched me yet, and damn, I wish he would. I just want to feel his hands on me.

"I couldn't turn this job down. I'm making over six figures here. I need this." *You. I need you.*

"Bullshit. All you need is standing right here in front of you. Are you scared? Is it the fear of commitment? Why the fuck did you run?" I want to cry. I want to scream at the top of my lungs. He's right. All I need is him, and he's the one thing I can't have. I turn away from him, knowing that I have to end this now.

"I'm not ready to settle down. I just need some time to figure out what I want," I lie, knowing good and damn well that what I want is standing only a foot from me. *Think of Todd. Think of Todd.*

"I think you've had enough time to figure out what in the fuck it is you want, Red. You lied to me the day you left and now, you're lying to me again." He didn't believed me when I told him I didn't love him. The thought is bittersweet. As much as I wanted him to believe it so he would move on, I wanted him to know that I did love him more.

"Say whatever you want. I'm not going to change my mind. See, that's what's wrong with you *bikers*." I say the word like it tastes nasty in my mouth-like it's a disgrace to even have it in my vocabulary. With images of Todd flashing fresh in my mind, I give him the coldest, darkest side of me. "You think you can just walk in here and take whatever you want. It's not gonna happen, Regg. Not now and not ever. Did you ever wonder why I never settled down with anyone in the club? It's because I know that life, and it's not something I want. Leave, Regg, before I have you escorted off the premises." I hope like hell Regg will just leave on his own. I am sure it will take all of the security staff and then some to forcefully remove him. And I am sure he isn't alone.

I hold his stare, keeping my face impassive. When I see the look of defeat creep into his eyes, I have to fight harder than ever to not tell him why I'm here.

"Are you with him?" he asks, shock evident on his face as if he's found the missing piece to the puzzle. I want to tell him the truth, but it seems I've found a way to get Regg to completely let go of me.

"What if I am?" I ask, throwing my hand on my hip for emphasis.

"If you are Red, then that's a game changer." His voice shakes with fury at just the thought of me being with someone else. This jealous side of him is new, and something I can definitely use to my advantage in this moment.

"Then consider the game changed." There. I said it. By the look on his face and the defeat in his eyes, I know that I've convinced him of my worst possible nightmare.

"I'm getting on a plane in an hour." He pulls a ticket from his wallet and hands it to me. My name is typed on the front of a first class ticket to New Orleans. "I want you to come with me. But, if I leave the state of Nevada and you aren't with me, you can forget I ever existed. I will disappear from your life, Red. Just like you disappeared from mine. And I won't come back." His words hold a promise that I know too well. He means what he says. This is my last chance to be with him, but some lives are more important than my own.

"Goodbye, Regg." His brown eyes hold me, staring deep into my soul. I feel everything inside me die when he forces a smile and mutters the last words to me I'll ever hear him say.

"Goodbye, Red." And then...he is gone.

I run to the bathroom, letting all the emotions I've kept in check pour from me until I'm nearly screaming with hurt. In my hand, I hold the ticket to my freedom. But, freedom isn't the only thing it possesses. It holds the key to a future that I once had at my fingertips. It's my journey back to a life that I never thought I was owed, yet God had somehow deemed me worthy of it. Now, it was just a piece of paper that would forever haunt me as being the closest thing to love I've ever had.

Visions of Todd growing old and Regg happily married are nothing but a blur now. I am not strong enough for this. If I told Regg, yeah, he might go to jail. But, I know deep down that he would rather spend the rest of his life behind bars than one moment knowing that I've sacrificed what we had for a problem that isn't even mine. Who am I to not let him be the man he is? Who am I for not bringing my problems to the one man that promised to take care of me? What does that say about how I felt about him? It is wrong of me to take on this burden. I remember the sadness I lived with on a daily basis thinking about what I put Luke through with my addiction over the years. Now, I am doing the same thing to Regg.

Sometimes in life, you do stupid shit. You make decisions out of impulse because you think it's the right thing to do. But living with the heartache of knowing that the woman you love didn't trust you enough to be a man and take care of her would hurt more than anything else. That's the kind of man Regg is. He doesn't need anyone handling his burdens because it is his job. And my job is to give him that burden with not an ounce of fear over what the outcome would be.

Shielding him from the truth might be protecting him, but it isn't love. It is cowardly fear of having something that belonged to me taken away. Telling him the truth and trusting him to handle it no matter the cost- that is love. And love is something I have for him- Devil's Renegades Regg. Jumping to my feet, I run from the bathroom with one thought on my mind- I have a plane to catch.

"Red! Where the hell have you been? I've been looking for you." Chip's voice stops me in my tracks and my mind works overtime to come up with a story to pacify him.

"I'm not feeling well, Chip. I need the night off." I hold my stomach, letting him think my red, swollen eyes are a result of vomiting.

"Damn, you okay?" I shake my head, squinting my eyes shut and grabbing the back of my dressing room chair as if the motion nauseated me further.

"I think I just need some sleep."

"Of course," he comes closer to me, a look of concern on his face. "Come on, I'll get one of the guys to take you home." He holds out my robe to slip my arms through before placing his hand on the small of my back and leading me to his office. Once inside, he picks up his desk phone, mumbling a few hushed words into the receiver. Turning back to me, he props up against his desk, surveying me. "You think it's some kind of stomach flu?" I've never seen the motherfucker be this nice and it has my stomach turning over, for real.

"Not sure. Maybe it was something I ate." I wish he'd just shut the hell up. Two guys walk in, and he motions for them to come closer. Does he think I have to be carried?

"I see, hmmm. You think it has anything to do with your visitor?" My head snaps up, as my stomach clenches in fear. "I think it does." He walks slowly over to me, picking up my purse from the floor. I try to snatch it from his fingers, but he's too quick. "What is this? A plane ticket to New Orleans? First class too, I'm impressed."

"It's not what you think, Chip. He left. He's gone and he's not coming back."

"So you aren't going to meet him?"

"No, I'm just sad to see him and I want to go home. Look, I've given you everything you asked for. You have no reason not to trust me." Anger builds inside of me. I'm getting defensive because everything he's accusing me of is true.

"You know what I think?" I stare at him, not really giving a shit what he thinks. "I think you're a liar. And I think you need something to help you remember where you belong." I jump to my feet, fearing that he will make a call to have someone hurt Regg. Big arms grab me, holding me down as he walks back over to his desk.

"Stop! Chip don't! I'll do anything, just please don't hurt them." He laughs at my state of panic.

"Come on, Red. You think I'd fuck with the brother of one of the most powerful MCs in the south? I'm not an idiot. So I took a couple of pictures...got a phone number out of a book. Luke's connections reach further than mine do. Charlie Lott would have my head if Luke asked him to." Charlie Lott- Luke's mob boss employer. He could make this all go away. All I have to do is find a way to make a phone call.

"I see your wheels spinning," Chip teases, walking towards me with his hands behind his back. "That'll stop soon enough. This is where you belong, Red. You've done a hell of a job. It's gonna be tough to replace you. But, you know too much for me to just let you go. Don't worry, though. I'll be sure to keep you happy." From behind his back, he pulls a needle and I feel my eyes widen at the sight of it.

"No!" I scream, but I'm silenced by a big hand that covers my mouth and holds my neck in a position that could easily cause it to break with one sharp twist. I thrash against the hands anyway, willing to die than be injected with what I know is heroin.

My arm is stretched out, exposing my veins and I blink rapidly to keep the tears from fogging my vision. I scream against the sweaty hand, begging him not to do this. Without a second look at me, he jabs me hard with the needle, and within seconds, everything goes black.

Chapter Thirty
Moving on

Regg

"Reggie, it's your play." I look over at my little brother, who is not so patiently waiting for me to make my next move in Checkers. I dominate this game usually, but today my head is somewhere else. I've been home for a week, and I convinced myself on the plane ride back that I was done. But since I got home, I've had this feeling like something is wrong and I can't seem to ignore it.

I tracked her down by pure fucking coincidence. Taylor, of all people, had gone to Vegas for a bachelorette party. She noticed Red's face on a billboard, and when I saw her in a bar a few days after her return, she told me to tell her congratulations. I didn't hesitate booking myself a round trip ticket and a one-way for Red. It was a waste of fucking money, I guess.

When I arrived in Vegas, Red's face covered the pamphlets in the back seat of the taxi. Once on the strip, she was on several big screens that read 'Hottest Show in Vegas.' I was afraid that she might be too caught up in the fame, but when I saw her face, I noticed the distance in her eyes. Then, she finally confirmed all my fears.

Luke was right- Red is a creature of habit. As soon as she got a chance to run back to what she's always known, she did. It was hard seeing her, but at least I have the peace of mind knowing that she isn't back on drugs. Out of impulse, I want to fuck everything that walks just to get her back in some way. She's moved on. Not only is Chip using her to promote his business, but he is fucking her as well.

I've been driving myself crazy. The guys have encouraged me to move on. Hell, some of the ol' ladies have told me it was time too. I can't get her out of my head, though. She is still the most important thing in my life, even if I'm not hers.

I ride a lot. I spend a lot of time with my family and too much time with the club. But, just like in my dreams, she's always there. I feel her behind me when I ride down the highway, even though I haven't had a bitch seat on my bike in weeks. I hear her laughter in the bars when I'm with the club, but they're ain't a soul in there that can hold a candle to her. I see her in the sad eyes of my Aunt Kathy who hurts because I hurt. And I smell her...everywhere. Her sweet scent fills my house and invades my thoughts, always leading me back to her.

Word spread across our small town that the most eligible bachelor in Collins finally found a woman, but was now available once again. I shit you not, I had bitches bringin' me casseroles and cookies like I am a widower or something. It was nice not having to cook though. I'd be eating spaghetti for my fourth night in a row very soon.

"Why don't you just go out on a date or something? Ain't that what you told me to do when my girlfriend dumped me?" I smile at Todd's advice. Smart little shit. It wouldn't be hard to find a date, that's for sure.

I call Luke, and find that him and some of the guys are at the only nightclub in Hattiesburg- The Library. The place is probably already crawling with pussy, which is exactly what I need to get my mind off of Red. Besides, the best way to get over one bitch is to get under another.

Sure enough, there's enough half-naked girls running around in here to give the Playboy Mansion a run for its money. They leave little to the imagination wearing skimpy dresses and shorts so tight you can see the outline of their pussy lips. I'm not complaining, I love trashy bitches.

It takes me a minute to realize the redhead approaching is not the redhead I want- it's Taylor. Maybe she bugged my bike with a tracking device or some shit. She always seems to pop up wherever I am. I give her a smile, and I imagine her panties melting from beneath her tight shorts as she flushes red. Her head dips self-consciously. She lacks the same confidence Red has, and it's somewhat of a turnoff for me. I like girls who like themselves. But, a change is what I need and change is what I'll get with Taylor.

"Hey, Regg," she says, leaning in close so I can hear her over the booming music. "I'm sorry about...you know."

"Yeah, I know," I say, cutting her off and motioning for the bartender to bring us a round. I'm sure Taylor will drink whatever I buy her. She's submissive like that. Red would have told me to go fuck myself if I ordered her a beer. She didn't settle.

Fuck.

I have to quit comparing everything to Red. I pass Taylor a beer, and just like I thought, she takes it with an appreciative smile and a 'thank-you.' When the one country song that plays every two hours comes on, I lead her out on the dance floor without question. She fits good in my arms, almost too good. I move her around the floor to the tune of one of George Strait's classics, then usher her back to the bar before the crowd takes over when some hip hop line dancing song comes on.

She likes when I put my hand on the small of her back, something Red once said she wanted to try, and then told me she felt like an idiot when I did it. Her exact words were, 'This is fucking ridiculous. Why do girls go crazy over this shit? I'm capable of walking on my own. I can live the rest of my life not having you usher me around.' I smile at the memory. It was her idea, not mine, yet she chewed my ass out like I forced her to do it.

"What's so funny?" Taylor asks, smiling up at me.

"Nothing. Let's get outta here." Out of spite, I place my hand on the small of her back again, guiding her outside to my bike.

"Where're we going?" she asks innocently, looking up at me with excited eyes. I'll regret this tomorrow. I'll hate myself for a little while, but I'll get over it. Everybody has their way of coping, this is mine. I answer her question, noticing how she seems to melt a little bit into the concrete at my words. She is the perfect one to use to get over Red.

"My place."

Taylor either really loves my house, or she's really good at acting. I learn that she's an interior designer, which makes sense from the disgusted look she gives my den. She tries to recover, but it's too late.

"I take it you don't like my collection of dead animals?" I give her a smirk and watch her die a little of embarrassment. Red would say it served her right for judging my home in the first place. At the thought of her, I clear my throat and continue, "The house has never really had a woman's touch." The only woman that has ever lived in my house is Red, and Lord knows she sucked at everything domesticated. Except for cooking. She could fry a damn good pork chop.

"You know, I'd be happy to help you out. I have some really nice pieces that would look great in here." Damn, is she always this sweet? I already have a toothache. Does the girl not have any grit?

"That would be great." I picture Red's face when she sees what Taylor's done and smile again. Even if she's living her dream with another man, it'd still light a fire under her ass to know another woman was here. That's the kind of jealous, territorial woman Red was. She wanted shit that didn't even belong to her.

"Come here," I say to Taylor, ready to move this along and get my mind off of *her*-the girl who's name I refuse to say from now on. At the sound of my voice, I see the need in her eyes grow. She walks towards me, ready to abide by whatever demand I give her. I take her face between my hands, noticing that her red hair is almost identical to *hers*. Taylor's features are softer; her smile nothing in comparison and when I kiss her, her taste is bland- like eating peas without salt.

I kiss her harder, catching her moans with my mouth. I pick her up and carry her to the couch. When she's beneath me, I know this is what I want. It's what I need to get over... she breaks the kiss, searching my eyes with big, green ones full of hurt. I hadn't even noticed how beautiful they are. I prefer hazel eyes though.

"You're thinking about her," she says, tracing my lips with her finger.

"I'm thinkin' about you," I lie, leaning back down to kiss her. She pushes me away, forcing me to sit across from her on the couch.

"My name's not Red, Regg. It's Taylor." Shit. I run my hands through my hair, already feeling the regret I thought would stay away until tomorrow.

"I really like you, Taylor. It's just gonna take some time. But I don't want to stop seeing you." I need her around. It might takes weeks, months or even years, but eventually, Taylor would be the one to help me get over *her.*

"Don't worry, Regg." She grabs my hand in hers, giving me a promising smile. "I'm not going anywhere."

Chapter Thirty-One
When Devil's Fly

Regg

Taylor and I are...friends. Close friends. I can't bring myself to fuck her, even though it's been over a month since her and I started talking. Nothing about her turns me on. She's more like a sister...that I kiss. It's fucking weird.

My man cave now looks like something out a of Southern Living magazine. She's trying to encourage me to start remodeling the rest of the house, but I'm not ready to become a complete douche, yet. My manly shit now sits in the upstairs den- a place I hate going because it reminds me of *her*. But, the newly renovated living room holds no memories of my time with her so that's where I spend every minute that I'm home.

Luke bought the bar he's been planning on building for years. He took *her* advice and set up shop near the university and got a liquor license and karaoke equipment. Most of my time is spent there when I 'm not at home or with Taylor. I finally broke down and hired some help at the farm, so I can devote more time to the club.

It took all of us in the club to convince Brooklyn not to go to Vegas and hunt *her* down. She eventually caved and respected my decision to just leave it alone. The club hasn't taken too well to Taylor. They claim she doesn't have the balls to be a part of the life. I could have said a few things about that, but I haven't. Luke and Ronnie helped persuade them though, and because she is with me, they are at least nice to her. It is all I can ask.

Todd tried like hell to like Taylor, too. But, she hates video games, doesn't give a shit about world history, has no knowledge of guns and thinks hunting is done inhumanely. He stopped coming around when she is over after that last one. Unless of course he is in camo and wants to brag about his latest kill. I love that kid.

I spent all day at the bar, getting ready for the grand opening in a couple of weeks. We've been going balls to the wall getting everything ready, and I am dead tired when I finally get home. I've been in bed for all of two minutes when my phone rings- Taylor. I go back and forth about whether or not to answer it, but I finally give in.

"Hey babe," I say into the phone, trying like hell to sound really fucking tired.

"Regg...I need to talk to you. Can I come over?" She sounds almost desperate. Because I'm too fucking nice of a guy, I agree.

"Yeah darlin', be careful." I hang up and throw on some pajama pants before stomping downstairs. She doesn't live far from here, only about ten minutes.

I put on a pot of coffee, and I hear her pull up as it's brewing. She must have already been on her way before calling. Am I that predictable? I need to work on being a better asshole.

I open the door, letting a very sad Taylor inside. Immediately my heart hurts for her. I don't love this girl, but I do care about her, and when she hurts- I hurt.

"What's the matter, babe?" I ask, ready to take her in my arms. She avoids me and walks to the kitchen. I watch as she pulls down the bottle of Jack from the cabinet and takes a pull straight from the bottle. This shit must be serious. I've never seen Taylor drink hard liquor. She pats her chest, urging the burn to hurry up and pass.

"I know you're going to hate me, but I couldn't keep this from you any longer. I just need you to hear me out first. Okay?" Uneasiness churns my gut and I nod my head. Hell, I don't have a choice but to listen, obviously.

"I love you, Regg. I've loved you since we were kids in high school." Oh shit. She's dumping me. How fucking shitty can my luck be? I can't keep a real girlfriend or a fake one. I knew I should have fucked her. "I thought that finally, we would be together. I didn't want you with Red and I was more than happy to see her gone from your life. I know that's awful, but it's the truth." She takes a deep breath, and I'm already anticipating her next words. *This just isn't working out. I've found somebody else. You've called me* her *name one too many times.*

"Just spit it out, Taylor. I'm a big boy. I can handle it." Tears fall from her eyes as she nods her head at me. Damn, this is really tearing her up. At least she feels guilty over it. The other one smiled the last time I saw her. I watch as she pulls a small, familiar box from her oversized purse.

"I found this hidden in the hollow neck of the wild hog in the living room. When I found out what it was, I kept it from you because I wanted you and I to have a chance at happiness. My guilt won't let me keep it from you one more second." I take the box from her hands, contemplating slapping her or kissing her. The key to why *she* left is in this box- one that I just assumed she took with her.

"I'm really sorry, Regg." She leans up to kiss my cheek before turning to leave. Apparently, She doesn't want to stick around to see my reaction to whatever is inside the box.

I sit down at the table, spilling the contents of the box in front of me. I pick up the pictures first. One is of Todd at football practice. The other is of him and that little bitch that left him for his best friend. Flipping them over, I don't see anything written on the back. I look down at the crumpled up letter that looks like it's been read a hundred times.

Red,
I asked you nicely and you refused. Did you really think I'd let you do that? You have two days to make your decision. If you aren't at Café Du Monde by noon on Wednesday, I'll break the boy's legs.
-Me
P.S. If you tell anyone about this, I'll do more than break his legs. I'll kill him.

Just like Red must have done, I read the letter over and over until everything around me becomes dark, and the only thing in my line of sight is the white piece of paper and the words scribbled on it. Fighting to keep my composure, I pick up my phone.
"Luke. We have a problem."

Luke assures me that he can have everything handled and Red back home by the end of the day with just one phone call. I don't need his assurance. I don't need his mob buddy either. Hell, I don't need Luke, but I would be a fool if I thought he would let me do this alone. An emergency meeting is called and it doesn't take long for a unanimous vote. Devil's Renegades will be flying out tonight to bring home what belongs to us- what belongs to me.

    We have enough club connections in the southwest to let other charters handle it, but this is a personal problem that is gonna be dealt with by the original charters that have been a part of Red's life for years. This goes far beyond mine and her relationship.
    People seem to move out of our way as we walk through the Louis Armstrong International Airport in New Orleans. We're not wearing leather cuts, but our soft cuts- t-shirts emblazoned with our patch- are worn with pride and leave no question as to who we are. The Devil's are going to Vegas, and we are bringing hell with us.

Chapter Thirty-Two
Dammit, Red

Red

Sometimes when I wake up, I eat oatmeal instead of cereal. Some days, I only watch infomercials on T.V. On Tuesdays, I shower. Sometimes I do it on Fridays too. It just depends on how I feel that day. That's about the extent of my life right now. It's been this way for over a month.

Chip comes to visit me every day. And every day he comes, he brings a bottle of orange juice and a syringe filled with heroin with him. I guess the orange juice is my treat for taking my medicine. I was able to fight him for the first week, but now, I anticipate him coming.

I need the drugs because it helps me forget that I'm alive. I've even asked him to up the dose, and he so kindly obliged. I thought for a while that I could find some way to escape. But, every time I tried I was caught. And every time I was caught, I was punished. Punishments consist of Chip using me as his punching bag because he is too big of a pussy to fight a man. Instead, he takes his anger out on a junkie. Me.

I noticed one time that one of the bouncers turned his back on the beating. I thought that he might be my saving grace. But I haven't seen him again after that night. I've given up on life again and I've stopped running. It took a couple of weeks for my ribs to heal from the last beating I took. After that one, I decided it was better to just stay fucked up than to spend days feeling like I was breathing through a straw.

Chip's nice enough to buy me cigarettes and allow me to have cable T.V. He kept my apartment too. At least he hasn't stopped low enough to force me to do anything with him. Although, I'm not holding my breath that things won't change. He often shows up just to sit and look at me. He takes that time to tell me what a pathetic waste I am, and how disappointed in me he is over my wasting all of my god-given talent.

He likes to watch me squirm, waiting for the needle that will take me to a place in the clouds. He wants me to ask for it, but I've yet to give in to that demand. I would rather shake, sweat and hurt than ask him for what I know is destroying my life- one injection at a time. Even if what he has to offer is the only form of coping with this life that I have left.

The only joy I have in life is pulled from my memories. I think of Ronnie's laugh, Brooklyn's scent, Possum's smile, Punkin's comments, Big Al's playfulness, Mary's accent, Kyle's favorite song, Katina's craziness, Pop's temper and Luke's brotherly love. But most of all, I think of Regg. Everything about our time together is it at the forefront of my thoughts. I think it's what's keeping me sane.

I think about the smile he gave me the first time I saw him. I think about his body and the way it seemed to be created just for my pleasure. I remember his laugh, and find myself trying to imitate it. I think of the way he made love to me, how I'd begged him to tell me he loved me and how he'd showed me in every way possible that love was something I would never do without, not when it came to him.

He is probably dating now. He more than likely has already moved someone in just to spite me. I'm sure he thinks of me often, but the memory fades when he looks into the eyes of the woman he now loves. I am happy for him. He always deserved something much better than me.

Life blends one day to the next. I'm living in a tunnel of darkness without a flashlight. Just when I think I've come up with a plan for escape, I'm taken back to the depths of hell that Chip has created for me. Like clockwork, he seems to know when my mind is capable of doing something to betray him. When I realize this, I start a diary.

Dear Diary,
It's me, Red. Just wanted to let you know that Chip has you figured out. So, I'm gonna write to you and tell you what my clear thoughts are for the day.
There is a fire extinguisher under the kitchen cabinet. Use it to knock Chip in the head with tomorrow. If one of his goons comes in with him, hit that motherfucker too.
Love,
Red

Dear Diary,
Well, that shit didn't work. Or I guess you just forgot to try it. Try not to puss out next time.
Love,
Red

Dear Diary,
It is confirmed. You are seriously a vagina. Grow some balls!
Love,
Red

Dear Diary,
You're an addict. It's amazing how much you want drugs more than you do freedom. I guess old habits die hard.
You're an idiot,
Red

I stop keeping a diary after that. It doesn't matter what I thought I could do. Knowing that Chip holds the key to my happiness, makes all thoughts of escape leave me. Chances are, I'll die in this shithole town, and I only have myself to blame.

Then, like an angel, the man that I thought might be my saving grace magically appears again. I don't know if he earned his way back in by beating another stripper within an inch of her life, or if maybe he's just been put on another assignment. But, he shows up again, and I notice a look in his eyes that screams at me to fight. So, that's what I do.

I've been fighting with my body, battling with my demons, and playing fucking rugby with my mind to keep me focused as soon as I regain consciousness. Today is day three of operation 'Red Fights Back' and it is working. Something in my gut tells me that today will be the day, and I am more than ready for it.

Above the stove are two cabinets that are never used for anything. Today, they house a small bag I've packed with a few days' worth of supplies. I only need a change of clothes, my cash stash, cigarettes and some Oreos. And I packed a can of Ravioli's too. I'm such a fat ass.

I don't know when Chip will show up, but I have everything in place for when he does. Clothes lay scattered on the bathroom floor, but they only appear that way.

They are laid out perfectly for me to just throw on in case I get a chance to run. I've practiced for hours and am thankful that no one was around to watch. My tennis shoes are just outside the bathroom door with a towel thrown over them. I've thought of everything- or at least everything I can in my current state.

Today, I'm not a junkie. I'm not some washed up stripper who is just gonna lay down and die. Today, I am a fighter. I will scratch, hit, bite, pinch, pull hair and do anything else crazy bitches do when they've had enough. And I've had enough of Chip.

***

"Hey gorgeous!" Chip says, looking entirely too fucking happy on a...whatever damn day this is. "Did you miss me?"

"Like the plague," I mutter, uninterested in his sweet talk. "Just give me my shit and go." I always say the same words, but it never works. Hell, it was worth the try.

"Well, I missed you." He doesn't even acknowledge my smartass remark, and I'm slightly offended. That was a good one. "You know, I'm going to break you one day, Red. One day, you're not gonna have that spark." Prior to today, if I had a spark, I wasn't aware of it. I was like striking a lighter that had been submerged in water for hours. Hey- that was a good one. I need to write that down.

"Reckon you could get me some crossword puzzles or a video game or something? I'm getting a little bored around here." He laughs at my requests, taking a seat on the couch across from me. Ninety percent of my time is spent in this recliner, wearing Regg's shirt and forcing food down my throat. No way was I going back to looking like a starved model. I'd die first. Hey- that's not a bad idea. If this doesn't work out, early death by starvation would be a good way to go. I need to write that one down too.

"If only I could trust you, Red. I would be able to offer you a life like you could never imagine."

"Yeah, well if grandma would've had a dick, she would have been grandpa." This earns me another round of laughter, and I roll my eyes. "Glad I can amuse you."

As always, pumping me full of dope is a challenge. When you shoot up daily, veins become weak and tend to collapse. Sometimes, it can be a bloody mess, and I mean that literally- not as a bit of Australian slang. This time is no different. I'm used as a pin cushion until the only vein that can be found is between my toes. I don't know why Chip doesn't give me powder, but I guess it's because he likes to torture. Fine. Whatever makes him happy.

Seconds after the heroin is flowing through my blood stream, I feel that familiar sense of warmth engulf me. My eyes roll to the back of my head, and I become relaxed and forced into a state of delirium. It may be bad for me. It may be the worse form of hell I've ever experienced. But this shit feels amazing. I'm falling through the air with nothing to hold on to, and I pray like hell that at some point, I finally hit bottom.

I land, and the thud I hear isn't me hitting bottom, it's the sound of the door closing. This is where Chip has fucked up. This is the silent message his bouncer has been giving me. Every time a needle is put in me, I guess they all go out for celebration. The man who usually guards my door, leaves and doesn't return for about an hour.

I've been building up a resistance to the drug since I found this out. Considering I only found out three days ago, I'm not sure I'm ready for this. But, the fear of staying here longer outweighs the fear I have of trying.

I'm fucked up. My body is struggling against the feeling of euphoria that is pumping its way through my system with every beat of my heart. But, like I said, today I'm a fighter. I want to give up when I see that Wheel of Fortune is coming on; it's the highlight of my day. I dig deep and find the will to get my sorry ass out of the recliner. I don't have much time.

Running... or skipping, maybe moon-walking, but in all reality- crawling, I make my way to the bathroom. Putting my clothes on comes as a challenge even though I practiced it to perfection. I pull on my tennis shoes, grab the bag above the stove, and slip out the front door of my apartment.

Now, I could run to a neighbors. I could call the police, or Regg or Luke, but I don't know who is on Chip's payroll and I refuse to blow this. If I'm caught, he might kill me this time. So, I do the only thing I'm can- I run.

Well, I don't run. I can't. I'm still too fucked up and everything I see makes me smile. It's so beautiful outside, and I have a desire to touch everything. Somehow, I make it to the parking lot, but I'm stopped by a black Lincoln town car that I recognize as one of Chip's. I open my mouth to scream. At this point, all I can hope for is that someone will hear me and come to my rescue.

The passenger door flies open and my angel, Chip's body guard, comes into view He's the most beautiful thing I've ever seen.

"Get in the car, Red!" he's yelling at me, and I take a moment to put my finger over my lips. Grabbing my arm, he jerks me inside. "Dammit, Red."

"What?" I ask, as he speeds through the parking lot and out into the street.

"I shit faster than you walk." What the fuck?

"Yeah? Well, what does that tell you about your digestive system? Sounds like you need to get that shit checked."

"Look, I'm taking you to a rehab place. You can check in anonymously, then call your family from there." Yeah, that isn't gonna happen. After Chip told me he wouldn't do anything to Todd or Regg anyway, there is no need for me to contact them. No way was I calling them in the state I am in. I would get clean first, then I'd go home, maybe. I'd call first. If Regg wasn't with anyone, then I'd go crawling back and beg for his forgiveness. But, I'll never tell him anything. I know beyond a shadow of a doubt that he would still hunt Chip down and kill him. I wasn't gonna let that happen. Not after everything I've been through.

"Thank you for this," I say, looking into his bright blue eyes. He's cute, in a scary way. He has a long, black beard, is built like a tank, covered in tattoos and his ears are pierced. He looks more like a biker than a body guard. "By the way, I didn't catch your name." He gives me a look, like he's deciding whether he should tell me who he is or not.

"Just call me Shark." Shark. I like that name. A word that would send most people running away in fear, yet here I am running away with him.

"Well Shark, I'm Red. It's nice to meet you." He gives me a smile, showing me his huge white teeth that are sharp and pointy- or maybe they're just normal. I don't know. I'm still fucked up.

"I know exactly who you are." Well, okay then.

Chapter Thirty-Three
Guns, Blood and Sock Puppets

Regg

"Where the fuck is she?" I roar into the face of the infamous Chip. This motherfucker looks nothing like a notorious drug dealer, he looks like a high school principal.

"I-I don't know!" I push the barrel of my stolen piece into the side of his neck a little harder. I'm not sure, but I think he just pissed his pants. His goons stand around the room, arms behind their heads as my guys hold them at gunpoint. A local support chapter hooked us up with some heat, and we are definitely using it to our advantage. "She left a week ago. I haven't seen her."

"If you don't have her, and you don't know where she is, then I guess we don't need you anymore." I back away from him, aiming the barrel of my nine straight at his chest. I see the worried look in Luke's eyes, but I ignore him. This asshole is fixing to talk, and he doesn't need his kneecaps to do it.

"Wait! I have a guy. He used to work for me. He's gone. MIA since the day Red went missing." Keeping one hand out in front of him for protection, he reaches over with the other and pulls a card from his desk, knocking shit over in the process. "His name is Shawn. He doesn't live far from here." I look down at the card that lists his name, his title as head of security and a phone number.

"If he don't answer, you're dead." I watch Chip's eyes grow in fear at my promise. I'll kill him and there isn't a Devil in the room that can stop me.

I dial the number, keeping my eyes trained on Chip while it rings once, twice...

"Yeah?"

"Is this Shawn?" I growl into the phone, daring the motherfucker to have my woman.

"Who is this?"

"This is Devil's Renegades Regg. We need to talk."

There's no point in meeting Shawn, because he tells me exactly what I need to know over the phone before I even ask him to. Apparently, he helped Red get away from Chip and drove her to a private rehab facility. The mention of the word 'rehab' has me training my gun on Chip once again. I'm given the address and a promise of help if we need anything else.

I'm torn between killing Chip and leaving to go get Red. I want to do both, but I know that once I pull the trigger, I won't be the only man that kills someone tonight. My brothers will react on impulse and shoot any witnesses left standing in the room. The music is loud, but I don't know if it's loud enough to cover six gunshots. We aren't really incognito either. Even though we all wore black, there is no denying that we're a gang or brotherhood of some sort. Too many eyes witnessed us coming into the club. After several minutes of thinking, I know that Chip has to die- it just won't be tonight.

"I'm asking you to let me handle this," Luke practically begs. I know his version of handling it. He gives Charlie Lott a call, Lott takes out Chip and in return, he inherits his enterprise. Everybody wins.

"I'm telling you to let Luke handle it," Ronnie says, coming to stand beside me. Well, I have my orders. I will not disobey my president. It isn't in me to deny this man the respect he deserves. He didn't get where he is not knowing what in the hell he is doing.

I lower my gun, handing it off to Ronnie.

"I only need a few minutes." Ronnie knows what I'm asking, and at the nod of his head, I get the few minutes that's due to me. This is for my brother. This is for my club. This is for my Red -the woman he tried to destroy. Everything fades to black. I let my desire to kill fuel me as I give this man not even half of what he's put my woman through.

The sound of my fists meeting his flesh is the only sound in the room. Lucky for him, he is unconscious by the second blow, but I don't stop. By the time they pull me off of him, he's almost unrecognizable. Charlie Lott won't have a hard time figuring out who the man that needs a bullet is. All he'll have to do is find the one that has a face that looks like it's been put through a meat grinder.

Luke makes the call and before we leave a team of men show up to takeover. I don't know what this will cost the club, but the favor is one we will be more than happy to repay. We'll be leaving Vegas in less than twenty-four hours. Our club will be whole, free and Red will be with us.

***

Green Acres is a weird fucking name for a rehab facility, and I'm surprised to not find the song playing over the loud speaker when I walk in. The place looks like a resort, and I'm sure Red is taking full advantage of it.

Shawn agreed to meet us here and now stands with me and my brothers on our mission.

I'm nervous to see her, but more anxious to have her in my arms. The sweet girl at the front desk nearly falls over when all of us walk through the door. When I ask for Denny Deen, she frowns and shakes her head, telling me that no one by that name is here. Shawn has me asking under the name 'Mary West'. When that brings me another round of bad news, I become impatient with our friend Shawn. He then tells me that she probably went in anonymously to prevent Chip from finding her. This leaves me at a dead end.

"If she checked in under another name, I can't tell you. We take the privacy act very seriously." I offer her my best smile, she doesn't budge. Luke steps in and offers his, she doesn't budge. When Possum's up, she caves a little, but doesn't tell us shit. I'm ready to choke the life outta this bitch. I bet she'd tell me then. Ronnie is on board with me, ready to get the hell out of Vegas and back home to real food. Priorities.

Just as I'm ready to hold her at gunpoint, laughter fills the lobby in front of us. It's a laugh I know all too well and one I've missed too fucking much. My beautiful redheaded woman is standing in the lobby less than fifteen feet from me. She looks amazing, her smile is genuine and on her hand is a sock puppet- go fucking figure. But, it's the shirt she wears that has me frozen. It's not just the way it clings to her great tits or the way the neck is cut out giving me a view of her amazing fucking cleavage-it's the words inscribed on the front in orange, glittery shit. PROPERTY OF REGG. My girl might have been through hell, but her Devil was here to save her, and she hadn't given up on me coming.

Chapter Thirty-Four
Making Memories

Red

Green Acres. What kind of fucking name is that? I've played the damn song in my head a million times, but haven't heard it once. It's so aggravating forgetting song lyrics and not having any way of researching them. Green Acres thrives on being a technology forbidden place, so there is no T.V., radio or computers. Some of the girls have stooped low enough to make sock puppets to entertain them with. I am one of those girls. I know it sounds stupid, but exercising our creative minds is one step closer in the healing process. Or, that's what in the hell the counselor keeps telling us.

I made a friend. Sherrie, or Chi Chi as I refer to her, was once a known affiliate in the club industry too. She wasn't a stripper, but she was a bad ass bartender who'd been able to use her skills to bring life to the terrible fucking kool-aid they served us in the cafeteria. She is also a victim of the sock puppet game that has become the highlight of our lives.

I'm clean. My withdrawals from the heroin were a hell of a lot easier to deal with here than they were at Regg's. They weaned me off of it slowly instead of forcing me to quit cold turkey. It cost me every dime I had, but the place was really nice with a pool, a workout room and a basketball gym that I use to dance. Of course, I have to make up the lyrics in my head, but I found myself and my spirit once again. And I'm pretty good at exotic dancing to the Green Acres theme song.

In my state of depression that always seems to come with the lack of drugs in my system, I find myself missing Regg more than ever. I've gone as far as daydreaming that I am his property and that his name is proudly worn on my back. During crafts one day, I even made a property shirt out of one of his old t-shirts. It is now my favorite and I wear it every day.

I'm walking through the lobby on my way to my support group meeting, sock puppet in hand and wearing my handmade t-shirt. Chi Chi is with me, proudly sporting her own sock puppet that has now just become a stab at the counselors and their boring talk. If they want to treat us like children, then why not act like children? They are making enough money that they shouldn't give a shit either way.

We're laughing about something stupid, as always, when I hear Chi Chi take in a sharp breath. Turning, I see that she has stopped walking and her eyes are focused on the front doors of the lobby. I turn to see what holds her attention and nearly faint.

Six members of the Devil's Renegades stand tall at the front desk, along with Shark who only has eyes for Chi Chi- unless he's looking at me like that, which I'm sure he's not because I hold the eyes of everyone else. One set of soft brown eyes pulls me in and almost has me floating across the room.

In all of his soft cut, blonde haired, brown eyed, six foot glory, stands the unmistakable Regg-my Regg. His fingers move with the urge to touch something. I'm sure it's me. He looks like he's fighting some kind of internal battle, and I know the moment it's won and which side is the victor. Closing the distance in only a few strides, I'm taken into arms I never thought I'd feel hold me again.

He takes a moment to just hold me, smell me and run his big, calloused hands through my hair. When he takes my face between his hands, everything that needs to be said isn't done verbally. I can see the relief in his eyes along with passion, victory and love. Unable to keep my lips from his, I claim his mouth-letting everyone know that this one belongs to me.

His taste is powerful, awakening something inside of me that I thought had died. We can't get enough of each other as we make out like two teenagers in a movie theatre- nothing but tongues and lips and horny passion. I want to fuck him right here in the lobby of Green Acres- theme song be damned.

After the sound of cleared throats starts to sound like the sounds of a ten year old dog with heart worms, he breaks the kiss, but keeps his face so close to mine that our noses touch.

"I love you, Red. And I'm here to take you home." I close my eyes at his words. Home. I'm finally going home. A place where Regg and I can pick up where we left off. A place that has been void of any woman other than me. "Tell me, Red," he demands, and I know the words that he longs wants to hear. But, I still owe him one from a long time ago. And today, I finally get a chance at payback.

"What in the hell took you so long?"

**

The best part about a ride is the gas station stop. When everyone gets off their bikes, lights up a smoke, cracks open a Mountain Dew and talks about the shit that happened while on the road. During that time, other shit always seems to happen to make life long memories with. I guess a ride, doesn't matter if it's by bike, car or plane, has the potential to make some pretty damn great memories. Ours started in the taxi ride to the airport.

"Sorry sir," the man with the strong accent says when he nearly brings us to our death at an intersection.

"If you do that shit again, you'll die an early death by dick strangulation," Big Al promises, causing all of us to take a moment to process his words. Now, my outlook on dick strangulation is just that- strangling a dick until someone dies. What he should have said was that he would strangle him with his own dick if he almost killed us again.

No...that wouldn't have worked either. Maybe he could cut off the man's dick and choke him with it if he almost killed us again.

"The motherfucker is gonna die if he don't get his shit in check." Big Al's words are said with enough determination that we all believe him- even though we can't stop laughing.

In the security line at the airport, Kyle gets to go through the TSA pre-check line. Possum, being the ornery ass that he is, doesn't understand why Kyle gets to keep his shoes on and he doesn't. It almost starts a war, I shit you not. It ends with Possum getting nearly thrown out of the airport and all of us apologizing on his behalf. Good thing they don't hold the middle finger motion to the same standard as they hold a threat. If that were the case, Possum would be in custody right now, and because his boys are ride or dies, they would all be in there too. Me? I am taking my ass to the house. With or without them. Call me selfish if you want to, but fried chicken and cornbread are in my very near future.

We have a layover at LAX. Unfortunately, LAX doesn't offer a smoke room, so off we go to the designated smoking area fifty friggin' miles away. If you're a frequent flyer, then you know that means that we have to go back through security. This time, we breeze through with only one security guard telling Possum to chill the hell out. I have a feeling they aren't in the mood to fuck around, and Possum is missing fried chicken and cornbread much like me.

The poor flight attendants on the flight from LAX to New Orleans will never forget the Devil's Renegades, I'm sure. By the time we board the flight, they are all pretty drunk. Prior to yesterday, neither Ronnie nor Possum had ever flown before. It is the funniest shit I've ever witnessed in my life. Picture two burly bikers holding vomit bags, shooting whiskey and still trying to pick up flight attendants between dry heaves and drinking, and you'll get the same vision I lived through.

We finally make it to New Orleans in one piece, and nobody gives a shit about the ex-junkie in the van as blunts are fired up and passed around. The PROSPECT driving is catching immortal hell and Luke is ill as a hornet because he doesn't smoke and he has to endure Kyle's version of *Milkshake* completely sober. It's a complete clusterfuck for everyone...well, not everyone.

Regg and I have claimed the back seat to ourselves. The laughter in the front of the van grows distant to us as we get lost in one another. Conversation is the last thing on my mind, but it's important that we get it over with now.

"I was never with Chip," I say, starting the conversation at what I feel like is the most important part. "I told you that to make you leave."

"It worked." Regg smirks at me and I'm glad he doesn't hold any hard feelings.

"I didn't tell you be-,"

"I know why you didn't tell me, Red," he says, cutting me off. "I know you did it because you thought it was the right thing to do. But, don't ever doubt my ability to take care of you. I'd rather give my life for you, than have to live one day knowing that you didn't trust me to protect you, or my family." I knew this. This epiphany came to me only moments after he left the last time I saw him.

"I know that now. Hell, I knew that then, but when I realized what I was doing it was too late."

"You want to tell me what happened?" he asks, and I wonder if he really wants to know the answer to that question. I know I'll tell him one day, but today is not that day. Plus, there is a burning question in my mind.

"Not right now. So, what about you?" I try to act like I'm not really interested, but his smile tells me that he can see right through my bullshit- just like he always can.

"What about me?"

"Did you find any…lovers while I was gone?" He laughs and it's one of those laughs that tells me he's fucking guilty. "What?" I yell, causing everyone in the van to turn around and look at us. They must realize what I've just discovered because they all turn back around- even Luke. Fucking traitors.

"It's not what you think." He's getting defensive, which means it's exactly what I think.

"Let me guess, fucking Taylor." A snicker comes from the front of the van and my suspicions are confirmed.

"Look, I didn't fuck her. We just hung out."

"Hung out? What do you mean y'all hung out?"

"I mean we hung out. Get off my back, Red. You had me convinced you were with another man."

"Get off your back? What did she do? What did y'all do? Did you kiss her?" I'm firing off questions left and right. I want to know the answer to all of them just as much as I don't. "Has she been to our house?" Regg runs his hands under his cap, letting out a breath that I guess he'd been holding. It is a fool move on his part. He's gonna need all the oxygen he can get because I am fixing to choke the ever-living shit outta him.

"Guys, I need a minute." I don't know what that means, but a chorus of 'I'm watching,' 'You got it brother' and 'Hell yeah' ring out through the van seconds before I'm on my back and he's on top of me, pinning me with his hips and shutting me up with his mouth.

I'm beating the shit out of his back when he grabs my arms and holds my wrists with one hand while he pushes up my shirt with the other. He kisses me deeper, finding my already hard nipple and rubbing his thumb over it until I'm leaning in to his touch. When I calm down, he breaks the kiss, whispering words across my neck as he kisses me between his promises.

"I only want to kiss you, Red." Teeth nip at my neck, and the sting is soothed with a flick of his tongue. "I only want to make love to you, Red." His hand covers my breast, squeezing it with just the right amount of pressure. "You are the only woman I want wearing my patch, sleeping in my bed and having my last name." He kisses his way up my neck then looks at me with eyes burning with desire. "I don't want anybody else. It's only you. Since that first night, it's only been you. Marry me."

What. The. Fuck. Did he just propose to me? I mean, I knew it was coming, but am I ready for this? I go through the list in my head, checking it off one by one.

Do I love him? Check.

Do I need him? Check.

Does he love me? Check.
Does he need me? Check.
Can I trust him? Check.
Can I trust him to not bring another girl into his home, kiss her, call her darlin' and introduce her to the club just because he thought I was living my dream with another man? We'll work on that one.
Can he take care of me? Check.
Does he make me happy? Check.
Has he proven himself to me? Check.
Do I want to marry this man that has devoted his time to me, sacrificed his life for me and just confessed his love for me?

You're fucking right I do.

But, I always imagined something a little more romantic than this. Maybe a sunset at the lake, or in a hot air balloon ride. Not like this.

"You just proposed to me, in the back of a van with six stinking men sitting up front, only minutes after you tell me you had another woman in our house?" His hips thrust into me, reminding me of what I do to him and another part of him that I don't want to ever live without.

"I asked you a question, Red. Now, either you can answer me willingly, or I can fuck it out of you." He smiles that panty-dropping, heart melting, has me already coming on the backseat smile of his.

"If I say yes, will you still promise to fuck me until I scream it over and over?"

"Yes." So the moment isn't romantic. So I won't get that hot air balloon ride. But, the thing about Regg is I know that if he thinks he is capable of doing something to make me happy, he'll do it. That's all anyone really wants in life, isn't it? Happiness? Well, I've found my happiness, and he wears a cut that says he is one of the Devil's

Renegades. So, upon my answer, not only will I become Mrs. Reggie Rawls, I'll become Property of Devil's Renegades Regg, Red.

"Yes, Regg. I'll marry you." And in this moment, I realize it's the only thing in life I've ever really wanted.

Epilogue

One week later

That's right. One week. That's how long it took me to undo everything Taylor had done. Who in the hell hangs pictures of trees on the walls anyway? You can look out any window of the house and see a shit ton of them. What an idiot.

Church was held the day after we got home. Luke was named the new Sergeant at Arms and was excited about his first job that will lead him to Tennessee. I will miss him, but I have Regg-the Devil's new Enforcer- to keep me company.

Enforcer.

That just sounds bad ass. Which is exactly what my future husband is.

The ceremony is being held at our house- if you want to call it a ceremony. It's more like a party. The dress code is leather, the decorations are non-existent and the yard has enough Harleys in it to start a dealership. It is my kinda place.

I am not dressed in leather. I'm wearing a dress that accents my ass, my legs and is about two sizes too small- just how Regg likes it. Oh, and the color? Fire engine red.

I wish I could tell you a whole bunch of romantic shit happened, but it didn't. Luke drove me around the house on the back of his bike to where Regg stood wearing his best ripped jeans and a black t-shirt. Catcalls rang out when I came into view and laughter replaced it when I nearly fell getting off the bike.

We didn't make up our own vows, we just let the President from a local Christian charter say them for us. We kissed in a very inappropriate way considering Regg's aunt and uncle were there.

But, when I felt the weight of that leather on my back for the first time, it was a feeling I'll never forget. Branding someone might sound demeaning to some. Wearing a patch that labels you as property might seem a little derogatory to most. But to a real ol' lady, it means that you belong. That you are spoken for. It means that in a world where dreams are shattered, hopes are lost and life has no meaning, you still have everything. You have the love of a man, the love of a family and the respect of many.

In my life, I've been a lot of things. I've been an orphan outcast, a private dancer, a well-known stripper, a star and a junkie. But, in all that time, there is only one place that I could call home. The club is my family and my home.

I might have been born Denny Deen, property of the state of Mississippi, but I'll die as Red, Property of Devil's Renegades Regg- the woman I was always destined to become.

The End.

Acknowledgments

Where do I start? Hmmm... Probably with the hubs. Regg...I love you so much. You have been my rock through all of this. Thank you for your support! I'm really gonna cook more and I'm gonna clean more too.

Mandy... You are incredible. Thank you for working with short deadlines and idiots like me.

Mom and Dad... I'm still the Phase 10 champion. Don't forget it.

Joanna... Thank you for all your support, advice and your shoulder. I love crying on it.

Kylie... I want you to sing Janis Joplin to me all the time.

Sali... You know. You already know.

Katie... Little momma... Thank you for talking to me, reading for me and listening to me bitch. #teamfsog

Amy... It's always been you.

Katelan... I'd fight for you any day.

James and Kathy...You guys are great.

My MC family, sisters, brothers from another mother, cousins, family and everyone who has supported me. Thank you.

Once again, if I forgot you, your name goes here_____.

Other books by Kim Jones
Saving Dallas
Saving Dallas Making the Cut
Saving Dallas Forever

www.kimjonesbooks.com
www.facebook.com/kimjonesbooks
@authorkimjones

Visit www.kimjonesbooks.com for an exclusive bonus scene from Red and Luke!

Made in the USA
Lexington, KY
05 February 2017